PLAY TO KILL

PUJA MUKHERJEE KHATTRI

Srishti
Publishers & Distributors

Srishti Publishers & Distributors
A unit of AJR Publishing LLP
212A, Peacock Lane
Shahpur Jat, New Delhi – 110 049

editorial@srishtipublishers.com

First Published by Srishti Publishers & Distributors in 2025

10 9 8 7 6 5 4 3 2 1

This is a work of fiction. The characters, places, organisations and events described in this book are either a work of the author's imagination or have been used fictitiously. Any resemblance to people, living or dead, places, events, communities or organisations is purely coincidental.

FOR ABHISHEK:

THE BEGINNING,
THE MIDDLE,
AND THE END

ADVANCE PRAISE

Play to Kill by debut author Puja Mukherjee Khattri is an unputdownable gripping crime thriller that keeps you at the edge of your seat because you 'don't know who is black, white or grey.' The fabric of the plot is intricately woven with threads of suspense, anxiety, awe, love, and empathy.

—**Lt Gen KJS 'Tiny' Dhillon**, *Former DG Defence Intelligence Agency and National Bestselling Author*

Nothing is more powerful than an idea whose time has come. Victor Hugo's words are spot on for *Play to Kill*, a book that will appeal to wide and diverse audiences. Moving from chapter to chapter, I could easily visualise it as episodes of a screen adaptation. From words on the page to scenes on the screen, Play to Kill needs to be read now!

—**Rannvijay Singha**, *MTV Roadies, MTV Splitsvilla, Shark Tank India and Mismatched.*

Play to Kill is a spectacular debut. Unpredictable, witty, and slick. I was hooked from the go and found myself rooting for Anya and Karan through all the twists and turns. This book is a must read, an instant classic.

—**Harman Singha**, *Writer & Actor, Entanglement, Arranged Couple, Potluck and A.I.S.H.A My Virtual Girlfriend*

Forget what you think you know about online games. Puja Mukherjee Khattri's *Play to Kill* plunges you into a high-stakes thriller where anonymous players wreak havoc on unsuspecting lives. With every turn, the Delhi Urban Crimes Team uncovers a deeper conspiracy, proving that in this game, no one is safe.

—**Abhishek Rawat**, *Actor, Kaamnaa, Married Woman Diaries and Agle Janam Mohe Bitiya Hi Kijo*

Razor-sharp. Fast-paced. Unpredictable. *Play to Kill* is a high-stakes crime thriller that will keep you guessing till the very end.

—**Anirban Bhattacharyya**, *Author and Television Producer, Savdhaan India, Crime Patrol and Fear Files*

ACKNOWLEDGEMENTS

It is often said that writing is a solitary process, but there are so many people who shape an author's perspective of the characters and situations that make the story layered and more interesting. And without these wonderful people, the story may never have made it onto the pages of a book.

I'd like to express my appreciation and gratitude to my literary agent extraordinaire, Suhail Mathur of The Book Bakers, for his immense support and guidance through the whole process. Thank you to the brilliant team at Srishti Publishers, Arup Bose and Stuti Gupta and to the many others working behind the scenes.

Reading was an inherent part of my childhood. Spending afternoons on the veranda reading with my sister, Aditi, while the grownups napped, saving my pocket money to rent or buy a book—most of my childhood memories revolve around books. Our parents, Sumitra and Trigunesh, gave us roots to keep us grounded while encouraging us to explore any and all opportunities we wanted to.

To the most important people in my life, Abhishek, Ananya, and Arnav—you give me hope even when all feels lost. Thank you for not letting me give up on my writing and for keeping me accountable to myself. Having children who read and think for themselves can be truly inspiring, and also humbling on many an occasion.

A big thank you to Simrita, Romi, Khevi, Mrs Hooda, Mimi, and Nafisa for being my greatest supporters. Without your unwavering support, this book wouldn't be what it is. Deepa Aunty and Ananya, thank you for always being there for me. You guys are the best!

To Dr Munisha Agarwal, thank you for helping me understand how much Neel's ear would bleed. Khevi and Sarfaraz, thank you for helping me figure out how Anya's jeep would keep her safe.

And finally, thank you, dear reader, for choosing to read this book. I hope it resonates with you.

Sometimes a pawn, sometimes a player.
We are all a part of the game.
The question to ask is: Are you playing or being played?

CHAPTER ONE

October 5, Kamla Nagar, New Delhi

Raina likes working in the middle of the night when the whole world is asleep, and for a very short span, it seems possible to have some control over her life. When the morning comes, the course of her day will be decided by others.

She completes the article, satisfied that she has earned enough to pay for the diapers that she'd order online. *Thank God for the Internet*!

She stretches her arms and looks around the room. Arjun, her husband, is sprawled across the double mattress on the floor, his hand touching their three-month-old baby, Navin's, tiny hand. Despite the 33-year difference between them, they have the same expression on their faces when they wake up in the morning—one that says they can't wait to take the day by the horns. She, on the other hand, would much rather hide under the covers until it is essential for her to arise.

Sleep is further delayed by thoughts of the years that have gone by. Arjun and she have been the best of friends for years. In the last decade, with no one else to support them, the sheer desperation to make their relationship work and survive gave their love an edge, an uncontrolled passion.

Raina reaches out for Arjun's arm over Navin's head and slowly drifts away to sleep.

She wakes up to the tantalizing aroma of piping hot, freshly brewed coffee and finds her mug on the kitchen counter. She takes her first sip with her eyes closed. *Sheer bliss!*

It isn't winter yet, and still there is the slightest nip in the early morning air. She smiles as she watches Arjun read out the headlines to Navin. The two men in her life are bonding over politics and sports. She watches them contentedly.

It is as though he senses her even before he looks up from the newspaper. It has always been this way—at school, later at college, and at work. The first time they'd met, she had been a gawky ten to his mature, cocky thirteen. They'd travelled on the same bus to school and walked together to their tuition classes.

The heavy stubble on his unshaven face makes him look like one of the brooding heroes from the romance novels she loves to read.

"Did you have a good night?" He pulls her close and wraps his arm around her waist so they can watch the sun struggle to make its way through the buildings around them.

"Fair enough," she replies. She then quickly calculates the dollar-to-rupee conversion rate and adds, "Enough to buy groceries for this week."

He groans. "I wish you'd stop putting it like that. We do have my pay cheque too," he says matter-of-factly, as he nuzzles her neck. She smells of sleep, exotic and mysterious.

"Yes, but we need to add some more money to our rainy day fund," Raina says.

"You do know we don't live in Mawsynram, right?"

"You're so funny, Arjun!"

"At the rate we're saving money, we may be able to retire in the next ten years."

"Not at the current inflation rate," she replies, sipping her coffee. "You aren't serious about retiring, are you? Navin will be about ten years old." She looks at the baby. He twirls his fingers, watching them fascinatedly.

"Only you could begin a beautiful day on such a note," he chastises softly and grins, knowing just how she'll react.

"I'm just being realistic; we really need to start …" She turns her face just in time to catch him trying not to smile. "Are you making fun of me, Arjun Singh Chauhan?" she asks indignantly. "Are you trying to get on the wrong side of the person who is going to pack your lunch? I have this sudden urge to cook *lauki*."

"Babe, save as much as you want," replies Arjun. "In fact, if it will make you feel better, buy some more medical insurance, but no more *lauki* this week, please."

Amidst the usual chaos of preparing breakfast and lunch, giving Navin his feed, and changing his diapers, the first few hours of the day slip by. By the time Arjun leaves for work, Raina feels slightly tired and crumpled. She lays Navin on the bed, hoping he'll nap for a while.

Two hours later, with most of her household chores done, she feels energetic enough to go shopping for groceries at the local Food Bazaar. Being a Wednesday, many products would be on discount.

On her way out, she stops to ring Mrs Sharma's doorbell. Over the years, the octogenarian has moved from landlord status to that of a favoured aunt and grandmother to Navin. Mrs Sharma's children and grandchildren are scattered across the globe and rarely have the time or energy to visit her. Mrs Sharma takes in Raina's attire and the determined expression on her face. She's dressed for her weekly fight, the old lady muses. After all, jostling the crowds for fair prices is nothing short of a battle. Raina asks for her grocery list. The old woman hesitates for a few moments before she finally gives in.

Raina reaches the store in time to beat the crowds. She is well acquainted with most of the salespeople and notices some of them at the far end of the store. She strolls through the grocery and personal care aisles to identify the best bargains, speaking to Navin in a low voice, asking for his opinion on sundry items, and he happily gurgles in agreement. She hears someone step up behind her. She hears a whisper and feels a prick on her arm. She turns around. "What the … ."

Her head feels weird—everything around her seems to be spinning. She tries to grab the pram and get away. She sees the orange T-shirts of the store's staff at a distance and tries to call out to them. There is a loud crash. The last thing she sees is the 25 per cent-off sticker on a bottle of Comfort, and then the store lights on the ceiling.

The store manager rushes towards the commotion and finds Raina on the floor. When she doesn't respond, he quickly calls for an ambulance. He sees Raina's phone lying next to her and quickly finds Arjun's number and calls him. He speaks haltingly, explaining who he is. "There has been an accident. Raina is hurt. I saw the medical card on her phone. We are taking her to St. Stephen's emergency room."

By the time Arjun reaches the hospital, Raina has been rushed in for scans and tests. He can only see her from a distance. She looks like she is sleeping. He is relieved to see there isn't a scratch on her. *After all, how dangerous could a bump to the head be?*

Arjun finds the store manager, and when the latter tells him that Navin wasn't with Raina, he relaxes a bit. He assumes Raina left the baby with Mrs Sharma. As he waits for a doctor or nurse to inform him of his wife's condition, he debates calling Mrs Sharma. If he calls her from the hospital, he'll alarm her with little reason, and if he doesn't, she'll worry about Raina being late. Finally, he decides to call her. He explains that Raina has met with a slight accident.

"Is Navin okay?" Mrs Sharma asks.

"Mrs Sharma, isn't Navin with you?" Arjun asks. His heartbeat echoing in his ears, he just knows that things are about to go from bad to worse.

"Mrs Sharma, I'll call you back as soon as I know something. Please try not to worry," he says, even though he knows she will.

The store manager stands only a few feet from Arjun, but as he walks towards him, it feels like a long distance. Arjun looks at the nametag. "Are you sure Navin wasn't with Raina today, Ramesh?"

"He wasn't with her when I reached her," replies the store manager. "I didn't see her enter the store. We'd just opened, and I was at the back. Let me call the store's security officer and ask him to go through the CCTV tapes." He turns away to make the necessary calls.

Raina and Arjun have a small but strong circle of friends—the kind you could trust when push came to shove. Arjun makes his first call.

Back at the store, the security officer watches the video again to confirm that Raina had indeed entered the store with the baby in the pram. He is unable to get a clear view of her in the FMCG aisle, but he does have a shot of someone pushing the pram out of the store. He checks the timestamp and finds that minutes after Raina entered the store, someone left with the pram.

***

October 10, New Delhi

There is nothing ACP Karan Singh Shekhawat loves more than driving through the capital city in the middle of the night. It's been a particularly nasty day, but then most days are, in his line of work. He checks his phone and sees four missed calls from his younger brother. He calls back. Abhi picks up on the second ring.

"What's up, Abhi? Everything okay at home?" Karan tries to sound casual even though he is sure something is amiss. In the past, his brother has preferred to avoid calling him, even if he was in trouble. Karan is more than a decade older than Abhimanyu—Abhi to his friends and family—but one would think they were generations apart.

"When will you get home?" Abhi asks impatiently.

"I am on my way and will reach in a few minutes. Are you okay?"

"Yes. This can wait till you get home." Abhi hangs up abruptly.

Before turning onto the side road leading to his home, Karan stops to speak to the beat constable in the PCR van parked on the main road.

Once home, Karan pauses at the front door. He takes a deep breath, inhaling the faint smell of the night flowers in the garden. He wonders how long it will take to resolve whatever trouble is brewing inside. He enters and finds Abhi sprawled on the low divan, watching a movie on the television. The seating arrangement has remained untouched for years. It works well, and Karan sees no reason to change it.

Along with a degree in commerce, Abhi is also pursuing a course in ethical hacking. The latter is on Karan's behest. Karan considers himself technologically disadvantaged. Of course, he uses the computer for work, to check his mail, and to chat with friends, but that is the extent of his knowledge. However, he does understand his brother could get into trouble for hacking into virtual spaces he shouldn't even know exist.

Abhi stands up to fetch a glass of water for himself and one for Karan. He clears his throat as he gets ready to ask Karan a question. Karan sips the cool water as he walks into his bedroom and places the glass on a side table. Abhi follows him. Karan decides something is definitely wrong, or it is 'take care of your elder brother day', and no one bothered to inform him. He removes his service weapon from its holster and places it in the electronic safe installed in the wall behind the bedside table. He stretches his limbs and lets out a deep breath.

"What did you want to talk about?" Karan asks.

"Do you remember the party I was telling you about—the one for which I was really excited?" asks Abhi, rubbing his hands together, fairly certain his brother won't like where this conversation is headed.

"What about it?" Karan sits down and unlaces his boots. If this is about a college party, things aren't as serious as he'd thought.

"It seems the venue for the party has changed," Abhi blurts out.

"Do you want me to drive you there?" Karan asks.

"Not quite. They changed the venue to Goa."

Karan chuckles, "That is going to be a huge Uber fare for you to pay."

"Bhai!"

"Did you really think I was going to say, 'Have a good time in Goa, Abhi'? Have you spoken to Mom and Dad about this?" Karan asks as he stretches out on his bed, hoping Abhi will take the hint and leave.

"No, but if you speak to them, they may agree."

Karan laughs. "You are asking one police officer to convince another to send his college-going son to Goa for a party! Abhi, what's wrong with you?" he asks, shaking his head.

"I didn't think you'd agree, but it was worth a try."

Karan can't help but grin. There is no one more hopeful in the world than a boy just out of his teens. "Forget it, Abhi," he says. "Now, let me get some sleep."

He has been on his feet the whole day, but sleep doesn't come easily. Though the Urban Crimes division of Delhi Police, which he heads, is still in its infancy, it is already making a name for itself. There has been no progress in the case his team is working on. There aren't any leads for them to follow.

In the last few weeks, several cases from across the city, and later, from other states, have found their way to his table. They have nothing in common except for the fact that the victims lost time, and that their urine and sometimes blood samples revealed the presence of a powerful benzodiazepine drug, Rohypnol. The drug is a powerful sedative but has gained notoriety as a date rape drug. However, in these cases, its use is peculiar. Fortunately, there is no sign of sexual assault in any of the cases. In fact, there are no obvious signs of a crime, other than the fact that the victims were drugged.

According to the doctors the team consulted, the drug usually takes about half an hour to take effect, and its impact could last for hours. However, in the cases they are investigating, the victims had been unconscious for no more than an hour. They were found in their cars, airport lounges, and even their own offices, with no clue of what had happened in the last hour. What they did share was a bewildering sense of confusion, low blood pressure and pulse rate, and an inability to put together a coherent sentence. Of course, the police only knew of the victims who were hospitalized. Karan wonders how many had simply shrugged off the effects of the drug to a bout of sickness. It is an odd caseload, not the kidnapping, extortion, and murder they usually deal with.

The first recorded case was that of a high-ranking advertising executive who was found in her car at the Mumbai airport parking. By the time the parking attendant found her, she was severely dehydrated and needed hospitalization. The doctor on duty had sent her blood and urine samples for several tests. The presence of Rohypnol in her system raised a red flag. Since then, every few weeks, they had added another case to their list.

No apparent motive or purpose had been detected in the cases as yet. Bank accounts had been checked, but there were no unusual withdrawals. Other than the glaring fact that they'd been drugged, the victims didn't seem to be harmed—until now.

Karan had insisted that instead of treating all the cases as a bundle, they investigate each one and see where it takes them, but the higher-ups in the force disagreed. So, they'd spent weeks trying to find common links between the cases and victims. However, how could one identify commonalities until each case was investigated separately? Wallets, watches, and jewellery had not been taken, which made the whole thing quite odd.

There was something capricious and almost whimsical about the cases, but Karan was glad he'd kept his opinion to himself because the latest case had led to the kidnapping of a baby and put the mother in a coma. It also explains the pressure being put on him to solve the cases before the media gets wind of them. *One case ... just give us one case that gives us some clear direction.*

***

12:45 am, October 13, New Delhi

The nightclub is abuzz with the 'who's who' of Delhi, and there is still a long line of hopeful guests outside. Anya can't wait to get out of the club. It is after midnight, and they've just finished shooting their piece. She looks out of place, not just because of her blue jeans and white shirt but also the impatience in her stance and the determination to leave before the party really gets started.

She catches Rohan, her cameraperson's attention and gestures a 'let's get out of here'. Though he continues with his conversation, he acknowledges her with a nod. The cameras and lights are packed away. She decides to carry the last bag out herself and smiles as she carries the heavy load without much effort. Her strength-training routine is paying off.

She passes the doorman with his impressive moustache and thinks of all the stories he'd have to share. Perhaps her boss would be interested in the idea of an episode about the city's top hotels, with a focus on the doormen, but that story is for another day.

She unlocks the network's red and black van and carefully places the bag inside. They always try to find a parking space that is well lit and close to the entrance, since one can never be too careful in this city. She can see the security officers from where she stands and isn't particularly worried.

As she locks the van, she hears footsteps behind her. Someone bumps into her. She feels a prick on her arm. She thinks irritably that it is a mosquito and tries to swipe it away. She takes a few steps and stumbles. One of the girls prevents her from falling. She wants to thank her but is unable to say the words.

When she opens her eyes, her head is throbbing, and she sees a soft, warm light. It takes her a few moments to realize she is sitting against the door of her apartment. A sudden wave of nausea hits her, and she shivers. *Did she pass out cold? How did she get home?* Rohan and Samaira would've brought her home—that is the only logical answer. *Then, why am I sitting outside?*

Anya manages to open the front door, though it takes longer than usual. She feels dizzy and wonders if it is the lack of sleep that makes everything look so hazy. The clock over the telephone tells her it is 1:30 in the morning. It hasn't been long since she left the hotel.

The shrill sound of the telephone shatters the silence; it seems louder than usual. *Why is Rohan calling on the landline?*

"Where have you been?" Rohan shouts into her ear as soon as she picks up the receiver.

The throbbing now turns into a full-blown headache. "I am at home. How did I get here?"

There is silence on both sides. "What do you mean, how did you get there?" asks Rohan. "We've been looking for you for the last hour. Do you know how worried we've been?"

"I don't know how I got home," Anya replied. "The last thing I remember is going to the parking lot. Oh no! The van! Was the van stolen?" Her head is pounding. "I've to go!" She hangs up just in time to get to the toilet to throw up.

She cleans up and changes out of her clothes into a comfortable pair of navy track pants and a grey T-shirt, softened with years of washing. The doorbell rings. She rubs her forehead and thinks that even outside the club, it's turning out to be an eventful evening.

Samaira stands silently as she takes in Anya's pallor. She raises her hand to stop Rohan from asking any questions. She helps Anya to the sofa in the living room and asks Rohan to bring her some water. The dazed look in Anya's eyes is unnerving. As an ER doctor, Samaira is trained to remain calm and notice all the little things that help make a quick but accurate diagnosis.

"Are you okay?" she asks, reaching out to hold Anya's trembling hands, which feel cool and clammy.

"I think so." Anya clenches and unclenches her left hand. "I don't know how I got home, Samaira. The last thing I remember is walking to the parking lot to put away the equipment." She pauses and asks, "Rohan, do you think I could've come home by myself and then forgotten?"

He puts a glass of water in her hands, hating the strain in her voice. This wouldn't be the first time she had lost a few hours. However, the last time was over eight years ago.

"No, I don't think so." He paces up and down the length of the long room. He decides he is going to deal with this absurd situation logically, like he does with most things in his life. "You couldn't have taken the metro at this hour. If you took a cab, then the security guard at the gate… That's it! I'll go check his register." He speaks more to himself than to the two important women in his life.

Samaira and Anya sit in silence until the bell rings. Samaira lets Rohan in. His hair looks tousled, as if he has been pulling at it.

"The night guard has a record of a car entering the colony," Rohan says as he locks the door. "The driver gave him your address. The guard saw you, too. He says you were asleep. Also, since there were 'ladies *log*' with you, there was no reason to be alarmed."

"Ladies *log*?" Anya asks.

"Yes, that's what he says."

"Maybe you met some friends, and they dropped you home?" Samaira suggests.

Anya shakes her head. "You know I wouldn't have left without telling you. Besides...."

"Did you drink anything at the event?" Rohan asks.

"I had coffee," Anya replies.

Rohan raises his eyebrows.

"My throat was hacking... I mean ... aching, and the bartender was kind enough to make me ... a cup." Anya takes another sip of water and swallows it slowly. Her throat seems to throb in rhythm with her head now. Her thoughts and words are getting muddled.

"Did you leave your cup unattended at any time?" Samaira asks.

Anya shakes her head. "You think someone may have ... added something to it?"

"It's possible," Rohan mumbles worriedly.

"Where is your purse?" Samaira asks.

"It was with me when I woke up. I checked—my phone and wallet were in it. Sorry about the hissed... missed ... calls."

"I need to check you, Anya. Rohan, can you bring my bag from the van?"

Samaira checks Anya's pulse and blood pressure. It's a little low, but Samaira knows that is normal for Anya. Her eyes are a little dilated, too.

"There aren't any scratches or bruises on me—I checked. I don't think I was molested either. My head is killing me," Anya mutters. The entire evening seems like a hazy dream. She tries hard to remember how she reached home but draws a blank. *Who brought me home? I wouldn't have left without speaking to Rohan or Samaira. Maybe I passed out? None of this makes sense. Unless...*

"I want you to give Samaira a blood and urine sample. Is that fine with you?" Rohan asks Anya.

"Yes, but I want to know the results—no 'protecting me from the truth' nonsense, okay?" Anya says. She leaves the room for a few minutes before returning to settle on the sofa. Samaira quickly draws blood from Anya's arm.

Anya's throat feels raw and throbs, probably from all the vomiting, and her stomach performs awkward acrobatics. "I think

I'm done with this day. So, both of you go home, and I am going to bed," she says as she gets up.

"We are staying the night," Rohan says. He turns to Samaira and quickly adds, "I claim the hammock for myself."

"That's not fair. You slept on it the last time," Samaira says indignantly.

Anya smiles and leaves her friends to argue about their sleeping arrangements. It is good to know that some things don't change in the world, even if her part of it feels upended. Before she goes to bed, she sends off a burn note. It is brief and sparse on details because the whole thing makes no sense.

The burn note is read within minutes of its arrival in the inbox of an obscure email ID. Within the next 20 seconds, it is burnt, leaving no virtual or physical trail. It starts a chain of actions, which will efficiently bear effect across the city and country.

CHAPTER TWO

The next morning, when Anya walks into the reception area of The Channel, there is hardly anyone around. Like most producers, she works simultaneously on several projects. Getting in a few hours of work at the start of the day when the office is almost empty helps her find her balance.

She and her team had spent the last few weeks travelling, and it is good to be back in the office. The series they're working on is not for the traveller who runs a Google search for weekend getaways, but for the discerning audience who believes that travel is its own reward. The first part of the series has already been shot. Now, the raw footage needs to be edited and put together as a four-part episode.

The nomadic camp at Sangla in Himachal Pradesh is worlds away from Delhi. It took them three days of driving on bumpy, and sometimes non-existent, roads to reach the location. The Kinnaur and Spiti Valley road trip had been an adventure and a journey in self-discovery. A strange sense of calm had settled on the production team, which was unique for such a long trip.

The Channel office is a second home to her. Her own small office is one of many that enclose an open space with modular workstations. Comfortable futons and easy chairs are strategically placed for people who want a break, a power nap, or just want to think before returning to their computers. The glass door gives her a clear view of her colleagues. Far ahead is a wall of windows that lets in enough light during the day to make it feel like she is outdoors. At night, it offers an incredible view of the sparkling city.

Her table looks crowded. The computer barely finds space with the travel books, notebooks, and sheets of project schedules that surround it. When she first came to work at The Channel, she was bothered by people who sometimes stopped and stood behind her to read as she typed at the keyboard. Over time, she has realized it is a widely accepted practice and, most often, a way to show support and appreciation.

***

While Anya enjoys her quiet time, Karan offers thanks to whichever god answered the collective prayers of his team. They finally have a lead in their case, though the details are sparse. From what he can understand, the victim had been left at her doorstep. This could be the break in the pattern they'd been waiting for.

Antara and Sameer have left to speak to the doctor who submitted the blood sample. Kabir and Imran are taking a deep dive into Anya Aulakh's life before he meets her. An hour later, Kabir places a file on Karan's desk. He looks uneasy. Karan knows this is never a good sign and opens the file. He is not sure if his laugh surprises him or Kabir more. The file holds a single sheet of printed paper. Karan turns it to find the back blank.

"I could add a lot of information we found related to her, like the company she works for and the work she does."

"But not about her?"

"Not directly. Every time I ran an internet search, I found information about things related to her, like episodes she has produced and this B&B in which she lives. Maybe I should have added that here," Kabir says.

"But nothing specifically about her?"

"Not even a photograph," Imran adds as he walks into Karan's office.

"How is that possible? You keep telling me there is always a virtual trail. To top it all, she works for a media channel. Those people are all about image."

"We found all the relevant details, like her IDs, in the official background check. Everything checks out. However, there is nothing remotely personal—not even an old college photograph posted on social media."

"Check her IT records on the police net."

Kabir and Imran exchanged glances. "We tried that too but came up against a very strong and tall wall," Kabir said. "There is a DNI status tagged to her name."

"A DNI?" Karan asks. His officers nodded. A DNI, or 'Do Not Investigate', can only be sanctioned by a handful of people in the country. It is offered as protection in the rarest of cases. *What has Anya Aulakh done to deserve it?*

"Is there any police case against her or filed by her?"

Kabir shakes his head.

"Fine. We'll work with this for the time being," Karan says, gesturing at the lone printed sheet in the file. *Interesting.*

***

Anya spends most of the morning with the editor. They ruthlessly work their way through the footage until both are satisfied with the first edit. It is now time to work on the rough script she has written for the Spiti episode. After about two hours, she rereads the edited script, the words conjuring up the experiences she wants to share with the audience. She pens down some notes on prospective advertisers she'll contact in a day or so. The organic flow of the episode will interest them, and the marketing team will be very happy with her. She stands up to stretch her limbs and make herself a cup of tea.

Ten minutes later, she is back at her desk, typing away. She adjusts the format for the next shoot. In about a week, they will be off to the Sundarbans. She has to use her time wisely so that all the work is completed before they leave.

Her phone rings, and she picks it up. The receptionist informs her that she has a visitor in conference room one. *Who is visiting her?*

As she walks towards the room, she realizes it is later than she'd thought. She looks towards the conference room and sees a man standing by the door. He isn't wearing the official khaki uniform, yet there is something about his stance that leaves no doubt in her mind. She can't decide if it is confidence he exudes or arrogance. Either way, he is the kind of person she steers clear of.

He watches her as she watches him, and Anya finds that a little unnerving. She enters the room.

He extends his hand and says, "Good afternoon, Ma'am. ACP Karan Singh Shekhawat, Urban Crimes."

Her pulse races as she shakes his hand. *What on earth is Urban Crimes?* "Anya Aulakh, Senior Producer. How may I help you?" she asks as she gestures for Karan to take a seat.

Karan expects Anya to be shocked or at least surprised to find a police officer at her workplace, but she seems calm. He waits for her to take a seat. Anya watches him for a moment or two, then sits down.

After a short pause, Anya repeats her words, "How may I help you?"

"That is usually my line," Karan says with a smile. "Your blood and urine samples were sent to a city lab."

Anya sits still, silently. *Have they found drugs in her blood? Is that why the police decided to pay her a visit?*

Karan believes silence is often the strongest tool an investigator has when he is looking for answers. People hate silence. Their need to break it usually offers a new direction in a case, and sometimes even a confession. This is one of the rare occasions when he's failed to elicit a reaction. She raises her eyebrows but only nods.

"May I ask why they were sent for testing?" Karan asks.

"Usually, it is to see if there is an infection of any sort in the body, isn't it?" she asks in return.

"Yes, but this was different." Once again, he waits for silence to work its magic.

Anya looks at Karan. His hair is cut short—not quite a crew cut but almost there. The slightest touch of salt and pepper at the temples gives him an air of experience and authority. She notices the sharp cheekbones and the cleft in his chin.

"Since I haven't got a call from the pathology lab and since a police officer is here to give me the test result, I assume there is something in my blood that shouldn't have been there?"

Karan finds her reaction interesting. In most cases, the victims were confused and upset. They demanded answers and vented their fears and frustration. However, for some reason, the woman before him did not want to discuss why her blood was sent for testing. That, in itself, is as interesting as the fact that she was drugged.

"Your samples had been submitted to one of the hospital labs, and we were notified about the results."

"Why?"

"Why?" he repeats.

"Yes. Why are the police interested in the results?" she asks.

"Your blood showed the presence of a drug. It is a powerful tranquilizer and muscle relaxant," he says in a low voice. As he'd expected, the information got her attention.

"You are saying someone gave me a sedative?" she asks, her eyebrows drawing closer.

"Sort of." He continues speaking, "Will you please tell me why your blood was sent for testing, and in what state you were found?"

Anya is quiet for a while as she tries to make sense of what the officer has just told her. She hadn't felt dizzy or uncomfortable during the shoot yesterday. *How was she drugged? Was it the coffee? Why would the police be interested in her blood* test? *Unless this had happened before.*

"This has happened before, hasn't it? Is that why you're here?" Anya asks.

"We can do this interview at my office if that's what you prefer. I thought you may be more comfortable in a more familiar setting," Karan says, looking around the room.

She is fairly certain he can't arrest her or interrogate her simply because a sedative was found in her blood, but she wants to be done with this interview as soon as possible, so she describes the whole evening to Karan. To give the devil his due, he listens patiently without interruption. Afterwards, he asks her several questions about any alcohol she may have consumed or any recreational drugs that she may use. After the third time he questions her about what she ate and drank, she begins to get testy.

"I've told you I did not drink last night. By the way, if you have my blood test report, it should give you the answers you want. This conversation is over. I'd like to leave now, otherwise let me connect you with the company lawyer." Anya walks towards the door.

"I'm not saying that you were drunk or that you use drugs—those are standard questions I need to ask you. What I'm saying is that someone gave you a concentrated dose of this particular drug," he says. "It would've left you unconscious in minutes, maybe even seconds, and the effect would've lasted anywhere between an hour to about ninety minutes." She turns around, and the expression on her face changes. He knows he has her attention now.

Anya walks back to the table, and somehow, the room feels smaller than it did a few minutes ago.

"I'll ask you again, why was your blood sent for testing?"

"I've already explained the circumstances of last evening," replies Anya. "My friend, who is a doctor, suggested that my blood sample be sent for testing."

Karan gestures for her to sit. "Please sit down." It is a request, but the steel in his voice is apparent. "Why didn't you go to a hospital?"

"Other than the glaringly obvious fact that I didn't remember how I returned home, there wasn't much that was wrong with me. I was nauseous, my stomach was acting up, and I had a splitting headache. That was about it."

"Why do you think this happened?" Karan asks, as his eyes follow every movement she makes. By now, Anya is pressing her hands together. She shakes her head.

"I don't know, but since Delhi Police is interested in me, it is obvious you know more about this situation than I do." She continues to meet his stare, waiting for him to speak.

Karan watches her for a few seconds before coming to a decision. He says, "For the last few months, there has been an increase in incidents where the victim has been unable to remember the crime or the criminal. The crimes are… strange. People have woken up in their cars, lost time, missed flights, and lost important documents—essentially, things that don't make sense to them. The only thing these victims have in common is the sedative that was found in their bodies. So, hospitals and labs across the country have been notified to report cases where it is found in blood and urine tests. Most of these cases were initially not reported to the police, quite simply because the victims couldn't remember anything."

"Like me," Anya adds.

"Well, yes and no. Yes, because you were given the drug, and no, because in each of the other cases, the victims were left in a car at an airport lounge or some other public spot. This is the first time someone was moved." Karan waits for the message to sink in.

"What does that mean?"

"Why did they risk driving you home? If all they wanted was to get into your house, they could've done that without abducting you. Were you carrying anything special last night, like papers, cash, or videos—anything that would be valuable to someone? Maybe a friend gave you something to hold onto?"

"No, my purse was on me when I woke up. Nothing seems to be missing from it."

"Is there anything missing from your home?"

Anya shakes her head. "Besides, I was left outside. They couldn't get in."

"Why couldn't they get in?" Karan wonders aloud. If someone had taken the time to drug Anya and bring her home, why leave her at the doorstep? He finds the whole visual creepy and disconcerting. *Maybe they were interrupted by someone. It would have been safer to leave her there than to be caught.*

"Are you married?" he asks, even though he knows she isn't.

"No."

"Boyfriend?"

She shakes her head.

"Maybe there is someone who has been trying to get your attention, but you've ignored them?"

"There is no one like that."

"There has to be someone who has taken an interest in you." He corrects himself, "No, not interested…this seems more of an obsession."

"I don't know why someone would do this," she says.

"You need to think about it," Karan says briskly, "because you are the only person who was drugged and brought home."

"I don't know…"

"Do you understand what you have escaped, Ms Aulakh?" Karan asks. "This person could have got you into your own home and had you at his mercy."

Anya gulps hard. "It wasn't just one person. Rohan spoke to the guard who was at the gate. He said I came back with a group of people that included women, too."

Karan stares long and hard at Anya. "A group?"

She nods.

"And you are telling me this now? It would've been nice if you'd started with that," Karan says irritably.

Anya stares at him, and before she knows it, she blurts out, "Is it just me, or are you always such a jackass?" Her eyes widen as she clasps a hand over her mouth, but it is too late. She closes her eyes for a few moments. So much for remaining calm.

Karan's eyes glimmer with humour. "I think it is fair to say this is a unique situation for me."

A smile barely tugs at her lips. "What now?"

"I'd like to see your house," he says. "This makes no sense. If they wanted to simply get into your house, they could have taken your keys or broken the lock."

Anya stares at him for a while and then shakes her head slowly. "It's not so easy to get into my house. It has a ... good security system."

Why did she hesitate on that word?

"I'd still like to take a look around."

"Okay," she replies unenthusiastically.

Karan hands her his card.

"My numbers are on the back," says Karan. "If there is anything else you want to add, or if something seems amiss—however small—feel free to call me."

Anya nods, stands up, and hands him her card.

"I'll speak to the night guard at your place. I want to see the neighbourhood around the time you came home yesterday."

"It was 1:30 in the morning."

Karan nods.

Anya stares at him. *This officer wants to visit me in the middle of the night? Well, at least he is committed to finding out what is going on.*

They shake hands. Karan is glad to feel the firm grip of her hand. He holds her hand for a few moments more than what he'd otherwise consider appropriate and watches her reaction. To her credit, she doesn't squirm or pull her hand away. Instead, she watches him. As he gauges her response, he smiles, realizing that she is doing the same. With a nod, he leaves the room.

He waits by his car. His partner, Antara, is supposed to meet him. He looks around and finds her standing at the other end of the parking lot. Karan walks across to see what has caught her attention. It is a jeep. They look at it in silence for a while. Then they walk around it, noticing the modifications made to it.

"It's geared up for some serious off-roading," Antara comments, and he agrees, taking note of the wide tyres and the snorkel. He peers in through a window and sees the roll cage and the three-point harness belt. *Who on earth owns the jeep? Indiana Jones?*

They continue surveying the vehicle before Karan begrudgingly leads them back to his car. Antara fills him in on her interviews with Rohan and Samaira. Their stories match that of Anya. Karan tells Antara about his interview with Anya.

"I'm going to speak to the night guard. Imran and Kabir will visit the nightclub from which she disappeared. I need you to find out who sanctioned the DNI and if we can get around it," he says, ignoring the blank stare she gives him. He knows the whole idea of the DNI is to protect Anya. It is so that people, even the police, can't look into her background. However, if Anya is the key to unravelling these cases, he'll do whatever it takes.

He notices someone walking towards the jeep. Since it is parked under the street light, he can see who it is. *No way!*

Antara follows his line of sight. "Interesting," she says.

"Maybe she is borrowing it," Karan suggests.

Antara rolls her eyes. "I'm going to pretend you did *not* just say that, Sir."

"She doesn't seem like someone who would go off-roading. She seems like someone who needs to be in control of things."

Anya doesn't look towards them, but Karan watches as her eyes sweep the area twice before she unlocks the vehicle and gets in.

"Does she know we're watching her?" Antara asks.

"There is no harm in our ensuring she gets home safely," Karan mumbles as he turns the key and follows the jeep. He sighs as he sees the flood of slow-moving traffic they have just joined. At least, there is no chance they will lose sight of her. Besides, the jeep stands apart from the other vehicles on the road. About thirty minutes into the drive, Karan's patience starts wearing off. The cacophony of horns can drive even the sanest of minds up the wall.

Antara's phone rings. She answers it and goes silent as she turns to look at Karan.

"What is it?" Karan asks, giving her a sidelong glance. He turns his attention back to the road. He hasn't seen the jeep for a while.

"Sir, I'd sent an update to the team with a picture of Anya and the jeep."

Karan nods for her to continue.

"Sameer is on his way to Gurgaon. He thinks he just saw someone who looks like Anya. He also described the vehicle."

Karan frowns at her words.

"He sent a picture to avoid any confusion." Antara turns her phone towards him. The picture is grainy, but there is no doubt that it's Anya.

"What the ... !" Karan exclaims, as he begins to keep an eye out for the next turn that would set them off in the opposite direction. "She knew we were following her. I can't believe she gave us the slip."

Antara decides discretion is indeed the better part of valour in this situation. She calls Sameer back and asks him to follow Anya.

"Tell *him* not to lose her," Karan says.

Antara knows that Karan takes pride in knowing the roads and side streets of the city like the back of his hand. In the years that she has worked with him, this is the first time someone has managed to give them the slip. An hour later, they park on the service road in front of the NSG headquarters. Sameer gets into the backseat. "We got here about forty-five minutes ago. She signed in at the gate. It looks like the guards know her."

Karan nods. "Sameer, we'll take it from here."

"Jai Hind, Sir." Sameer salutes and leaves.

Things are getting curiouser and curiouser. Karan forces himself to relax. Waiting is a crucial part of their job. Half an hour later, they watch Anya's jeep leave the gates. He follows at a safe distance. The traffic is still heavy, but at least they're moving at a good speed. Eventually, Anya turns into the AWWA complex opposite the Taj Palace Hotel, parks under a street light, and walks into a café.

Karan watches her settle down at a table by the glass wall and speak to the server. She gestures towards the parking lot. Ten minutes later, the server walks up to Karan's car window. "Sir, your order is ready," he says and leaves.

"I like her," Antara says with a wide grin and exits the vehicle. Karan shakes his head and follows.

Anya waves towards them. She stands up, shakes hands with Antara, and introduces herself. Before Karan can get a word in, three large cups of coffee and thick sandwiches are brought to the table. "If you are a vegetarian, we can change the sandwiches," Anya offers genially.

Karan stares at her openly. She has showered and changed into blue jeans and a grey T-shirt. *Has she been visiting a boyfriend?* The thought irks him, more than a little.

"Thank you. This is fine," Antara replies. "How are you?" she asks.

"I am just a little confused with yesterday's events, but otherwise alright."

"I'm glad to hear that. I'm sure Karan Sir explained things to you; we still don't know what this is all about. So, I cannot emphasize how important it is for you to be careful."

Anya nods and takes a bite of her smoked chicken sandwich.

"That's an interesting vehicle you have," Antara says.

"Do you like it?" Anya smiles broadly. "You are welcome anytime you want to come off-roading."

"Why a jeep?" asks Antara. "In fact, why this particular jeep?"

"I wanted something I could drive anywhere I wanted to," replies Anya. "I bought it cheap at a military vehicle auction. The modifications cost me more than the vehicle itself."

"But well worth the money," Karan adds.

"I think so," Anya replies.

"Why did you give us the slip from the office?" he asks abruptly.

Anya frowns. "The slip? I noticed you somewhere close to Dhaula Kuan. I thought you may want me to stop. It made sense to stop somewhere we could eat."

Karan stares at her for a while.

Antara watches them reach an uncomfortable impasse. She is unsure of what is going on, but if they're all going to work closely on this case, the sooner they get along, the better. Once they finish their food, Anya and Karan argue over the bill.

"I decided to stop here. So, this time I'm going to take care of the bill," Anya says.

"This time," Karan repeats.

They walk Anya to her car. When she unlocks it, Karan holds the door open for her and closes it safely behind her. He gestures for her to roll down her window and bends a little, so that he is inches from her face. "I'll see you later," he says in a low voice.

She nods, unsure of whether it's a promise or a threat.

"Did you smell it?" Karan asks Antara as they watch Anya drive away.

"Her perfume?" Antara asks in surprise.

"No, the smell of gunpowder. She'd taken a shower, but her hair still had that unmistakable smell."

"Are you sure?"

"Quite sure. I think she was using the firing range at the NSG."

"Why would they let her do that?" asks Antara. "How many civilians do we know who fire at the NSG range?"

Karan shakes his head. "I don't know any."

CHAPTER THREE

It is well past midnight when Karan finds himself outside The Tri, taking in the details of the red brick building, built in the quintessential Laurie Baker style. After speaking to the guards on duty at the gate, he walks through the colony.

Anya is something of an entrepreneur. She works at The Channel and owns The Tri. The high-end B&B, though a bit odd, seems to work well with people who want some quality time away from the maddening crowds, without leaving the city. The Tri can't be booked online, and there is a stringent background check before a booking is accepted. Karan can see why. Anya lives in the basement of the building, and the manager lives on the ground floor. He handles the day-to-day running of the B&B with his girlfriend. A stay at The Tri doesn't come cheap.

Why would someone pay so much money to stay in an obscure B&B in the city?

There is no information about Anya's family, and beyond the last decade, they haven't found anything about her. Karan wonders if she has some skeletons in her cupboard that may be ready to come out. On the surface, there doesn't seem to be anything out of the ordinary about the building, but a closer inspection reveals that the gardens are well-maintained, and the path that runs through them is lined with stones that glow in the dark. Somehow, the sound of the breeze is louder in this part of the colony. *Perhaps it is because the building is at a corner.*

Anya's basement apartment is barely visible from the entrance gate. The steps that go down to her doorstep are smartly recessed away. One could easily walk past the gardenia bushes and miss her apartment. When he reaches her doorstep, the light over the door comes on. *Smart.* He rings the doorbell. *Who on earth would choose to live in the basement?* There is no sound from inside the house; he hasn't even heard the sound of the bell. He wonders if it is working and if Anya has fallen asleep. Then the door opens. He takes in her damp hair, grey T-shirt, and black track pants. Her hair is rolled into a bun, and there is a chopstick sticking out of it.

For a split second, he is distracted by his reflection in the large mirror behind her. When his eyes return to hers, he finds her watching him.

"May I come in? It's awkward to have this conversation on your doorstep."

She watches him for a few moments before nodding and letting him in. He places his helmet on the wall table under the mirror, next to a blue glass bowl full of keychains. He walks past her, taking in the clean smell of a late-night shower. Her living room is a bit of a surprise. It looks neat and tidy, almost untouched. The neutral colour of the walls and upholstery is balanced by the jewel-toned cushions and the large blue carpet.

As she closes the door behind him, the folksy tune of a fiddle fills the room, as does the story of the Galway Girl. Anya picks up the remote from the console table and turns down the volume.

The computer is on, and in front of it is a corkboard with papers and photographs pinned to it, but most of it is cast in shadows. Next to the table, hanging from adjacent walls, is a hammock. *Not the most conventional space.* He sees some movement in the shadows through the sloping glass window behind the hammock. It is dark, but he can see tall trees swaying in the breeze. At the far end of the property, he thinks he sees a waterfall amidst a bamboo grove.

"Do you want to see it up close?" Anya asks. Instead of walking towards the front door, she walks past him to a floor-to-ceiling bookshelf. The shelf moves out of place and opens noiselessly. She leads him outside and walks over to sit on the wooden bench at the edge of the garden.

The stone path Karan had seen from the gate weaves its way through the small garden that is edged with tall bamboo trees. He walks slowly, taking in details. He enjoys the thrill of walking into something unexpected. The path curves gently, adding to the illusion that the garden is bigger than it is. A candle burns somewhere amidst the trees, giving out just enough light to add to the mystique.

The gentle gurgling of water grows louder as he approaches the end of the property. He stands in front of the waterfall for a while before he turns around to look at the building. He can now imagine the view the guests are treated to. He walks back. This time, he pays attention to the thick grass and the small pond to his left. "What is this place?" he asks as he sits down next to her. There is a faint glow on her nape. *Odd place to put a design on a T-shirt.*

"I'm sure you've done your research on me, and you know I own it. I found this plot. By some weird surveying error, it is triangular. I got a bank loan, bought it, paid my loan off, and now own it, fair and square."

After a few minutes of silence, Anya leans back, trying to forget the happenings of the night before and wishing she could transport herself to a simpler time—when her worries revolved around making a home out of a piece of land that had lain empty and unused for several decades.

Anya tells Karan about the first time she'd heard about the plot from an architect who'd joked about it at the DDA office. She was there to collect information about an upcoming luxury condominium project. When she spoke to a few realtors, she was told the land was not worth investing in, as, according to Vaastu, a triangular piece of land was inauspicious. The more people tried to dissuade her, the fonder Anya became of her pet project. Buying the land turned out to be the least of her problems. The city was more than happy to get rid of the property at a ridiculously low price.

"I had a business plan, but for it to work, I not only needed the finest minds but also needed them to charge me very little money," she adds. "Then we were in Ahmedabad for work, and at a pizza joint, I met a group of NID students. The pizza was awful, but I came back to Delhi with a host of ideas to work on. My next stop was at IIT Delhi and then the SPA because the creative genius of the idea needed the right technology to make it possible. At that time, I was living in a *barsati* close to the university."

She skips telling him how her assignments at The Channel, freelance writing, and the construction of her home led to a year of five-hour nights. It also meant that while it was being constructed, she'd lived on *dal-chawal* for months on end. Fortunately for her, meals at The Channel were catered, and so she became the hardest-working employee the company had ever seen. Late nights and sleepovers at the office were common.

The Tri is the culmination of the efforts of some of the brightest young minds in the country. They had considered and incorporated traditional, contemporary, and experimental techniques and materials. *It was a chance for them to prove themselves*, she reminisces.

In the months after her father died, she'd often wished she could crawl into a burrow and hibernate. Sometimes, Anya wonders if that instinct had led to the design and structure of her apartment. Of course, the final-year students from the School of Architecture and Environmental Design couldn't wait to try light tubes and daylighting to bring natural light into the basement space. Her home looks and feels bigger and airier than it is. The fact that her electricity bills stay low is an added bonus. Of course, ever so often, one of the institutions that helped build The Tri continues to send students or visiting faculty her way, but that is hardly a downside for the kind of home they built together, she tells Karan.

"That's quite a story," he says when she finishes. "But where does the DNI come in?"

"What's a DNI?" she asks.

Karan explains with exaggerated patience, but she just shakes her head. "There must be something wrong with your system," she says.

"The DNI is placed when you are, for whatever reason, valuable to someone in the department," Karan adds.

"Well, there is no one in my life who'd do that. The Tri gets guests of all kinds—politicians, celebrities, even cops. Maybe one of them requested it. This is the first time I'm hearing about it."

Karan decides to let it go for now. "Do you want to take a walk around the colony?"

"Now?"

He nods. "Maybe you'll notice something I didn't, like a CCTV or a neighbour who comes home late."

"Okay," she says, leading them back into the house. Karan takes in as many details as he can. *Neat, sparse, and purposeful. The front and side doors seem particularly heavy.*

He peppers her with questions, and she answers them. He realizes it is not as if she holds back answers, but more that she carefully weighs her words before saying them.

"You don't like the police much, do you? Or is it just me?"

"I am a single woman who lives alone in Delhi, and the cops in this city don't have the best reputation. So, yes, I like to keep my distance."

Karan sweeps a hand through his hair. "With great power comes great responsibility."

She narrows her eyes. "Did you just quote Spiderman?"

"More like I quoted Stan Lee. Or perhaps the French National Convention."

She watches him for a few moments before nodding and opening the door. "Touché!"

He picks up the helmet he'd left on the table. "What kind of holster do you prefer?" he asks.

She freezes. There it is—the brief, split second of indecision when the brain has to decide on whether to invent a lie or tell the truth. It isn't the eyes or the hands that first give away a lie but the sudden stillness of the body, as if all energy is directed to answering the question.

"Holster?"

"Yes, holster. You were at the firing range today, weren't you? So, I assume you have a weapon of your own; otherwise, what is the use of keeping your skills sharp?"

She nods. "How did you know?"

"When we met earlier in the evening, your hair had the slightest smell of gunpowder."

She replies, "It's a Walther PPK, and I have a licence. I prefer an ankle holster."

"May I see it? It has nothing to do with the case. I haven't seen a PPK in a while."

"Wait here," she says as she goes into her bedroom. She returns with the gun, still in its holster, and puts it on the table.

Karan removes the weapon from its holster. Weighing about half a kilogram, the pistol is lighter than most. It looks well cared for.

"This Neoprene holster is a good choice for a concealed weapon," he says. "Does it belong to you or your father?"

"The licence is in my name, but it belonged to him."

"Do you know why it is called the PPK?" he asks but doesn't wait for her to reply. "It was called the Polizei Pistole Kriminal—the 'policeman's pistol'. 'Kriminal' in German means detective. It's, of course, James Bond's choice of concealed weapon, with good reason." He places the gun back into its holster. "Why did you give us the slip on the road today?"

Anya huffs, "I didn't give you the slip. I was driving home, and on the way, I called a friend to check if the firing range was available. It was, so I changed direction."

Karan tsks. "There is no way to turn off that main road."

"True, but you can enter the residential colony adjacent to the road. It is big enough to warrant several entry and exit gates, so I just drove through."

Karan considers her point. "Hmm... Smart. However, the road mostly houses gated communities."

"Everyone knows you only need to know a name and the right address. It's not like the guards accompany you to the doorstep." Anya brings out a road map of that section of the city on her phone and shows him three residential enclaves she prefers to use.

"Sneaky and smart," Karan says. "Can I see your phone?"

Anya gives him a grim look. "In this day and age, asking someone for their phone is like asking to sift through their life."

He smiles and gestures for her to hand it over. "Unlock it."

She complies, just to see where all this is going. He dials his number, and the first few bars of 'Dancing in the Dark' play from inside his jacket. He waits a few more seconds before returning the phone.

"My number is now Speed Dial 1," he says. "If you have an issue or something feels off, just call. The second number on speed dial is that of the officer who will join you tomorrow as your intern." He hands her his card.

"I already have it."

"Memorize the number. I'll wait for you to memorize it," he adds.

Anya huffs but takes the card.

"Like I said, if anything feels off, call me. We'll not meet unless something comes up. In case you're being watched, we don't want to tip them off."

"Okay."

"I know your friends stayed over last night. Will they come over tonight?"

"No, I'll be fine," she says. "This house is extremely secure."

Karan doesn't look convinced. "It's not the house I'm worried about," he says as he rubs his face with his hand. He hasn't told her she'd been drugged with Rohypnol. Or that last night, Rohan and Samaira had noticed two wet patches on the driveway. This morning, his officers had found traces of blood there. It seemed like someone had tried to wash it away in a hurry. A closer examination of the garden had revealed more blood in the flowerbeds, and they'd found a small piece of flesh in one of the larger pots.

"Could you give me the clothes you were wearing last night? The crime scene team may find something. You haven't washed them, have you?"

"No. I'll get them for you," she says and leaves the room.

Karan looks around. He is tempted to walk over to her computer table. That part of the room holds more details about her than any other. Strangely, the battered boxing bag in the corner looks right at home.

Anya walks back and hands him a cloth bag with her clothes.

"I'll make sure the clothes are returned to you after they've been through them."

"It's okay, I don't want them back."

"Is your T-shirt one of those glow-in-the-dark ones?" he asks, gesturing at it.

Anya looks down at her T-shirt. "No, why?"

"Then, maybe the tag glows in the dark?"

She pulls at the small tag. "It doesn't look like it."

"Can you turn off the lights for a minute?" he asks.

She switches off the lights in the room. He stands near the mirror by the front door. "Stand with your back to the mirror, and turn slightly."

"What the..." Anya murmurs. He is right. There is a glow on the nape of her neck, but it's not her T-shirt. *It's her!* "What is that?" she asks, shocked.

"Do you mind if I check?"

"I'd mind if you didn't check!"

Karan gently moves the T-shirt away from the nape of her neck. A simple spiral design glows on her skin. "It seems like a temporary tattoo," he says.

"So, last night...."

"Hmmm..." Karan replies. *Were all the victims marked with a temporary tattoo? Or was something different about Anya's case?*

"Were the others also marked like this?" she asks.

"Not that we know of, but it's worth looking into."

She hesitantly touches the tattoo.

"Is your skin irritated there?"

"No, but I am. The idea of someone putting it when I was unconscious is a bit...disconcerting."

"Disconcerting?"

She nods.

"Are you always this careful with your words?"

"Usually."

"So, you calling me a jackass today was unusual."

"Quite unusual."

"May I take a picture of the tattoo? You've bathed twice, if not thrice, since last night, so I assume there is no trace evidence to collect, but we'll still give it a go." *Someone had their hands on her when she was unconscious.* The thought makes him want to punch something, or someone, hard.

He takes out his phone, chooses the camera app, alters the settings, and takes a few pictures of the tattoo. Next, he takes out a thin plastic envelope from his wallet, removes the sterile film inside, and places it against the tattoo. After a few moments, he gently removes it and places it back in the envelope. He hands Anya his phone. "Does the design mean anything to you?"

Anya looks at it and shakes her head. "Do you think it is symbolic? Does it mean my life is spiralling out of control?"

"Don't read too much into it," he says. "We'll find out what is going on. In the meantime, I need you to be cautious and continue as if the incident from last night didn't leave a mark on you." He winces. "You know what I mean."

"Can I take this off?" she asks, rubbing her nape.

"Anya, it's harmless. If you still want to remove it, use a damp towel. Just don't rub it until the skin is sore."

She looks unconvinced but stops rubbing the back of her neck.

"That's all then," Karan says as he picks up his helmet.

It feels oddly like she is being dismissed. "Excelsior!" she says.

He looks at her for a few seconds before nodding. "Upwards and onwards!" he adds with a quick grin.

CHAPTER FOUR

Her doorbell rings a little before six in the morning. Anya peeks at the security monitor discreetly hidden behind a shelf. *Hadn't Karan told her he wouldn't be in touch unless something came up?* She opens the door, a mix of curiosity and worry bubbling inside her. "Is something wrong?" she asks him bluntly.

"Good morning to you, too," he replies.

She lets out a breath of air. "Good morning! I thought we weren't going to meet unless something came up. Since you are dressed like an internet technician, I guess this is important." She moves aside to let him in and then notices the tall, slim man standing a few steps behind him.

"Anya, this is Kabir," says Karan. "He'll be assigned as an intern to you. I've spoken to Mr Shah. It's all sorted out with HR."

Anya reaches out to shake the officer's extended hand before remembering the sweaty boxing wraps on her hands. Instead, she just waves.

"Can we sit?" Karan asks politely.

"Sure." Anya gestures towards the sofa and sits on the adjacent chair.

Karan begins to explain about the traces of blood they'd found on the driveway and the blood and flesh they'd uncovered in the bushes. "We sent the flesh for analysis; it seems to be part of a human ear."

Anya's eyes widen. "Do you think I bit someone's ear off?"

"No, no. There was no blood on you, your clothes, or your doorstep. The part of the ear we found seems to have been bitten off by a bird. The bite mark suggests that it was probably a predatory bird. I sent Dr Samaira the analysis, and she said you may be able to add something to it."

"A bird bit off the ear?" Anya repeats.

"Well, a part of the ear. Whoever it belongs to would've needed medical attention, so we are contacting hospitals and clinics in the area."

"He is back," Anya mutters and stands up.

Who is back?

"Stand near the door for a while, and when I wave to you, you can come over," she says and opens the side door. The officers look at each other before following her.

"Do you think the shock was too much for her, Sir?" Kabir asks, wondering if the woman had lost her mind.

"Let's just wait and see," replies Karan.

Anya sits down on the wooden bench, and a few seconds later, a large bird—a falcon—swoops in and perches on the table next to her. The falcon lies flat on the wooden surface, almost looking docile.

"Hey there! When did you come back?" she asks the bird as she gently strokes its feathers. She continues speaking for a few more minutes before she waves the officers over. In a low voice, she explains that about two years ago, when the falcon was young, he had crashed into her garden while trying to catch his prey and had hurt his wing.

"I didn't really do anything other than give him a place to recover," she says. "He keeps coming back, off and on. I haven't seen him in months. His mate lives in one of those trees." She points it out to them. "Apparently, they mate for life. She doesn't come down here like he does. Do you want to touch him? His feathers are soft."

"No, I like my ears the way they are," Karan mumbles. "Do you think he'd attack if he thought you were in danger?"

"I don't know. It's not like he is a guard dog. Besides, he has never done anything like this before," she says as she continues to pet the bird. "You think he could have?"

Karan watches the bird bask in the attention she gives him. "Yes. This could be one of the reasons they left you outside your door."

"One of the reasons?"

"Dr Samaira asked the lab for a more detailed blood report. Last week, you started on an antibiotic for a throat infection. She thinks it may've weakened the impact of the anaesthetic. Maybe you struggled with them, and the falcon decided to protect you."

"Did you hear that? The cops think you are a hero." She removes her hand. The bird sits up and looks her in the eye before flying off.

As they walk back into the house, they are suddenly showered with tiny leaves.

"What the…" Kabir says as he looks up.

"He likes to do that," Anya says.

"I think I'm going to enjoy working with you, Ma'am," Kabir says.

"Anya," she corrects him, and he responds with a thumbs-up sign as they leave.

"Saved by a bird," Karan says. "That's definitely a first," he adds as he starts the bike. "Keep a close eye on her, Kabir. Something about this case seems off."

"They've never moved anyone before; they have just left people where they drugged them, Sir," Kabir says. "Well, not that we know of, but then, Raina and Navin's case doesn't fit the profile."

Kabir has zeroed in on the most troubling detail of Anya's case. *Why bring her home?* The more Karan considers it, the darker the answers become.

"Is she being watched after she leaves work?" Kabir asks.

"Hmm," Karan replies. "But we can't get too close. Make sure you do a deep dive at her workplace—check colleagues and clients. If you need an extra set of hands, speak with Abhi. We'll catch up at the end of the day."

***

The Urban Crimes team is about to start eating dinner at Karan's home when Kabir walks in, puts down his laptop bag on a chair, removes his shoes, and slides onto the diwan. "I'm officially taking back everything I said about the private sector," he mumbles.

"And here I was jealous of him working at The Channel," says Antara. "They even cater meals for employees, Sir."

"I ensure all of you are fed too," Karan counters and then gestures at Abhi with his chin. Abhi cajoles Kabir to wash up and join them for dinner.

It is after Kabir has finished his first *kathi* roll that he finally speaks. "Anya was not very happy when her boss told her she'd mostly be staying in the office for the next few days. He asked her to think of it as a creative challenge, but she didn't like it. So," he continues, "she goes back to what she calls her drawing board. She looks at some sheets of paper that were pinned to the board on her wall. Then she makes a dozen calls while Rohan and I enjoy an amazing breakfast. Did you know the company feeds its staff?"

"I'm feeding you too," Karan interrupts, and Kabir grins.

"Anyway, she comes out of her tiny cabin with a smile on her face, and Rohan asks me if I've ever experienced the lull before a storm. I say, yes, many times. You know how we have a quiet period, and then there is barely any time to come up for air. Apparently, she's had a 'Living Solo' web series in mind for a while. It is essentially ultra-short videos for people who've just left their parents' nest and are ready to fly solo. We made videos of everything, from buying insurance to fixing a leaking sink and figuring out your way around an MCB to creating an emergency fund. At the end of the day, Rohan told me she had sponsors lined up for each episode even before we started shooting. Every episode ends with practical advice from an expert. Karan Sir, she has a cyber expert from the CBI for the internet security video."

"Anything suspicious at her workplace?"

"I had my ear to the ground and heard a bit of gossip. She rose up the ranks in the company fairly quickly but chooses to stay away from the limelight. She has no enemies—more like a few annoyed colleagues who think things come easily to her. From what I saw, it's because she does a lot of research and has a knack for gauging what viewers want to see. She promised to let me have a few hours with her computer tomorrow."

"Where are we on the other cases?" Karan asks Antara. He'd spent most of the day at the Police Commissioner's (PC) office. Since finding connections between the victims was a dead end, he wanted to take a different approach to the cases, but some of his seniors disagreed.

"Nothing, Sir. We went through three more cases, detail by detail, but nothing stood out. Also, I think most of these people just feel they were fortunate not to get into too much trouble and don't really want to revisit the whole incident."

"The *raat gayi, baat gayi* syndrome," Imran mutters. All eyes turn to him, and he swallows hard. "Sir, when surgeons do a bowel resection, they run the guts, as in they check every part of the intestine until they're sure there is no reason for concern. We've run the guts of all these cases. These are ordinary people; nothing really stands out. There is nothing we found that connects them."

Karan nods and turns to Sameer, who smiles. Every time Imran explains a case from the point of view of another profession, the team knows he is dating someone in the field. His euphemisms give his colleagues a window into his life.

"So, surgeon, huh? Anyone we know?" Sameer asks, and the rest join in.

The banter continues for a while until it loses steam.

"We're going to take a new approach now," says Karan. "Maybe this is something we should've done to begin with instead of clubbing all the cases together. We take each case individually and do a deep dive. Choose a case or a person you think is likely to open up to you. There is an undercurrent here that we can't see, but its presence is felt sporadically and across the cases. Let's find out what it is."

"If people's lives weren't at stake, there is an odd, playful feel to the whole thing," Antara says. She quickly corrects herself. "I don't mean there is anything playful about drugging people, but like most of the victims in the cases said, they got away virtually unharmed."

"Unfortunately, that is not true in Raina's case," Sameer says. "It's been more than 10 days since Navin was taken. How does one look for such a small baby? Showing his picture around won't really help. Raina is still in a coma. That case is not like the others."

"I agree, Sameer," Antara says. "I think Mrs Naugiyal's case also stands out, not because of the actual drugging but the fallout from the whole episode. She may have lost a large international contract because she missed her flight and the following meeting. I spoke with her today. There seems to be trouble brewing in Almora. Someone tried to sell a plot of land and faked her signature. The sale didn't go through, but the situation with her in-laws is tense."

"For the next few days, we only focus on these two cases, and let us see where it takes us," Karan says. He then proceeds to fill them in on his visit to Anya's home the night before, and then again with Kabir.

"Saved by a bird? I can officially say I've never heard that before," Antara says with an impish smile. "But then, before yesterday, I'd not seen anyone give Karan Sir the slip in Delhi traffic."

"I told you how she did it. It was an extremely smart way to get out of a jam," Karan concedes, but the team won't let it go.

After the rest of the team has gone home, Karan sits in his study, going through the two cases. Mrs Naugiyal's husband, an air force officer, had died in a crash. The loss had left the family devastated. She'd eventually picked up the pieces of her life and gone on to create a unique brand, Forest Garden.

The business focuses on products made with ingredients sourced from forest gardens across the country. The company created a forest garden in Almora and set up a manufacturing unit. The venture is both popular and profitable and generates employment for the villagers. On the surface, she didn't seem to have any enemies, and her brand is unique enough to stand apart from her closest competition. Nevertheless, where there is money, there is motive. The new detail of someone trying to sell a piece of land added another element to the mix. Karan still can't figure out if it was her professional or personal life that prompted someone to drug her.

Raina's case was troubling because Navin was taken, and her condition still didn't show any improvement. While her husband, Arjun, seems genuinely upset, there is something that lurks beneath the man's obvious pain. Karan would have to gain his confidence. *I can't help someone who doesn't want to be helped.*

This is the worst part of his job. Years of experience can help him identify a disaster in the making, but most often, people don't want to listen to good old-fashioned advice. A long time ago, he'd accepted that there is only so much he can do. However, with a child missing, he is willing to pull out all the charm and wit in his arsenal.

***

Anya's phone beeps a message as she plots the storyline for the videos they will shoot tomorrow. She glances at her phone distractedly. Her fingers still hover over the keyboard, but they stop typing.

ACP Shekhawat: *All quiet on the western front?*

Intrigued, she picks up her phone.

Anya: *Let's hope it doesn't come to that.*

ACP Shekhawat: *So, you've read the book or watched the movie.*

Sorry, that was not the best starting line then.

Let me try again. All okay?

Anya: *All okay. I'm surprised you've read the book.*

ACP Shekhawat: *You don't have a very high opinion of police officers. Or is it just me?*

Anya: *Neither. It's not the kind of book people usually pick.*

ACP Shekhawat: *Growing up, my mother had 'a book a week' rule. At least one book had to be read. If it was more than half an inch thick, she gave us two weeks.*

One summer, I only read historical romance, just to irritate her.

Anya: *What did she say?*

ACP Shekhawat: *She told me it'd improve my powers of description.*

BTW, Kabir says he has newfound respect for the media. He had no idea they worked so hard.

Anya: *He is a very convincing intern.*

Fair warning, if he continues to work like he did today, he's quite likely to be offered a job.

ACP Shekhawat: *I am sure he'll be glad to know he has an alternate profession.*

Anya: *Is there anything I can help with?*

ACP Shekhawat: *Tomorrow, he'll need to check your computer and phone. He may need some time with your devices.*

Anya: *Okay.*

ACP Shekhawat: *Goodnight.*

Anya: *Goodnight.*

At a little past one in the morning, Anya's landline rings. Groggy with sleep, she manages to somehow pick up the phone.

There is a strange hush at the other end. "What do you want?" someone asks in a low voice.

He repeats the question before she mumbles, "Wrong number," and falls back into deep sleep.

CHAPTER FIVE

"Can you read out the basic details of the case again, Antara?" Karan asks as he drives them to Mrs Naugiyal's store.

"Two months ago, Mrs Naugiyal was at the airport, T3, to take a flight to Paris. She had a Park N Fly booking. The parking attendant found her unconscious in the car and notified the security team. Initially, they thought she was fast asleep, but when they couldn't wake her up, the emergency medical team was called in." Antara reads some more before continuing. "She began to regain consciousness in the ambulance. Unfortunately, that was not the end of her troubles. She suffered a respiratory attack and had to be hospitalized for several days. When the police finally spoke to her, she didn't remember much—just arriving at the parking lot, someone helping her, and then waking up in the ambulance. Her bags were untouched. Nothing seemed to be missing."

"Go back to the parking attendant's statement. He said the engine was off, and the windows were rolled up. It would have been quite warm inside the car. So, she probably didn't sit voluntarily in her car like that. In her first statement, she mentions someone helping her."

"But not in the later ones. Do you think she is hiding something?"

Karan shakes his head. "No, I think in her first statement, she mentioned what she vaguely remembered. Later, she probably dropped that detail because she wasn't sure. I found a similar trend with some of the other victims I spoke to. I think she parked the vehicle and got out to take her bags from the boot. She was drugged, 'helped' back into the car, and then they walked away."

"They didn't take any money or valuables," Antara says. "They just drugged her and left her there. That is strange. We went through the CCTV videos from the parking lot. The parking attendants have a specific route they follow. There is a clear ten-minute period when someone could have approached Mrs Naugiyal without being seen. The cameras are basically placed to keep track of cars coming in and out of the parking area. Only three cars left a few minutes before the attendant found her. However, that would mean they knew that she was going to the Park N Fly level."

"We need to find out who was privy to that information. They were probably there before she arrived. Let's request for the Park N Fly bookings for that day," Karan adds as he parks close to the store.

Antara wanders through Forest Garden. It's the kind of place you can't leave without buying something. Beeswax candles share space with smooth rocks with Buddhist prayers carved on them. She walks past shelves full of organic soaps and oils. The large stained-glass window at the entrance is painted with a bright and cheery sun, and as the morning light filters through it, the floor seems to come alive in vivid colours.

"Would you like a cup of tea?" Mrs Naugiyal offers. She looks calm and graceful in a blue paisley saree. Her short, straight hair frames her face perfectly.

"That'd be really nice," Antara replies, and they follow her out to the small patio in front of the store that has been converted into an outdoor café.

The three of them sit quietly, drinking *tulsi* green tea.

"How are you?" Karan asks. Even though she looks composed, she is clearly tired.

After a few moments of silence, Mrs Naugiyal says, "The children and I are fine. Things seem to go quite well for a while, and then something or the other comes up. My in-laws think I should move back to Almora."

"Is that what you want?" Karan asks.

She shakes her head. "The kids have a good routine here; they go to good schools. They've finally settled down. The Forest Garden has come into its own. It's pretty much taking care of itself."

"How did you come up with the idea of creating the Forest Garden?" Karan asks.

"It was really Ravi's, my husband's idea. We bought a few acres of barren, overgrazed land outside the village. It had to be landscaped to increase the amount of rainwater collected on the land. How much do you know about permaculture?" she asks the officers.

"Not much really," Karan replies with a smile.

"Well, without going into full-on lecture mode, as the kids call it, permanent agriculture works with nature and its rhythms. There are multiple layers of plantings that are used to create a sustainable ecosystem. There are fruit trees of varying heights. Then you have the shrubs and bushes that thrive in the dappled light. There is, of course, ground cover and vegetables that grow underground. However, before all this can be designed and laid out, you've to increase the available ground and surface water, which is where the landscaping comes in. The rainwater and water from streams that come into the forest are encouraged to meander through it. It creates pockets of stored water. It took about two rainy seasons for the water table in the area to rise, and soon, the villages around us noticed a difference. Now, there are four forest gardens in the area. We source a fair amount of our products from them. It's a win-win situation."

"Were there any apparent problems when you started the forest garden—perhaps when you bought the land?"

"The whole area was barren and unused for a long time. The people we bought the parcels of land from were rather glad to get rid of them."

"Now that the land is giving back, perhaps they've changed their mind," Antara suggests.

Mrs Naugiyal shakes her head. "Almost everyone we bought the land from is employed in the food forest. We also try to give back as much as we can to the community. Our forest garden and the others that came up after are the best thing that has happened to the area in a long time. For me, the kids, and Ravi's parents, it's what keeps us going."

She sees the sceptical expression on their faces. "Why don't you visit Almora and get a feel of the place? I don't know why I was drugged or who tried to sell the land, but I don't think it has anything to do with the forest. In fact, whoever tried to sell the land was rather foolish. Ravi set up the forest garden in such a way that the land could never be sold, in part or in whole. Faking the papers and my signature is useless."

"Yes, I think we'll plan a visit to your village soon," Karan says. "Do you remember anything else about the incident at the airport?"

She shakes her head. "It's just a blank. After I got out of the hospital, everything seemed to pass in a daze. The kids were so upset. I tried to get back to our usual routine, and maybe, I just let it get buried with the humdrum of daily life."

"You were going to France for a business meeting, weren't you? Did your company lose money or a contract because you missed it?"

"Yes, I was going to meet a few companies that were interested in our products. Fortunately, they understood the circumstances. Forest Garden didn't really lose out on the contract in which we were interested. We had already sent gift hampers of our products, and the businesses seem happy with our products. God willing, we'll soon be exclusively supplying to a chain of spas in the country."

"Are there any competitors you're worried about?"

"To be honest, we are a niche business. Not only do we sell organic products, but the fact that we source ingredients from forests seems to be our biggest appeal. Besides, the target audience is large enough to accommodate us and our competitors."

"Do you use the Park N Fly often?" Karan asks.

"Yes, it is convenient. I don't fly very often, but when I do, the Park N Fly just makes sense. Do you think that has anything to do with this whole situation?"

"We're just looking into all the details," Karan says. "So, is this something that people around you know about?"

"I guess so. At least the staff and my friends and family know I don't like waiting for a cab."

Karan nods. "We'll be in touch. I'll need to speak with your accountant and see the land deeds for the forest garden. Please email me the details at your earliest. Also, we'll give you a call before we leave for Almora."

"I'll ensure that the manager at the forest is ready for you. In fact, you should stay at our house there. It is small but comfortable, and you'll get a better feel of the place. Though I'm not sure if my in-laws will be willing to talk to you."

"That's fine. If anything comes to mind, please give us a call," Antara adds.

On the drive back to the office, Antara checks in with the others.

"No hospitals and clinics around Anya's place admitted anyone with an ear injury that night or the next day."

"Ask Dr Samaira to have a look at the piece of the ear we found. She works in the ER. She should be able to tell us the kind of damage the bite could have caused. Also, ask Kabir to get some of the staff from the local police station to speak to chemist shops in the area that are open 24 hours. They may have some CCTV recording to help us."

"That may take a while." Antara sighs.

"Yes, sometimes it does, and sometimes we hit the jackpot with the first interview."

***

"May I speak with you?" Kabir asks Anya as he closes the door to the small editing room.

Anya glances at Rohan and nods. "We can speak here—far more privacy than anywhere else in the office."

Kabir remains quiet.

"I trust him completely," she says as she looks at Rohan.

"I didn't mean ..." Kabir starts to reply.

"It's fine," says Rohan. "I can get us some coffee while you both talk."

"No, Rohan. She is right. It is better you hear this too," Kabir says as he sits down on the narrow wooden bench placed against the back wall. "I went through your computer. It seems all clear—no bugs or viruses. Do you use a programme that lets you access the computer from home?"

"I beg your pardon?"

"Some computer programmes allow you to access your computer even when you are away from your workplace. Do you use a programme like PCAnywhere or GoToMyPC?"

"No. If I've something to work on from home, I use my laptop. Why do you ask?"

"Five days ago, someone used your system well past midnight. They bypassed the password setting."

Anya looks at Rohan. "That makes no sense. My work isn't secretive. Besides, my office computer only has files for my projects."

"I know. I went through your files; it's just work stuff. Since someone did think it was worthwhile to get into your computer, I expected to find some spyware, but I didn't," Kabir says.

"Isn't that a good thing?"

Kabir shrugs his shoulders. "I don't know. Either whoever was snooping found what they were looking for or..."

"Or?"

"Or they were just checking. The largest folder on your computer is for a photo and sound library. It was one of the files that had been opened. Do you have any idea why?"

Anya and Rohan exchange another confused look.

"The library? That's strange. It's just a bank of visuals and sounds that Rohan and I collect."

"Do you use it for your work?"

"Yes and no. We own the library, and sometimes, The Channel uses our visual and sound collection. You can access the library online, too. Rohan, can you show him?" Anya asks.

Rohan opens a website on the large screen in front of them. "We've a wide range of images and sounds and a steady clientele that uses them. They are mostly used for advertisements. It is not something someone would break into her computer for—you can access the library online. Of course, if you wish to use a photograph or sound, you'd have to pay a fee."

"May I?" Kabir asks, and Rohan gets up so Kabir can sit in front of the computer. It takes him a few minutes to navigate through the library and understand what it offers. The pictures are mostly of inanimate objects.

"I assume the people in these pictures agreed to be photographed?" Kabir asks.

"Absolutely. We have waivers and details of every person we have in the library. However, most of our photographs are of locations and objects."

"What if you don't have permission to photograph someone?"

"That's simple," Rohan says. "We make sure bystanders are out of focus."

"Late last night, you received a phone call on your landline. I was wondering what that was about," says Kabir.

"Last night?" Anya asks him. "I went to bed at about eleven and woke up a little before six. I didn't speak to anyone on the landline."

Kabir wonders if she is lying. "Anya, the call was received by you. It lasted for less than a minute."

"Anya is a sound sleeper, Kabir. It's quite possible she could've picked up the phone in her sleep and not realized," Rohan adds.

Both men look at her. Anya tries to concentrate and then closes her eyes. "I thought it was a weird dream as it made no sense."

"What did the caller want?"

"I don't know. This morning when I woke up, I had this vague recollection that the phone had been ringing."

"I ask this because the call was made from the junction box close to your home."

"What? You mean like when the lineman checks to see if the telephone line is working properly?"

"Yes."

"Someone was calling her in the middle of the night and was probably on her street?" Rohan asks as Kabir gets up from the chair to return to the bench behind them.

"Yes. I checked and found that you received a similar call the night before you were drugged," says Kabir.

Anya shakes her head. "I don't remember getting a call yesterday or on that day. In fact, almost no one calls me on the landline. The only reason I have it is because it is complementary to the internet connection. I can count the people who have that number on one hand."

"Don't get stressed out about this," says Kabir. "In your own time, if you can relax and try to recollect what the caller said to you, it may help. Don't force yourself to remember. That will just frustrate you and make it worse."

"You think this person has called me at least twice, and it could be why I was drugged." Anya runs a hand through her hair. "I just woke up feeling uneasy—the way you wake up from a dream you don't remember, but it just makes you feel uneasy."

"I am serious, Anya. Just relax. It'll come to you at the right time," Kabir assures her.

"What if it doesn't?"

"We'll figure it out. In the meantime, I want to install a recorder on the landline," he adds.

She nods but doesn't look entirely convinced.

"I don't remember answering either of the phone calls," she says. "That's crazy, Rohan."

"Not really, Anya," Rohan says. "It happens to us all at some point or another. Let's get back to this." He gestures at the video on the large screen. "The buzz around the office is that Mr Shah may want to create a full-length web series based on your short videos. What do you think?"

"It should work if it's funny enough to connect with our target audience." She glances at Kabir. "What were the five things that you had trouble with when you moved into your own place?"

"Getting a maid to clean the place, shopping for groceries, the sink that would leak even after three plumbers fixed it, insurance, and wondering why there was so much dust on every surface," Kabir replies promptly.

Anya thinks about it. "That's really good. Can you create a survey on the website that asks the same questions? Let's see what other issues we could consider." She has a general idea of the storyline that could work for the web series. Now, it would be great if she could just slip in the core issues without making it sound like an advertisement or a sermon.

***

By late afternoon, most of the Urban Crimes team was back in their offices. Antara and Imran divided the CCTV recording between them. It was going to be a slow, tedious process but a necessary one.

"The car could've had a first-aid kit," Antara remarks without taking her eyes off the large screen in front of her.

"Wouldn't the person have been bleeding a lot for a first-aid kit to do the job?"

"Dr Samaira said, considering the part that was bitten off was mostly cartilage, the bleeding wouldn't have been as much as a wound in the fleshier portion. She thinks it may not have needed stitches. Of course, ideally, the bitten-off part should have been stitched back on because the cartilage will not grow back on its own."

"So, there is someone out there whose ear is missing a small part. At least, when we see him, he'll be easy to identify," Imran adds with a grin, his eyes still trained on the screen.

"Let's find him first, Imran," Antara replies.

Three hours later, they've still not found the person they are looking for. Antara pulls out the lists that the local police station has sent them. The constable had asked each of the 24-hour chemist stores in a five-kilometre radius to pen down sales made that night.

She peruses the list until she finds what she is looking for. There were three medical stores that sold antiseptic solution, sterilized cotton, and medical gauze that night. She circles the details and hands the sheet to Imran.

"Have a look at these three stores again. I'm going to go check in with Karan Sir."

Their offices are on the second floor of an old colonial building in Civil Lines. Karan's office shares a side door with the team that is always left open. Antara pauses momentarily at the doorway. Karan waves her in and gestures for her to take a seat next to Sameer.

"I had a chat with Arjun," Sameer says. "He can't think of anyone who would want to hurt Raina or Navin. We are missing something. Between the two of them, Arjun and Raina earn pretty well. I would've expected a couple like them to live in a better apartment. Their place is basically a *barsati*. Usually, students or people who are just starting their careers live in a place like that. The couple gets along well with the landlady, so perhaps that is why they choose to live there." Sameer hesitates and adds, "Arjun was quite irritated when he realized we were looking into their background. I think he is going to complain to you."

"Good. People are likely to give away more details when they are irritated or angry than when they're guarded."

"Do you think he is worried about what we might find in their past?"

"It could be so. Maybe he is more scared of his past than this whole situation."

"Scared enough to not help with the investigation? How much worse can it get?" Sameer asks sceptically.

"Start a new file on Navin's case, Sameer. Start from scratch—the way you would deal with a kidnapping."

"Do you think the local station missed something?"

"No, I think they were more focused on the presence of Rohypnol in Raina's body. Instead of handling this as just one of the Rohypnol cases, we investigate it as an abduction. When we are done, let the chips fall where they may. Antara and I have opened a file for Mrs Naugiyal's case. You and Imran investigate Navin's case. Like I said, we treat them as new cases and work them from the ground up. As always, we look at all the angles—work, family, and friends," Karan says.

Sameer nods in agreement.

"Sir, Kabir called a while back," Antara says and fills him in on the details.

"She doesn't remember picking up these calls," Karan repeats.

"It could happen. After a long day at work, most of us are groggy at that hour," Antara says.

"Hmmm," Karan replies, lost in thought. *Calling from the junction box is old school but just as effective.*

"She received a call the day before she was drugged. Maybe she is hiding something?" Sameer suggests.

"Maybe," Karan replies. "Kabir said there was no spyware on her computer. I find that strange. What better way to snoop into her affairs? Antara, ask Kabir to send me the link to this photo library,"

Karan adds. "Let's get back to work. I'm going to start with Mrs Naugiyal's financial statements."

Antara smiles. "Better you than me, Sir. I don't know how you manage to go through it all without getting your brain warped."

He didn't have to tell them that the numbers gave him a crucial angle to every case, every story. They never lied, and when someone manipulated them, it was as clear as day.

"Any word on the DNI?" he asks Antara.

"I'm working on it. It turns out it was requested by the Ministry of Women and Child Welfare," she says and sees the concern on his face. "I thought that was odd, too. I'm surprised you haven't already got a call about my looking into the DNI."

Karan shakes his head. "It is a pretty smart way of going about it and gives them time to figure out our interest in her. We should see some response in the next few days."

After spending several hours with the Forest Garden's financial records, Karan is ready to call it a day. His phone chimes a message.

Anya: *I can't understand why I don't remember taking those calls.*

Karan: *It's okay, don't worry about it.*

Anya: *It's weird that this person was so close to my place.*

Karan: *Don't overthink it. Call me if anything feels odd.*

Anya: *Like everything right now?*

Karan: *We'll figure this out. How many businesses do you have?*

Anya: *?*

Karan: *The photo library has some great reviews.*

Anya: *Yes, it's fun and brings in some money.*

Karan: *I'm sure it does.*

Anya: *You think this is maybe about money?*

Karan: *Probably not, but it makes sense to have a clear picture of what we are dealing with.*

Anya: *I do have my fingers in a few more things, all on the up and up.*

Karan: *Why don't you have a look at your financial statements and see if anything seems off?*

Anya: *I'm mostly a silent partner—emphasis on silent—but I could go through the account statements. I'm going to get back to work now.*

Karan: *Take care.*

Anya: *You too.*

***

Anya is fast asleep when the telephone on the bedside table rings loudly. It is after the twelfth ring that she finally reaches for the receiver, her mind still groggy with sleep.

"Hello," she says, forcing herself to pay attention.

"Anya," Samaira's voice comes through the line. There are a few seconds of static. "Come quickly. Rohan was in an accident." With a click, the call ends.

What the—

CHAPTER SIX

Samaira's cell phone number is out of the coverage area. Cursing all the network providers of the world, Anya jumps out of bed, pulls on the first pair of boots she finds on the shoe shelf, grabs a jacket, and picks up the messenger bag she left on the side table, all the while redialling Samaira's number. Now, it's busy.

"Calm down, Anya," she repeats the familiar mantra. "You won't be of help if you start panicking."

She walks down the lane to where her jeep is parked, gets in, and forces herself to take the time to ensure the three-point harness is secured. As she starts the engine, she hits Speed Dial one. Karan picks up on the second ring. She blurts out the details and tells him she is headed to Samaira and Rohan's place.

"Anya, just wait there, I'll send a PCR van to their place. I'm coming over."

"Karan, I'm already in the car, just getting out of the colony."

"Take the main road. I'll be right behind you," he says as he gets dressed and shakes Kabir and Abhi awake.

"I'm coming with you, Sir," Kabir says, pulling on his shoes. "Abhi, wake up Sameer Sir and Antara Ma'am."

Karan is already driving out of the gate, and Kabir rushes to catch up with him.

"It could be nothing," he mumbles under his breath.

"Let's hope you are right," Karan says as he puts his foot down on the pedal. The roads are well lit and look desolate—not even a street dog is in sight. He takes a side lane to get to the main road. A vehicle approaches from a distance. "I think that's her."

Before he can say another word, he hears the growl of a powerful engine come alive. There is a black SUV that is speeding onto the road. Its headlights are off. At the intersection, just as Anya's jeep drives past, the SUV crashes into its rear left side. Karan almost stops breathing as he watches the vehicle flip, land on its roof, and then flip back. To his surprise, the SUV does not speed off, but the driver gets off and starts walking towards the jeep. The tyre iron in the silhouette of the man's hand has Karan hitting the lights and siren.

By the time they reach the jeep, they can only see the rear lights of the speeding SUV in the distance.

"I'll report it in," Kabir says as they get out of their vehicle.

Karan approaches Anya's jeep. Fortunately, the tell-tale smell of spilt petrol is missing. He stands next to the driver's side and gently knocks on the window. Anya grips the steering wheel tightly in her hands as she turns to look at him. Karan gestures for her to lower the glass. She nods and complies.

Karan takes in her pallor and searches her for any obvious signs of injury. "Are you alright?"

She nods slightly. The harness and the bucket seat have done their job and held her securely through the crash.

"How many fingers am I holding up?" he asks.

She looks at him closely, a faint smile on her face, "You aren't holding up any fingers."

Karan smiles back. "Any aches and pains? Let's make sure it's okay for you to move."

She nods and gently stretches her neck from side to side. "My neck feels a little strained, but I don't think I banged my head. Was I driving too fast? I thought I was only doing about 50 km/hr. I didn't even see the other car in my rear-view mirror." She watches his face for a few moments and then remembers why she is out so late. "Rohan?"

"Kabir is checking," Karan replies. "I'm glad you called, but I wish you'd waited for me to get there or to confirm the situation."

Anya nods and then winces at the effort. "It was stupid," she agrees.

Karan's eyes narrow in suspicion; he isn't used to people agreeing with him so readily. He looks away from her and up and down the road. "There isn't much traffic right now, but we should get your jeep off the road."

"Yes, I think I've had enough off-roading for today," she says as she tries to remove the harness.

"Let me do that," Karan says, noting her trembling hands. He opens the door and unlocks the harness. "I need you to check again for aches and pains before getting off."

Anya takes a few seconds. "My neck is a bit strained, but that is to be expected." She picks her bag from the passenger seat, slips it over her shoulder, and gets off. Her movements are slow and deliberate. She stops by the open door and turns to touch the harness, pats the steering wheel indulgently and sighs. If it had been any other vehicle, the whole situation might have been quite different.

"Thank God for off-roading," she mumbles in a low voice. "I should park to the side," she says as an afterthought, finally noticing the awkward position the jeep sits in—in the middle of the road.

"I'll deal with that. Right now, I need you to come with me," Karan says as he gestures towards his vehicle. She lays her hand on the hood of the jeep and stands there for a few seconds before turning to look at Karan.

"This was a dumb thing for me to do," Anya says as they slowly walk towards his car. "I should have realized it."

"Your concern for your friends was a priority. Did the call come on the landline or the mobile?"

"Landline."

Karan isn't sure if she is in a daze or in deep thought, but before he can ask, she requests, "There is a pouch taped to the underside of the driver's seat. Can you get it, please?" She rubs her forehead and adds, "At the back, under the seat, there is a gym bag. Please get that, too."

"Sure, no problem."

Kabir walks towards them. "Rohan and Samaira are fine. They're obviously worried about you," he tells Anya and then turns to Karan. "They want to come see her."

"Ask Antara or Sameer to pick them up and bring them to my place. I'm going to take Anya to Ajay's clinic," he says.

Kabir nods. Tonight's incident changes things. They can't afford to use her as bait. In fact, her case, like Raina and Baby Navin's, seems more personal and reeks of desperation.

Two hours later, when Karan finally goes to bed, his mind is full of the strange details of the evening. It had been a long day, and he should've fallen asleep as soon as his head touched the pillow, but a while later, when Abhi stood at the door, Karan sensed his presence before his brother had an opportunity to call out.

"What's wrong?" Karan asks, and Abhi gives out a muffled yelp.

"That's just creepy, Bhai. You scared me," he says, walking in.

"You are the one creeping around the house, and I'm scaring you?"

"Your friend can't sleep," Abhi says in a low voice.

"And?"

"She is also mumbling. I heard a little of what happened. Maybe she isn't taking the whole thing as well as you thought she was."

"Why are you waking me up and not Antara? Maybe she'd like to speak to another woman."

"Maybe," Abhi replies, "but I also noticed how you look at her."

Karan considers a series of choice words for his younger brother, but he settles. "Cheeky fellow! Go to bed." He pulls on track pants over his boxer shorts and makes his way to the guest room.

The curtains at the door are drawn, but Karan can see Anya sitting on the bed with her knees against her chest, her arms tightly wrapped around her. She is as close to the foetal position as one can get sitting up. She rocks herself very gently. Karan is certain she isn't aware of her body's involuntary movement to soothe itself. Her fists clench and unclench sporadically.

She is about to have a full-blown panic attack.

Karan knocks on the door, keeping his eyes on Anya. She looks towards the door and nods. He enters the room. The lights in the room are turned off, but Antara has left the lamp in the corner on. Karan sits on the small settee next to the bed.

"This is stupid, isn't it? I came out without a scratch. You and I know things could've been far worse," Anya says. "Still, I can't seem to stop it." Her eyes look wild. "I'm *not* a victim. I refuse to be one."

Karan's eyes widen, before he forces himself to relax. Her vehement need not to be seen as a victim suggests this is not her first time.

"I'm so tired, Karan, of all the hiding and surviving. I don't think I can do this anymore. One way or the other, I'm done," she says forcefully.

"Do you want to talk about it?"

He is glad to see her roll her eyes.

"You've researched me. You know you can trust me," he adds. He smiles at the surprise on her face. "I've seen some of your office files; you research virtually anything and everything. Why would I be any different?"

Her fists clench and unclench as she comes to a decision.

Karan decides to help her along. "You're hiding from someone—that is apparent." He watches her face for cues. "You live in a basement apartment. That is as close to burrowing into the ground as one can really get. You have no social media presence—not a single selfie in cyberspace. You're definitely hiding. As long as you haven't killed anyone or intentionally damaged lives, anything you say will stay between us."

Anya looks at Karan for a long time. He knows if she is going to talk, he can't crowd her.

"I didn't kill anyone. I'm just trying to survive."

"From what I see, you're doing more than just surviving. Professionally, you are at the top of your game; you play by your own rules. Personally, you have friends who are closer than most families are, and I haven't even begun to explore the many pies you have your fingers in."

Karan says the last bit with a smile. Anya's breathing is still erratic. She looks lost and dazed before she begins to speak.

"My father was an army aviation officer. He died in a crash just after I finished college. I was supposed to go to Mumbai for my Masters, but everything changed with his death. My mother decided to move us all to Hisar since my parents hail from there. This was the first time we were going there in years. There was some problem between my father and his brothers.

"We'd been there only a day before I was told I was adopted. This was strange because I resemble my father. It turned out my parents had trouble getting pregnant, and they adopted me. My brother was born a few years later. My father never differentiated between us. My mother was a different story, but I'd always assumed it was a gender thing." Anya shakes her head. "Anyway, it was late in the evening, and my brother came into the room we were sharing and told me I had to leave. My uncles were planning to marry me off to someone they owed money to. I didn't believe it, so we eavesdropped on their conversation with my mother. I had no choice but to leave. I changed my clothes, wore my sneakers, picked up my still unpacked backpack, took a servant's cycle, and left."

Karan knows she is skipping vital bits but doesn't interrupt her.

"I knew there was an hourly bus to Delhi," Anya continues. "Fifteen minutes after I left the house, I boarded it. At that time, I was interning at The Channel. I don't know why I went to the office that night instead of the *barsati* I shared with a friend."

Karan considers her words before he asks a question, more to slow down the rush of her narrative than anything else. "You knew there was an hourly bus to Delhi?"

For the first time since he entered the room, Anya relaxes. Her hands are no longer fisted. "My father made us play these games. Initially, it was a way to keep us busy and out of trouble, but later, it just became a way of life. Whenever we walked into someone's living room, we learnt to take in all the details, like the décor and those giveaway signs of the life people lived that made one family different from another. When we'd leave, he'd quiz us about them."

"Quiz you?"

"Most *fauji*-s collect curios from places they've been to. Then there are mementoes with insignias that are great clues to where an officer was posted—stuff like that. My father would insist we always know the entry and exits from our neighbourhood and the cantonment. I think it was his way of helping us settle down. It worked out well for us. Before we arrived at a new city, my brother, Vikram, and I had a fair idea about the place. Settling in was easier."

"I guess this story does not end there."

Anya lets out a deep breath. "No. I continued working at The Channel as an intern and then got a job with them. I was in touch with Vikram, so I was sure going back was never an option. My mother thought I was headed to Mumbai for my post-graduation. They checked there. I kept my head down and continued working and living. Rohan and Mr Shah are the only ones who know what happened that night."

She pauses, then continues. "About two years later, we were in Chandigarh on a shoot. I didn't want to go pub hopping with the rest of the crew and was on my way back to the hotel when a cop stopped me. He said there was an arrest warrant out for me. Like an idiot, I didn't resist or even question the fact that he was alone and without a constable or another officer." She shakes her head. "I made the mistake of getting into the vehicle. He didn't take me to the police station; instead, he stopped at a deserted corner and started questioning me about some papers he thought I had. I had no idea what he was talking about, but I guess he didn't like my answers. He thought burning me with a cigarette might help persuade me. You can guess how that situation went. Anyway, a little later, another police van drove up and a constable got out. I took a chance and ran. By the time I reached the hotel, my feet were all cut up. After that, I knew I had to vanish, at least in name."

His eyes flicker to her feet. The light from the lamp in the corner is just enough to illuminate the tell-tale circular scars. He struggles to rein in the anger he feels surge within him.

"You changed your name?"

She nods. "Mr Shah had some contacts that could make me disappear on paper. In the real world, it was up to me to keep as low a profile as I could."

"That is why you have no social media presence."

"That, and I stay out of any kind of spotlight and just live my life. I have trouble trusting people. After the Chandigarh incident, Vikram told me an old school friend of mine had seen me in town and called our mother. Apparently, she'd told family friends and relatives I'd run away from home and that she was desperately looking for me."

"What about the papers the officer was questioning you about?"

"Vikram had no idea, but he knew everyone in the house was desperately looking for them, too."

"Why would they think you have these papers when you left home with virtually nothing?"

"That is exactly what I thought. I just want to be left alone. You don't think today's incident has anything to do with it, do you?"

Karan mulls over the whole situation before he answers, "No, it doesn't seem like it. Do you remember what the late-night caller said to you?"

She shakes her head. "It's all a blur. Like I told Kabir, I thought it was an odd dream." She sees the concern on his face. "It is important, isn't it?"

"It'll come to you in good time," he reassures her. "I know you've not had the best experience with the police, but you *have* to take a chance on someone, sometime in life. The Urban Crimes team will get to the bottom of this situation. For now, we need you out of sight. The official story is going to be that you're admitted to a hospital. I'd like you to stay here until we figure out what is going on."

"I want to help. I'm done with playing the victim."

Karan nods. *It is interesting the way she begins to panic and then reins in those wild horses just before they get loose.* "For now, all you need to do is sleep."

Anya nods but still sits in the same position.

"May I hug you?" Karan asks cautiously.

"Why?"

"You look like you could use a hug. Besides, I need a hug after the day I've had." He stands up and keeps his arms by his sides.

She watches him for a while before getting off the bed. "You are an odd one."

"Usually, people call me 'weird'. 'Odd' is a nice change."

"I'm odd, too," Anya adds absentmindedly as she puts her arms around him and holds on. She isn't sure if it is the simple act of comfort that breaks through her defences or the day, or maybe it's just her, but she finds tears rolling down her cheeks. She gives up trying to control them and sobs silently.

Karan holds on as her body shakes violently with the sorrow it purges. When she stops, he pulls out a handkerchief from his pocket and hands it to her. Anya takes it and wipes her face.

"Go ahead, blow your nose," he says.

She pulls a face. "I'm going to go wash my face."

When she returns, Karan is still there.

"You need to sleep."

"I know."

"You're safe here. No one is getting past us."

"I know," Anya repeats as she sits on the bed. She seems to be weighing her thoughts. "Can you sit with me for a while?"

"Sure." Karan looks around the room and chooses the easy chair in the corner. He picks up a book from the side table. *The last thing Anya needs is for him to watch her fall asleep.* He glances up from the book to see that she has pulled her sheet up to her chin and is staring at the ceiling.

"Kabir has been through your work computer and your laptop," he says. "Both show signs of someone snooping. Have you worked on anything confidential or been privy to information that may be profitable in some way?"

Her eyes narrow. "Like corporate espionage? Do you think I'm a spy?" she asks with a laugh.

Karan smiles. "No, more like you may know about a product launch or marketing plans. Some of your programmes are sponsored, aren't they?"

Anya shakes her head. "No, nothing like that. My computers hold information important to the projects I work on. So, yes, they are important to me, but I don't see why they would be of interest to anyone else."

"Let's go back, say, a month from today. Can you make a list of everything that has happened and everywhere you've been?"

"It won't be a very long list. I am usually in the office or on a shoot."

"How about the other pies you have your fingers in?"

"I'm mostly a silent partner. Do you really think it may be related to one of them? My name isn't associated with any of those businesses."

"Yes, but somewhere there will be a record, won't there?"

"Yes, but…Okay, I will work on the list."

"I'd also like Kabir to check your home computer, so if you can give us the keys to your home and the PIN for your number pad, we'll get that done tomorrow."

Anya stares at him thoughtfully.

"We won't snoop around or anything," he reassures her.

Her eyebrows rise. *Of course, he would; that's his job.*

"We can be on a video call while Kabir checks your computer," says Karan.

"My home computer is not connected to the internet," says Anya. "There is no way anyone had access to it."

Karan frowns. "No net access?"

"It has stuff from my earlier life. I'm not going to take any chances," she says with a note of finality.

"It's not a problem. Kabir will be extra careful. Just give me the keys."

"You can't enter the house without me."

"Don't be ridiculous, Anya. There is no way I'm letting you anywhere close to your home or office. You need to trust me to do the right thing."

Anya shakes her head as she sits up. "You don't understand. You can't enter my place because I am the key."

"What?"

"The number lock is more for show than anything else. It's a biometric lock."

"Is there no way to get around it?"

She shakes her head. "The lock uses more than one biometric identifier."

"Who all knows this?"

"No one, not even Rohan and Samaira."

Karan shakes his head. "No. Someone else knows it. This could be why they drugged you and brought you home." Her expression hasn't changed; he realizes she has considered this possibility. "What makes your home so valuable that it would need a lock like that?"

"Nothing, other than the fact that it is my space," says Anya. "I told you the design of the house was finalized after inputs from several experts. This was part of the security bit. Besides, if someone wants to see the apartment, all they have to do is make an appointment through any of the institutes I consulted with back then."

"Back to my question, how many people know about the biometric lock?"

"In theory, anyone who takes the time to research The Tri could put two and two together, but they'd have to dig really deep. I contacted the student who designed the doors as his final-year project and the institute where he was studying. Nobody has contacted them about it."

She burrows her face in her hands. "What is going on?"

Karan is fairly certain Anya has no idea why her life is being turned upside down. *Someone was rummaging through it, looking for something. But what?*

In all the cases, except for Anya's and Raina's, the victims had shared a fair amount of information on social media. However, to dig into the lives of these two women, one would've had to get close enough to know Raina's routine and details about Anya's home. Karan is pretty sure there are still things Anya is keeping from him, but after her past experience with the police, he can't blame her. *Trust has to be earned, and the process can't be rushed.*

"Do you think he could still be watching my place?" she asks him.

Instead of replying, Karan merely watches her and then gives in. "I don't think so. I think this was the desperate act of someone who realizes he can't get his way. You were lucky to have been driving your jeep—it is designed to withstand abuse—which, surprisingly, means that this fellow didn't do a proper background check on you."

"If you hadn't come when you did, he would've finished off the job," she says, her face bereft of expression.

"Probably."

"So, he thinks getting rid of me will solve the situation. No one will find what he is looking for?"

Karan nods.

"Then it can't be my relatives from Hisar."

"Probably not."

Anya gets off the bed and slips her feet into her boots. "Let's go get the computer and anything else you need from my place. Let's do it now when no one expects me there."

"Are you sure?" Karan asks. "You need your rest."

"It looks like I'm not going anywhere for the next few days, so I'll have plenty of time to rest."

Karan scrutinizes her for a few more moments before standing up. "You are crazy, and I'm crazier to go along with this."

"But it makes sense, doesn't it?"

"It does. Let me get Kabir and Antara. It's not quite the quiet entrance I would've preferred, but we'll work quickly. When we get to your place, I need you to pick up anything you may've collected in the last month—information, souvenirs, photographs, everything. We'll bring it all back here." He looks at his watch. "We should hurry if we want to finish before daybreak."

"If you want, we can enter without being seen. There is a hidden gate to get into the garden."

Karan stares at her for a few moments. Something tells him The Tri holds more secrets. He hopes none of them have brought trouble to her door.

An hour later, when they return, Anya can barely keep her eyes open.

"Don't take this the wrong way, Anya," Antara says as she walks into the house, "but I'm really glad you have a minimalist approach to life. Otherwise, we would've been combing through your stuff for hours."

Anya smiles and shrugs her shoulders. "It's just easier to have less stuff."

Antara nods and holds the door open so Kabir can bring in the computer. "I switched off the data on your phone and took out the SIM. You can access the internet on your devices only after I install a VPN."

Anya didn't really care about all that. She has sent off the burn note she needed to, and Mr Shah, Rohan, and Samaira are the only people who know why she is out of circulation.

Off and on, for years, she'd yearned to get away from it all. To stop rushing, to stop moving. To just stop. *Perhaps this is providence.* She slips into bed and into a deep sleep.

Antara closes the door to Anya's room and walks into the living room to find the team together. "You still haven't told her about the Rohypnol?" she asks Karan.

"We haven't told anyone, Antara. We're definitely not telling her, at least, not right now. She has a hard enough time trusting people. Imagine how she'd react if she knew."

"That is exactly what Dr Samaira said."

"Rohypnol can be crushed and dissolved into a drink, added to food, and also be snorted," Imran says.

"Those three options are out, so that leaves…" Karan lets the team fill in.

"She was injected," Imran adds.

"Probably outside the club," Antara concludes.

"Alright, let's get some sleep," says Karan. "Imran, in the morning, I want to see the CCTV recording from the chemists you decided to focus on. Sameer, check with your sources about any talk on the streets of a special, fast-acting Rohypnol. My contacts haven't come back with anything. What about the phone call she got tonight? We have the recording, don't we?"

"I'll begin working on it first thing tomorrow," Kabir promises.

CHAPTER SEVEN

The next day, the team begins work later than usual, but by afternoon, they are at full speed. As usual, Karan's home office doubles up as their second office. When Anya sleeps through breakfast and lunch, Karan asks Antara to check on her a few times and misses the meaningful glances the team shares.

Kabir isolates the background sounds from the call that had come on Anya's landline the night before. The caller played a recording of Dr Samaira saying those words on several different occasions. The 'come quickly' bit is most probably from the ER at which she works.

Someone went to a fair amount of effort to get Anya on the road last night. Karan reviews all the details from the night before and the last few days but still doesn't find any promising leads.

Kabir has sent him the cleaned CCTV video from the chemist. Karan watches it a few times, zooming in and out when a young woman arrives and leaves the store. He can't see her face or whether she is accompanied by anyone. When she'd come out of the store, her bag was slung across her body, and her hands were full of things. She'd probably been in too much of a hurry to wait for the shopkeeper to put them into a paper bag. Even though the video is slightly clearer now, her face is mostly turned away from the camera. It's not enough to print a photograph to show around.

And then, he sees it and wonders how he had missed it in the first place.

Kabir watches the expression change on Karan's face. "Do you see something, Sir?"

Karan says, "Come and have a look."

They watch the video, and then, once more.

"It's not enough for an identification sketch or photograph," Kabir mumbles.

Imran enters the room and stands next to Kabir. He watches the video with them.

"She is a Tempest girl."

"What?" Kabir asks.

"I keep forgetting you didn't study at DU. The pin on her bag is a Miranda House pin." Kabir points to the clasp. "She could be an alumnus, but I'd bet she is still in college." He looks at his watch. "By the time we get there, the office, and more importantly, the canteen, would've closed. The chances of the canteen staff recognizing her are obviously higher than the office clerks."

Karan nods. "So, you people are on this first thing tomorrow. I don't want to scare the girl off. Just get the basic details, and we'll go from there. Make an appointment with the college principal. That way, you are sure she'll meet you. Make sure she doesn't feel like you are a threat to her student."

"We could say she may've been a witness to a crime but is unaware," Imran suggests.

"Good idea. Also, ask her not to mention your visit to the girl as it could interfere with her recollection of relevant details—that sort of thing," Karan says and turns back to the screen. "Good catch, Imran!"

"But you caught it first, Sir," Imran counters.

"It took me a while. You caught it on first glance."

Imran grins at the acknowledgement.

As the two younger officers descend the stairs, Karan hears Imran promise Kabir a visit to all the popular spots in North Campus.

***

Karan has barely caught a glimpse of Anya today. He is fairly sure this is by design and not a coincidence. After all, his home is not so big that they do not see each other. She hasn't stepped outside the house, but no one can blame her if she just wants to be left alone for a while.

Kabir talks to the team about the new project she is working on. The last three meals they'd eaten had been more than 'just edible', which was their standard fare. In fact, the food was downright delicious. Instead of scarfing down meals the part-time gardener and cook usually left for them in the kitchen, the team had actually set their work aside to enjoy their food. For a change, there hadn't been any shop talk at the dining table.

"You can't keep hiding like this," Karan says as he knocks on Anya's open door after dinner.

"I thought that was the idea," she replies from the workspace she's created in a corner of the room.

"Hiding from me, I mean, the team, is not necessary."

"I didn't want to get in the way," she says.

"You aren't in the way," he insists. He sees the disbelief on her face. "In my experience, when people share a secret they've kept for a really long time, they are either relieved or feel a lack of control."

"I guess you're not wrong," she replies.

"But I'm not right either?"

"I don't know." She shakes her head in resignation. "I've been trying to hide, go unnoticed for so long that this whole situation is unnerving. I'm used to dealing with things on my own, so invading your space and life is unsettling."

"I've been thinking," he says. "Antara is going to Almora. We usually prefer to use the buddy system. That way, we always have a backup. However, things are developing with the other cases. I can't go along, and neither can any of the others. I was wondering if you'd go with her."

Anya narrows her eyes.

"I assume you brought your weapon when you went home," says Karan.

Anya nods. "If you want me to leave, it's okay. I'll make the necessary arrangements."

"I don't want you to go, but you need to get out of the city for a while, away from all this, and I don't want Antara going by herself. So, it works out well for everyone."

She gestures for him to sit. *It would be nice to just get away from everything for a while, but—*

Karan watches Anya as she considers the possibilities. "Everything we talked about—your father and your family—is between you and me. The team knows nothing of it. If it doesn't have anything to do with the current situation, it is up to you to decide what you want to share."

"You're sure Antara will not mind me tagging along?"

"It was her idea."

"It's tempting. You knew I'd be tempted."

"I know you're all for facing the situation head-on, but it is okay to just go away for a while. Maybe the time away will offer a different perspective. Don't forget, I need you to prepare a detailed list of everything that has been going on in your life from before you left for the Spiti trip—even things you might consider mundane."

"Alright. Are we driving down to Almora? Where will we stay?"

"Antara will coordinate the details with you. I think she wants to leave early tomorrow. Both of you can borrow my car."

Anya's eyebrows rise. "I got the impression you are particular about your vehicle."

"Just go with her, and carry your weapon," he huffs as he gets up.

"I wanted to thank you for everything. I know this whole situation has put a spoke of sorts in your wheel—investigation-wise," she clarifies.

"A spoke in my wheel?" he asks. "We'll just have to see about that. Antara will brief you about the reasons for going to Almora. She is going to depend on you to keep your eyes and ears open. You see and note a lot that others may miss, so don't forget to discuss anything you find interesting with Antara or with me."

"Do you think my going will actually help?"

"I do. The kind of information we're looking for is unlikely to be volunteered; it's a more 'read between the lines' kind of thing." He watches her for a few more moments before adding, "I'm not trying to get rid of you."

"Okay."

"Just like that?"

"Yes. Why not? You don't seem to be the kind of person who deceives."

"When the circumstances require it, I can deceive with the best of them, but not with you," he says.

"Are you feeling bad for me, ACP Shekhawat?"

"Not even a little, Ms Aulakh."

"I just wanted to thank you and your team with a little something, but I wanted to talk to you about it first." She explains that a friend owns a food delivery service that delivers meals across the city, and she wants to gift the team a subscription for six months.

"You don't have to do that. We're just doing our jobs."

"In my case, you and I know you've gone beyond doing your jobs. Next, I've heard of third-degree torture, but I've never seen it inflicted on food. Your gardener has a green thumb, but a cook, he is not. Please let me do this for you. The deliveries cover breakfast and lunch. The food arrives in insulated bags that are easy to carry and put away." She opens an app on her phone and hands it to Karan.

He shakes his head. "This is too much."

"It's not. I'm a silent partner in the company. Besides, I assure you that by the time the six months are up, you'll end up recommending the company to everyone you know. That's free promotion for us."

He grins. "Okay, set it up, but you really don't owe us anything."

"If you say so," she says with a smile.

"What language is that?" he asks as he carefully listens to the song playing on her laptop.

"Thai."

"Nice voice."

"I'm glad you think so. I don't think I could be friends with someone who doesn't like Jeff," she says with a smile.

"Will you share your playlist with me? You don't have to if you don't want to," he adds. He'd noticed the impressive speaker system in her home and was sure music was important to her.

She considers his request longer than he expected her to.

"It's not like I am asking you to share your bank statements with me," he says.

"That would be less personal. I'll share mine if you share yours," she says.

"Done!" Karan says, taking out his phone and touching the screen a few times to share his playlist.

***

"They say, you can only be betrayed if you first trust someone," Karan says to Arjun, watching his expression. "You can't be betrayed if you don't trust, can you?" He'd convinced the man to let Kabir stand guard outside Raina's room while they had a cup of coffee in the hospital cafeteria.

Arjun's face remains expressionless. He looks as though he has aged years in the last few days.

"There is something going on with your lives that you aren't telling my team," Karan says. "You have near-perfect identities, and yet, your background stories are weak. Until about ten years ago, neither Raina nor you existed in the real world. I must give you, or whoever created those identities, credit because they're nearly perfect. However, you can lay a meticulous paper trail, but you cannot create memories for people. Your neighbours from Agra don't remember you or your family. The fact that over the years, someone went to inquire about your family was something that people remembered. That was a good touch."

Arjun remains silent, his expression impassive. His hands are placed on the table, fingers interlaced.

"Do you even want your son back?" Karan asks and is glad to see rage in Arjun's eyes. "And yet, you remain silent." He decides to lay his cards on the table. "So, your past terrifies you more than the prospect of it grabbing your son."

"If our past had anything to do with Navin being taken, believe me, neither Raina nor I would be alive. Both our families take pride in zero tolerance for indiscipline, and we've been more defiant than they'd ever accept. We chose our life partners; that is, after all, an unpardonable crime," he says bitterly.

Arjun had done his due diligence too, and it told him the ACP could be trusted. However, after years of maintaining an illusion, it was difficult to say the words. "If they knew where we work and live, that would be the end for us. Even though Raina is in a coma, we are both alive. Well, Occam's razor."

"Hmm," Karan replies. "Do you think we could have a look at your home? We're going to the store from where Navin was taken, so we'll be in the area."

"Sure." Arjun takes out a key chain with several keys from the front pocket of his jeans and hands it to Karan.

"I'll make sure they're delivered back to you by tomorrow. How many sets of keys are there?"

"Only two—mine and Raina's. Hers are still in her purse—I checked."

"Can you help me understand your usual routine as a family—people you interact with regularly, that kind of thing?"

It takes Arjun a few minutes to give Karan the details he wants. Then, Karan begins questioning him. They go over every little detail until he is satisfied.

"I have to ask this, and obviously, I need honest answers. Have either you or Raina had an affair, a passing love interest?"

"Absolutely not. Fidelity is not something you need to question in our relationship. When you have a lot going against you, life has an odd way of strengthening your relationship."

"Anyone who may've taken an untoward interest in either of you or maybe as a family?"

"To be honest, we're too busy creating a life for ourselves. We travel frequently. Raina keeps a close eye on our finances. She tries to keep us prepared for any emergency. Except this one," he says, shaking his head. "I don't think either of us could ever see this coming."

"No one could have," Karan reassures him, though he is not entirely convinced himself.

"You own an apartment in Noida, don't you?"

"Yes. It's an investment. We took possession a few months ago. It's already leased out as a corporate guesthouse."

Karan nods. "Good decision."

"It was Raina's idea; I can't take much credit. Our landlady was quite unhappy with the whole thing. It took Raina and me a few days to convince her we were not planning to move out."

Karan refers to his notes. "Mrs Sharma?"

"Yes, nice lady. She used to be a chemistry teacher. She is retired now. Her family is mostly abroad. Her kids are in the US and in Australia. She is sort of Navin's adopted grandmother," he adds with a slight smile. "You'll probably meet her when you go to our place. Let me just explain how we lock our doors."

Arjun explains the sequence in which the locks were to be opened.

"You obviously put a lot of thought into this," Karan says.

"But at the end of the day, it was worth nothing."

"I wouldn't say that, Arjun. Like you say, you don't think Navin's kidnapping has anything to do with your families; we'll be as discreet as possible when we take a glance in that direction." Karan can see Arjun getting worked up. "There will be no mention of you three; it'll be from afar on a completely different pretext."

Arjun nods even though he looks far from convinced. "If you find anything to suggest they may be involved, I'll give you the names you need to investigate, but not unless there is no other option left."

Karan wants to press on, but he can see the man isn't going to see reason—at least, not till they find some concrete evidence. "I'm told you've been essentially living in the hospital since all this started."

"My work keeps my mind off things, and our friends have been rallying for us. I haven't been home since it happened."

"Since we'll be going there, is there anything I can send over for you?"

"That's okay. I had a friend go home and pack a bag for me."

"Okay, then," Karan says as he stands up. "By the way, do either of you know someone called Anya Aulakh?"

"Sorry, I don't think I've ever heard that name. Is she connected to the case somehow?"

"Not really, just another case that seems similar. We'll keep in touch," Karan says.

Kabir and he spend the next few hours in Arjun and Raina's home. They put on protective gloves before opening the locks in the sequence Arjun had described. The heavy doors of the house are not the kind they usually see in *barsati*-s. Kabir takes photographs of the house before they begin to go over every inch of it. They find everything one would expect to find in the home of a young family.

In the *puja sthan,* Karan finds a well-thumbed copy of the Gita, and in it, a faded blue inland letter. It was from Arjun's mother, warning him to stay away from the family if he wanted a future with Raina. She had used the names they had chosen. *Interesting.* He looks for a return address and finds the space blank. While Kabir moves on to speak with the neighbours, Karan stops to speak to the landlady.

Her living room has the appearance of a store full of curios. Mrs Sharma is pleasant and hits all the right notes with her concern, but she seems a little too interested in the details of the case. Morbid curiosity is not a crime, and unfortunately, Mrs Sharma isn't an exception.

What is it about human psychology that makes us consume and then share stories of the trials and tribulations of others with such pleasure?

"My son is settled in the US and is a doctor. My daughter is in Australia and is an engineer. Serious careers," Mrs Sharma adds.

Karan nods as his eyes sweep across the room again. He sees lots of pretty things but no trace of the people who make a life rich. It is no wonder that Arjun, Raina, and Navin are important to her.

He asks her some questions about their routines, and she helps fill in some of the details. Mrs Sharma doesn't seem as upset as he'd expected, but then people react differently, Karan reasons. He drinks a cup of tea with her and leaves.

After speaking to the neighbours, Kabir waits outside the house, hoping to speak with the maid who works for both Mrs Sharma and Arjun and Raina. He knows domestic help has a unique window into the lives of those they serve. They see and hear more than most people think and are good at reading between the lines.

By the time Karan comes out of Mrs Sharma's home, Kabir has started talking to the maid, and he notes down her address and mobile phone number. Karan walks up to them but doesn't interrupt the officer. Karan's phone chimes softly, but his focus is on the young maid. Neatly dressed in a *salwar-kameez,* she has a small tote bag slung from her shoulder. She holds three thick envelopes in her hand. As she speaks and gestures animatedly, Karan notes that two of the envelopes are airmail, probably headed to Mrs Sharma's children, and the third is a registered letter headed for domestic post.

The maid speaks about Arjun, Raina, and Navin with apparent affection. Raina pays for her children's education and for the family's medical insurance, she tells them. Before she leaves, Karan asks her if Mrs Sharma writes a lot of letters, and she nods in reply. The maid jokes that she can now hold a letter in her hand and calculate the exact postage it needs—both domestic and international.

"Madam is very careful. All letters are sent by registered post," she adds.

"It's nice to see people writing letters," Kabir says as they get into the car. "Emails are quick, but receiving a physical letter is something else."

Karan agrees. "I don't think her children come to visit often, so I guess the letters are important to her."

Kabir nods in agreement. "Sir, tomorrow I want to go back to the Channel office and continue with the internship. That way, things won't look suspicious."

Karan nods as he keeps his eyes on the road. "You can also keep an eye on how Anya's colleagues respond to her absence. Check her computer again. Maybe we missed something. Let's schedule a call with the team at eight."

At the next traffic light, Karan checks his messages. He reads the one from Anya first.

Anya: *About to reach Almora. Small request, is it okay if we stay the night at a hotel I want to write about?*

It'll also give us an opportunity to speak with some locals.

Will mention this plan to Antara only if you're okay with it.

Karan likes the plan. In fact, it is like the one Antara and he'd agreed upon, but Anya didn't need to know that.

Karan: *Hi, Anya.*

Glad to know you both made good time getting there.

Message me the name of the hotel. Have fun.

His phone chimes again before he can put it away.

Anya: *You too.*

He is tempted to reply but thinks better of it.

"Where do you want me to drop you? Your bike is still at my place," he asks Kabir.

"I want to spend some time on Anya's computer and devices, so if it is okay, I'll go back with you."

"Any news from Sameer and Imran?"

"When I last exchanged messages with Sameer Sir, they were waiting to speak with the college principal. After that, they planned to go to the office and then the canteen."

Karan smiles. "There is a much better chance of the canteen staff recognizing her than the office people."

CHAPTER EIGHT

As they drive towards Almora, Antara notes how Anya seems perfectly at ease. She is not averse to talking but definitely prefers to observe rather than speak.

They stop twice during the eight-and-a-half-hour journey from Delhi. Anya recommends both *dhabas,* and much to Antara's surprise, the owners and staff recognize her. The ease with which she chats with them obviously comes from frequent visits.

"You don't like cops, do you?" Antara asks when they set off again.

Anya stiffens just a little. "Why do you say that?"

"People we meet when we investigate cases give off a vibe. Some seem innately guilty, some are fearful, and others show apparent disdain."

"What kind of vibe do I give you?" Anya asks.

"You aren't particularly comfortable with the police. If I had to guess, I'd say, at some point, you've had an uncomfortable run-in with them. Add that to the fact that you have a DNI tag. Obviously, you have stuff going on in your life. Initially, we thought the reason you have the DNI may have led to your situation. Karan Sir does not think so. He is probably still looking into that and will take some heat for it," Antara says as she looks at the other woman. Anya looks at Antara and nods as the officer continues speaking.

"To be completely honest, I didn't know of the concept of the DNI until we met you. It's the same for the others. Karan Sir says this is only the third time he has heard mention of a DNI and the first time he has actually met someone with that tag. You are not politically linked or have any obvious police connections. So, I'm guessing someone is protecting you for the simplest, most basic reason."

"And that is?"

"You need the protection, and you are valuable for some reason."

Anya nods. "When you handle cases, do you suspect everyone?"

"That is usually how we're trained to think, but the Urban Crimes unit has a slightly different way of doing things. Karan Sir insists we go in with an open mind. It's true that, most often, family and people close to the victim are connected to the crime, but if we follow this as a paradigm, we're likely to miss out on other important details."

"So, no one is above suspicion?"

"Yes. Then we check and double-check details. Usually, we work with a partner, but we make sure the rest of the team is in on all details. That way, the chances of missing out on a lead or not making a connection are reduced."

"Does being a cop make you naturally suspicious of people?" Anya asks.

"I guess it does," Antara says. "I know you don't like cops, and I don't blame you; there are many on the force who are in it for the wrong reasons. However, you can trust the Urban Crimes unit. Don't just take my word for it—our actions should suffice."

"If it is fine with you, I asked ACP Shekhawat if we could stay tonight at a hotel I'm going to write about. The magazine will pay for our stay, and we can relax before you start with your investigation tomorrow."

"Sounds good to me. I thought he asked you to call him Karan," Antara says.

"He did, but honestly, I don't know if that's okay. He is investigating my situation, so that is a professional connection. However, I've been living in his home for the last few days, so that makes things personal."

"You like clear boundaries."

"Doesn't everyone?"

Antara smiles as she continues to watch the road. She would bet a month's salary that Karan's interest in Anya went beyond the professional connection, but he was unlikely to admit it. It is just as well because Anya seems to shy away from personal connections. The woman is an interesting bundle of contradictions. She is friendly, yet maintains a certain distance. According to Kabir, other than Rohan, Dr Samaira, and her boss, she keeps most people at arm's length.

"I am hoping to get at least two articles out of our stay tonight," says Anya enthusiastically. "I write a regular feature in an in-flight magazine."

"What do you write about?"

"The section is called 'High Tea.'"

"No way! You write 'High Tea' for *Fly with Me*? I love that column. In fact, I've a friend who flies with that airline, and she usually gets me a magazine every month. You know, when you write about a place in the city, the team usually goes there."

"Really?" Anya asks, giddy joy bubbling inside her that her writing had connected with the readers.

Antara laughs. "I think we're going to get along just fine. Go ahead, call the hotel."

She wonders if Karan had known that she'd get along so well with Anya. She is the only woman on the team. On most days, it makes no difference to her, but occasionally, it's nice to have another woman to talk to.

***

At eight in the evening, Karan is still in his home office. He taps his pen against the file he is reading and looks around the room. Other than Antara, the rest of the team is there.

"Sir, should we set up the call?" Kabir asks. "Antara Ma'am requested an audio call as her network isn't great there."

Karan nods and reaches for his notepad to pen down the details the team has to share. Kabir links his phone to the speaker on Karan's table and then connects the call. The team quickly exchanges pleasantries with Antara, with more than one officer commenting on her accommodation for the night.

"Antara, we'll let Sameer and Imran start first because they seem to have made the most progress," says Karan.

"Yes, Sir," her voice comes through clearly.

Karan nods at Sameer, and he begins his briefing.

"We met the Miranda House principal, and as expected, she wasn't particularly happy with us. That is, until we mentioned we belonged to the Urban Crimes team. Apparently, the principal is good friends with Karan Sir's mother. After that, things moved along smoothly. While she couldn't recognize the student, she put us in touch with department heads and the office staff. As expected, it was the canteen staff who recognized her. Ipshita Kamra is a third-year sociology student. She is in the debating society and lives in Karol Bagh. I'm sending everyone a profile that Imran put together," he taps on his phone. "Now, the question is, do we surprise her or call her, make an appointment, and then keep her under surveillance? We did a quick deep dive through her social media profiles. She is quite active online and was generous enough to keep her security settings open, so we can pretty much walk through most of her life." He nods at Imran to take over.

"She is part of the inter-college scavenger hunt team that competes twice a year, and I think she is part of the original group that started it. Believe it or not, the hunt gets a lot of sponsors—big ones. We all know that means a lot of money is involved," Imran adds.

"Do you think her being at Anya's place has something to do with a scavenger hunt?" Kabir asks.

Sameer shrugs his shoulders. "Sir, from what we found on her social media posts, she isn't averse to taking risks, but we don't know if this is part of a weird scavenger hunt."

"How about we put her under surveillance, physical as well as electronic, and then make contact? Let's see how she reacts," Karan suggests.

"That makes sense, Sir," Antara agrees.

"In the last few weeks," Imran adds, "most of her posts have included a cousin who is visiting from the US. Usually, she posts daily, but she didn't post anything last week. Then the day before yesterday, she posted something college-related."

"Do you have this cousin's name?"

"Yes, Sir. He is 23-year-old Neel Kamra. We are also following up on him."

Karan nods. "Antara, how was the drive up to Almora?"

"Interesting, to say the least. Now I know why you decided to send Anya with me. Still waters run deep." Antara goes on to describe their journey to Almora. "We arrived at the resort, which is gorgeous. Our room has a floor-to-ceiling glass wall that faces the forest." She pauses for dramatic effect and lets the rest of the team sigh. "Anya is working on two articles, the first being, wait for it, 'High Tea' for the in-flight magazine."

"No way!" Imran interrupts her. "That column doesn't carry the author's name, and I've spent months trying to find out who writes it."

"Well, I saw the writer in action," says Antara. "She has this unassuming way about her that gets people talking. The funny thing is, when you observe her, you realize that she doesn't really say so much, but the genuine interest comes through and works wonders. So, we went in for the high tea that this place is known for. Now, I am a nice person, so I'll not torture you all with what we ate. Other than a group of elderly ladies, we were the only ones there. And this group take their high tea seriously. The manager of the hotel personally oversaw how the tea was poured. It turns out they have a permanent fortnightly reservation there. We caught snippets of their conversation and hit the motherlode. The senior Mrs Naugiyal was also part of the group. There was some discussion about the daughter-in-law, how she would soon get married and take the grandchildren away, and how she should be brought under control. If you heard the conversation, Sir, you'd think we lived in the medieval age," Antara huffs.

"Anyway," she continues, "the senior Mrs Naugiyal ended the conversation with the declaration that she has requested Mataji to look into the matter. Anya managed to get the ladies talking, got their permission to take some pictures for the article she is writing, and we got to hear a few more of those inside details."

"Mataji?"

"I guess there is a local temple here where people go and make requests and tie a thread—that kind of thing."

"But what kind of request is she making?" Sameer asks. "The kind people make to vent their frustrations or the kind that would put a spanner in Mrs Naugiyal's business?"

"I don't think the gods decided to drug Mrs Naugiyal and put her in the hospital, but a family member may've decided to take matters into their own hands," Kabir says.

"Tomorrow, we'll go to the forest garden and also meet the family," Antara says. "Let's see what more we find."

Karan nods at Kabir, and he proceeds to describe their day to the rest of the team.

"Those CCTV recordings are going to be a pain to go through, Sir. The quality of recordings outside most stores is usually poor. I don't think most of those lenses are ever cleaned."

"If you were kidnapping a child, would you walk out of the mall with the pram or go down to the parking lot and drive out?" Karan asks as he flips through the file in front of him.

There is silence in the room.

"Driving away is more inconspicuous," Karan says. "Yet, the security guards and the local police were looking at CCTV recordings for someone with the pram. I assume there is a reason for this?"

"Yes, Sir," Kabir replies. "The parking area doesn't open that early in the day, which is why they were only looking at the exits someone could have walked out of."

Sameer shakes his head. "No, I think Sir is right. Just because the parking area was not open doesn't mean that the parking bays were not in use. It just means that the attendant was not there. Besides, even if the parking was closed, the service elevator stops at the ground floor, close to the parking area, for delivery trucks. Let's say they drove out of the parking lot, or the vehicle was parked in the delivery area. What are the routes they could have taken?"

"The parking has only one entrance and exit, and the service elevator can also be accessed from the same road," Kabir says as he looks carefully at the rough sketch he's made.

"Then, only check the CCTV recordings that would cover that road. Ask Abhi to help you if you need additional eyes," Karan says. "Sameer, when will you reach out to Ipshita?"

"I thought tomorrow morning, Sir. Or should we do it tonight and see how she reacts?"

Karan nods. "Are you set to keep a track of her calls?"

"Only track right now, Sir, not listen in," Imran replies.

"Okay, throw in the pebble, and let's see how things ripple. Set a time and place to meet her, and keep a close eye on how she reacts. Let's try not to make her defensive and see how it goes. Let's call it a day now. Antara, enjoy Almora, and stay safe."

***

Anya decides to treat them to a little R&R. While she gets a head and shoulder massage, Antara chooses to pamper her feet. The officer leans back in the lounge chair as the masseuse works wonders on her feet. Later, they sit back, watching the glittering night sky through the glass wall.

Anya's phone chimes with the arrival of a message.

ACP Shekhawat: *I hear you both had a productive time at high tea.*

Anya: *Glad to help.*

ACP Shekhawat: *Need the password for your desktop computer. Kabir has cleared the laptop and iPad.*

Anya rubs her forehead absentmindedly.

"Problem?" Antara asks.

"No," Anya says. "Karan wants the password for my computer. I mean, ACP Shekhawat," she corrects herself.

Anya: *Please ensure that the computer is not connected to the internet at any time. This is important to me.*

ACP Shekhawat: *Okay.*

Anya: *Any chance someone could check on the state of repairs for my Jeep?*

ACP Shekhawat: *Should be ready in a few days.*

There've been no visitors to your home. I'm told guests to The Tri continue to come and go.

No sign of your winged friend when I stopped by there today.

Anya: *Okay, good. Thanks.*

ACP Shekhawat: *Are you okay?*

Anya: *Much better than I thought I'd be.*

This trip may've been just what I needed. Thanks.

ACP Shekhawat: *Plus, you get two articles out of it.*

Anya: *There is that.*

ACP Shekhawat: *Why do you write an article every day for a content generation website?*

Anya: *It's extra money. Why would I refuse the work?*

When she doesn't receive a reply from Karan for a while, she types out another message.

Anya: *This company gave me work when I really needed it. While I was building The Tri, I mostly lived off my freelance income.*

Karan isn't sure how to respond to this level of loyalty.

ACP Shekhawat: *So, Antara got to enjoy high tea with you, and if I know her well, she'll convince you to let her read your article before it's published. What about my treat for getting you to go on this trip?*

Anya: *We'll see.*

ACP Shekhawat: *Really? You're going to be cryptic with an Urban Crimes officer?*

Anya: *I'll take my chances. How are things going with you?*

ACP Shekhawat: *Good.*

Anya: *Okay, then goodnight.*

ACP Shekhawat: *Anya.*

Anya: *Yes?*

ACP Shekhawat: *The password?*

Anya: *Didn't I send it to you?*

ACP Shekhawat: *No.*

Anya: *You're persistent. Sending you a burn note.*

ACP Shekhawat: *Goodnight.*

"There is a nice chill in the air today," Antara says as she wraps her arms around herself.

"It is supposed to get colder tomorrow," Anya says. "What time do you want to start?"

"After breakfast."

"Perfect."

***

Ipshita Kamra agrees to meet Sameer and Imran at a café adjacent to the college premises. A little digging reveals that the owner of the café is her boyfriend. The officers arrive ten minutes before the decided time. Given the décor and furniture, it is apparent that the owner takes the café's connection to Miranda House seriously. Ipshita is standing behind the counter.

"Ipshita?" Imran calls out, and the young woman nods and walks towards them. She gestures for them to take a table closest to the counter. Her friend continues working, but his eyes are on them.

Imran makes the introductions. They wait for her to take a seat before they settle down.

"You said this was about a crime I may've witnessed? I'm quite sure I would've known if I had done so."

"We think you may not have witnessed the actual crime but may've run into the criminal." Imran goes on to describe her late-night visit to the chemist and the customer who had walked out of the pharmacy when she had entered it. He asks her for details that she may remember from that night. Ipshita relaxes visibly as she talks to them.

"May I ask what you were doing there so late at night?" Imran asks.

"We were playing a game, and my cousin got hurt, so I went to buy bandages and stuff."

Imran looks at Sameer and then at Ipshita. "It was quite late, well past midnight. What kind of game? I hope you weren't racing."

"Nothing like that," she says with a shake of her head. "It's like a mystery game. We had to find someone—that kind of thing. It was quite bizarre. My cousin is in town and wanted to try this game I play. Anyway, things were going well until he was attacked by a bird. It bit his ear."

"A bird bit your cousin's ear off?" Sameer asks, looking suitably shocked.

"Well, not his whole ear, a small part of it," she explains.

"But still ..."

"Exactly," Ipshita says as she nods.

"So, were you trying to catch the bird? Was this like a bird hunt or something?"

"No. The game is a role-play thing, and the bird came out of nowhere."

"Can you tell us a little bit about your game?"

"It's like an online mystery game, but it's played in the real world. You have to find someone or something. There are clues, but most of the work is done together as a team. I guess it is sort of like your investigations, but more fun, of course."

"Of course," Imran agrees.

"I hope your cousin is better now," Sameer says.

"Oh yes, much better, but at that time, we were really panicking. I mean, the game started off well, but suddenly, everything started to go wrong."

"Everything?"

"Yes, we couldn't complete it," Ipshita says as she turns to look at the man behind the counter.

"Sir, were you also playing?" Imran asks, and the man just smiles and shakes his head.

"No, he is not much of a mystery game player. It was just me and Neel with the others." Ipshita says.

"How many players in total?" Sameer asks.

"Including me, four."

"Can you give us the address where the bird attacked your cousin? We'd like to check the place out."

"Sure, but we don't want to complain," she says.

"That's nice of you, but we still want to check it out. I've never heard of a bird attacking like that," Sameer says.

"Exactly, right?" Ipshita says.

"Our office is not too far away from your college." Imran hands her his card. "If you could please come over, we'd like to show you some photographs. You may recognize the man you crossed paths with as you entered the pharmacy. This is related to a string of car thefts in the area, and this is the first break we've caught."

Ipshita takes the card and reads the details on it. "Fine. Is it all right if I bring my cousin with me? However, he won't be able to identify your man."

"That'll be fine. What time can we expect you?" Imran asks.

"My last class gets over at noon, so I can come after that."

"Okay, we will see you then," Sameer says as he stands up. "By the way, what is this game called?"

Ipshita hesitates before replying, "PTK. You can check out the website online."

"PTK?" Imran asks.

"Yes, it's an online and offline game."

"Thank you so much for your help. In case you have any trouble finding our place, just call Imran for directions," Sameer says. He nods at the man behind the counter, going about the chores of a barista, but whose attention is still on the three of them.

"Let's take a walk," Sameer says as he walks past their bike. "So, what do you think?"

Imran shrugs his shoulders. "I can't tell if she was lying or telling the truth."

Sameer nods. "Don't give yourself a tough time about it. As police officers, we'd love to claim to be lie detectors, but it's not always so. What is the most difficult lie to catch, Imran?"

"The one that is mixed with the truth, Sir."

"Exactly. Most of what she said seemed to ring true, but…" he looks at Imran to continue the line of thought.

"But there was something there that made her uncomfortable."

"Fortunately, we recorded the conversation, so we can play it back as many times as we need to," Sameer says.

"Do you think she was telling the truth about the game? It did sound like it. So, Anya got caught in some kind of game. That's odd."

"The whole thing is odd, Imran. Let's go back. I've seen enough," Sameer says as he begins quizzing Imran about the places and people they'd passed on their walk around the perimeter of the college premises.

After returning to the office, they review the video captured on Sameer's pen. Karan makes them rewind it a few times before saying, "You are right, Imran. It isn't easy to catch the parts where she is lying."

"So, she is lying, isn't she?"

"She is lying, or let's say, she's trying to cover something up, but a lot of what she is saying is true, or at least, it's her version of the truth. Her body language is a little stiff in the beginning, but that's to be expected. Most people are not comfortable talking to the police. However, she gets comfortable as the conversation goes on, and there is a slight change here." He clicks on the mouse to replay the section.

"For a few seconds there, she folds her arms in a defensive position, but she unfolds them just as quickly. Then," he says as he moves to another section of the video, "here, she clenches and unclenches her fist."

"Repressed aggression. Isn't that what it usually indicates? But why? We didn't take a line of questioning that would be considered threatening," Imran says.

"Frustration often resembles aggression. There is something about the game she doesn't like answering questions about."

"And with good reason, Sir. The website and the game are called Play to Kill. As threatening as the name sounds, it gets weirder. May I?" Imran gestures at Karan's laptop, and the senior officer moves it towards him. "Your system is secure, and even if someone were to trace the IP address, it would show this computer somewhere in Eastern Europe. Play to Kill, or as Ipshita called it, PTK, is pretty exclusive—you've to receive an invitation to be able to register on the site. The registration does not come cheap, and there is a waiting period."

"So, does that mean we can't access the game?"

"Have a little faith, Sir." Imran logs in to the website and turns the laptop screen towards Karan. "There are several levels to the game. Now, most of the games are the kind of mystery and detection games you would expect to find on such a site. I think as a player progresses through the levels, they get access to the real-world games that Ipshita mentioned. I had a quick look at the setup of the site. It is a little strange—the code isn't consistent. I need to spend more time on it to figure out why."

"What do you mean by the code isn't consistent? Are some parts more secure than others, or is there a variation in the coding style?" Sameer asks.

"Both," Imran says.

"Both?" Karan and Sameer ask in unison.

"Okay, dig deeper, Imran, without setting off any red flags. By the way, how did you manage to get us access to the game?"

Imran rubs his nose. "I remembered a gamer friend who likes this kind of thing. It turned out they have a PTK membership too, so I asked for their user ID and login details to take a peek."

"I assume your friend is a woman," Karan asks, his fingers steepled together.

"Why would you assume that, Sir?" Imran asks with a small smile. He then sees the expression on Karan's face and stands tall at attention. "Yes, Sir."

"Be careful. I don't want our snooping around the game to place her in danger. Understood?"

"Yes, Sir."

"Let me know when Ipshita gets here. Keep your tone cool and confident, with the slightest touch of intimidation. We want her to cooperate," Karan says as he dismisses his officers.

He goes through the deep dive report into Ipshita's and Neel's social media accounts.

Neel's posts seem normal for a twenty-something, premedical student in the United States. Ipshita's account is more active, and there are several posts daily. Karan pens down his thoughts on a notepad as he peruses through the virtual lives of the cousins.

He is still going through PTK when he hears snatches of conversation from the team office. Karan looks at his watch. It is past noon. Ipshita is on time. Karan wonders if this is a good sign. God knows he needs one at this awkward, nascent stage of the investigation. His phone signals the arrival of a message.

Sameer: *Interview Room 1?*

Karan: *Yes.*

CHAPTER NINE

"I've never been in an interrogation room before," Ipshita says as she looks around the well-lit space. "Is that actually a two-way mirror?"

Imran smiles. "We call it an interview room. We need to ensure we get all the details, so let's get started." He steadily guides her through the conversation they'd had earlier before he begins questioning her in detail.

"So, just to summarize, you were playing this game, PTK, when your cousin was attacked by a bird, and you had to go to the pharmacy."

"It sounds pretty bizarre, doesn't it? But that's what happened. The bird just ripped a part of his ear, and it was bleeding. I went to get basic first aid—cotton, bandages—before we took him to the hospital. Of course, the trip to the hospital turned out to be pointless because all they did was clean up the wound again and bandage it. It couldn't be stitched up. He will need plastic surgery once he returns to the States. Though, between you and me, I think he has changed his mind about it. It looks pretty cool. Do you want to show me any pictures of this person you want help identifying?"

"Yes," Sameer says. "Imran, show her the CCTV video we have."

They watch the video several times, but when Imran stops it, Ipshita shakes her head. "Sorry, at that time, I was kind of oscillating between anger and panic. I wasn't really paying attention to the people around me."

"Ipshita, at that time of the day, there would've been very few cars parked on the road, and traffic would've been minimal. Do you remember seeing any vehicles on the street? Just close your eyes for a few seconds. Give yourself a little time to recollect."

Ipshita sighs and closes her eyes. It takes her a little while to start talking. "You're right. The street in front of the pharmacy was virtually empty. When I walked back to the car, I think I passed a dark SUV, possibly black. The street light was the kind that gives out a yellowish light, so I'm not sure of the colour. I think it was a Range Rover, but it didn't look stolen. I mean, there were people in it, and it looked like they were having a good time. I remember thinking that at least some people were enjoying the evening."

"What do you mean exactly by 'good time'?"

"There was music playing, and I may have smelled alcohol and food. Anyway, I was in a rush, so I didn't think much of it."

"How do you play PTK? I thought you said it was online."

"It is mostly online, but as you progress through the levels, the lines between online and real world get a little mixed up."

"I'm sorry, I don't understand what that means," Sameer says.

"PTK is basically a game about finding people and things," Ipshita explains patiently. "I first heard about it a few months ago on a scavenger hunt. I thought it was just one of those online detective games—the kind where you find clues and objects in a virtual game. But it is far better and more exciting. I think it is something that is going to catch on fast." She notices the interested expression on the officers' faces. "If you are interested, I can show you my journey in the game."

"That would be great," Sameer says, glancing towards the observation room.

Ipshita takes her iPad out of her bag, and with a few swipes, she opens the webpage to the game. "My account shows my entire journey through the game. It does a phenomenal job of showing how I progressed and how I can improve my score."

Imran and Sameer get up to stand behind her chair so that they can get a clear look at the screen.

"My first *real* challenge was to find this person." She clicks on a link, and a picture of a young woman comes up. "This one wasn't easy because the image search websites on the internet did not come back with results. However, I have a friend who is studying AI and cybersecurity, and he said he could try writing a programme to help me identify her."

"Is that how you found her?" Sameer asks.

"No. I didn't need that because this picture was taken on a smartphone. So, all I had to do was pull up the EXIF info, use the location information, and I knew where the picture was taken."

"So, that helped you locate her?"

"That was just the starting point. It gave me clues about the kind of person she is. The photo was taken in a bowling alley. So, I thought it was likely she had gone to the stores at the mall where the bowling alley is located. Anyway, one thing led to another, and I found her."

"Found her?" Sameer asks curiously.

"I mean, online, of course. I guess they have a database of these pictures that helps people develop their skills."

"Skills?" Imran asks.

"Yes, like tracking and stuff. Anyway, most of the levels are online, and each time a player is successful, they get a reward."

"Like points or a change in player status?" Imran asks.

"No, like a gift card. This game isn't cheap. The registration fee is high to keep non-serious players off the game. However, if you do well, you can earn back your registration money in no time."

"Non-serious players?"

"Yes, players who don't have the basic instinct or don't want to put in the effort to play the game properly. A lot of the initial games involve finding information, people, or things online. Very few players rise to the levels that offer IRL games."

Imran nods in understanding and resists the urge to push that line of interrogation right now. *Timing is everything in an interrogation.* Karan repeats this during investigations, time and again.

"How much does the registration cost?" Imran asks.

"It was ten thousand when I joined, but when I registered Neel, it had increased. Of course, because of my player level, his registration was free."

Nothing in life is free. 10k for registration on a gaming site sounded insane to Imran, and yet, to this college student, it seemed like no big deal. "What is your player level?"

"I am a Level 4 player," she replies with a smile.

"How many levels are there?"

"I don't know. As you move up, you gain access to new levels."

"So, what was your challenge in this game?" Sameer asks.

Ipshita looks a little conflicted. "I can't really talk about it. I signed a non-disclosure agreement."

"Really? An NDA for a game? That's quite interesting," Sameer says to Imran.

"I thought only businesses and companies did that with confidential information. Does an NDA hold true if it breaks the law?" Imran asks Sameer curiously.

"I guess that is a matter for the lawyers to sort out," Sameer replies, his focus completely on Ipshita.

"I didn't do anything illegal," she insists.

"Then just tell us what the game was," Imran encourages.

Ipshita looks at Sameer, then Imran, and then at Sameer again and huffs. "There is nothing illegal about the game. Think of it as a play but with the stage set in the real world. Of course, the characters are just that—characters."

"So, what were the characters in this game like? Was the game fun or challenging?"

"Both. We had to find this TV producer who is selling secrets of national security. Then we had to gain access to her home, but her place has biometric security, so it couldn't be done without her presence."

In the observation room, Karan stills at the nonchalant way in which Ipshita speaks about Anya.

"So, how did you gain access to her home?" Imran asks and then mentally kicks himself for jumping the gun.

"We didn't. The door to the apartment wouldn't open. Then, Neel got bitten by the bird, and all hell broke loose."

"So, you couldn't complete the game?"

"No," she says with a shake of her head.

"I still don't understand how you were going to get into the woman's home," Sameer asks.

"Yes, that part was interesting. We drugged her with a sedative and then drove her home. Then, technically, we should have got access to the place."

"You drugged her?" Sameer asks.

"Obviously, we didn't 'actually' drug her," she says, air-quoting. "It's all part of the game."

"Once you were there, what were you supposed to do? What was the next step in the game?"

"We just had to put a pen drive into her computer to delete all the information she had stolen."

"But considering how tech-savvy the game is, can't that just be done online? Why would the game need you to go there physically?" Sameer asks.

"The character this woman was playing is smart. So, she saves the information she steals on this computer that is not connected to the internet."

"Really?" Imran asks. "I mean, most computers nowadays require an internet connection for the initial setup procedure. And who doesn't use the internet?"

"Exactly, right?" Ipshita raises her hand as if to high-five Imran and then puts her hand down.

"Let's go back to the part where you drugged her," Imran says.

"Supposedly drugged her, okay? PTK tries to give the game a real feel. This woman passed out like that," Ipshita says as she clicks her fingers. "But I don't know why, she started to wake up much sooner than the others."

"The others?" Sameer asks in a blasé tone.

"Yes, most of the IRL games use a 'sedative'," she says as she air quotes the last word.

"How do you sedate a person? I mean, do you add something to their food or drink?"

"No. The supplies they provide for a game include a tiny syringe with the sedative in it. Each player has a role to play, and the details are only known to individual players."

"Supplies?" Imran encourages.

"Yes, the things we'd need for the game. This one had a pen drive that I was supposed to use on the computer. Another player gave the woman the sedative. Each player has their own role to play."

"What about the car that you were driving?"

"It belonged to one of the players. You should try playing the game to get a feel of it."

"Are you sure this woman was a character in the game? What if you picked the wrong person?"

"I don't think you understand. This isn't some random game like in that old movie, *The Man Who Knew Too Little,* where you just pay a fee and join a game. A lot of work goes into each game. You are chosen to be part of a team based on your performance in earlier games and how you work with other players." She sees the doubt on their faces. "This game was preceded by several others. It took us weeks to find this woman simply because she has no social media presence. Can you believe that? What kind of TV channel producer has no social media accounts? You won't believe the extent to which we had to work to find her. Then we had to find the perfect place to sedate her, drive her home, and get rid of the secrets she had stolen. Someone went to a lot of trouble to create such a detailed scenario. I mean, I had no idea people used biometric locks for personal use."

"You say she started to regain consciousness."

"Yes! We never expected that. You should've seen how we panicked because she was not supposed to remember any of it. We knew she was acting, but the gameplay required her to be unconscious through the whole thing. We would've lost the game if she had woken up. Then, of course, everything became chaotic with the bird biting Neel."

"Do you have any idea what sedative was given to her?"

"I think it was just saline. The rest was good acting."

There is a knock at the door before Karan walks in. He doesn't say anything to Ipshita, just nods at Imran and stands behind his officers.

"Ipshita, let me just get the order of events right," Imran says as he refers to his notepad and carefully goes through each detail.

Ipshita listens and nods ever so often. Sometimes, her eyes drift to Karan. After Imran finishes with his questions, Ipshita says, "I thought I was here to identify the man driving the vehicle I walked past that night."

"You've helped a lot with that investigation. It turns out the vehicle was not stolen. You saw the owner's son and his friends that night," Karan says. "But this game that you described..." He looks at Imran.

"Play to Kill, Sir."

"Right. Play to Kill— that's an interesting name."

Ipshita sits up. "It's just a name. It's like saying 'play to succeed'. The 'Kill' part of the name is more like how you say you killed something, like you smashed through a challenge or a target. We aren't shooting people or killing them. It's just a game!"

Karan nods slowly. "I was wondering if the game has a reward system," he asks.

Ipshita remains silent for a while. "Yes, it does, but players earn it; it's not something that is just given away. We had to find this woman, and believe me, it wasn't easy with the most basic information they had given us, and that, too, was IRL."

"So, did you get the reward?" Karan asks.

"No," she shakes her head in dismay, "we didn't finish the game."

"But no one could've possibly imagined this strange sequence of events occurring. Shouldn't you all have had another chance?"

"I thought the same, but PTK has a policy that if a mission is unsuccessful, it is closed. No other team can play it either."

"How long have you been playing this game?" Karan asks casually.

"A few months," Ipshita says with a flip of her hair.

"How long have you played at a level that puts you in contact with people in the real world?"

"About two months."

"And each time the person was sedated?"

"The actor," Ipshita corrects him.

Karan smiles. "The actor, as you said, is sedated, right?"

She nods in response. "This was the first game that I've left incomplete on this level."

"Can you go through the gaming site and tell the officers which games you have been involved with, especially at this level?"

"I think I've spent enough time here. I'm going to go now," Ipshita says as she pushes her chair back.

"Have you heard of the drug, Rohypnol?"

Ipshita's expression is blank. "Like the date rape drug?"

"Correct. That is the drug you gave the woman in your game."

Ipshita shakes her head vehemently. "No, that's not true. It's just a game."

"Play to Kill may be a game to you, but to that woman, it is not," Karan says and waits for the implications to seep in.

Ipshita sits still for a few moments, and then she shakes her head again. "No, it's not possible. It's just a game."

Karan continues to watch her, waiting for the cold reality of the situation to sink in, but it doesn't.

"No. It's a game I've been playing for months. It's just clean fun, nothing else."

"In how many of your games have you sedated a person?" Karan asks, but Ipshita seems lost in thought.

"No." She shakes her head. "This makes no sense. Why would anyone use a date rape drug? In the games I played IRL, there was nothing suspicious, no one touched a player in an odd way, if you know what I mean. Besides, many of the actors were men. There was nothing sexual about the games."

"Rohypnol is a sedative. It's been misused far too often for sexual assault, but essentially, it is a fast-acting sedative." He didn't mention that the formula that the game used was more refined and shortened the sedation period significantly. "Where did you get it?"

"It was in the game supply pack, I swear. The first time I saw it, I thought it looked like something out of a child's toy set. The syringe is barely the length of my small finger." She raises her right hand to illustrate. "The needle part is just about a centimetre, maybe even less. It is easy to hide in your fist. It looks like a prop for a drama. It isn't real. You've got this whole thing wrong."

"Ipshita," Karan says, "you seem genuinely shocked, but the fact is the woman you drugged is not an actor. She is, as you said, a producer with a television channel. She was taken from outside the hotel where her team was shooting at and brought home. The fact that she has a biometric lock on her door should tell you how seriously she takes her security. The fact that you were unable to get inside her apartment was sheer luck. This woman has been having nightmares at the mere thought of what may've happened. Do you understand what I'm saying?"

Ipshita's face pales. "We weren't going to hurt her. It's just a game," she says in a low voice as she holds her face in her hands. It takes her a few minutes to speak again. "She wasn't a part of the game? Are you sure?" she asks, raising her head slightly. Since she is looking at Imran, he shakes his head. "Did we pick the wrong person? I mean, was the actor there, and we missed her?" Ipshita mumbles, still unwilling to read the writing on the wall.

Imran looks at Karan, who nods.

"I think you picked the right person, except for one crucial detail. She wasn't playing the game."

"How's that possible?" Ipshita shakes her head and then freezes.

Finally, Karan thinks to himself.

"In all the IRL games I've played, is it possible that the people we drugged were not actors?" she asks in a hushed tone and looks at the officers for a response. "No, no, no! And on top of that, I've dragged Neel into this. The minute he saw the syringe, he looked extremely uncomfortable about the whole thing. Oh no! Are you going to arrest me?" she asks, panic-stricken.

"No, we're not, but we need your help to figure out what is going on with this game."

"You won't arrest me?"

Karan shakes his head. "Not if you can help us."

"I'll help," she replies quickly.

"Tell the officers everything you know about Play to Kill, and I do mean everything," Karan says as some colour returns to Ipshita's face. "Go through every detail, however insignificant it may seem. Call home and let your family know you'll be a little late. Don't tell anyone about meeting us, okay?"

"Okay."

"You also need to continue playing, except now, one of the officers will monitor the game."

"Since Neel got hurt, I haven't had time for PTK. Besides, I've been busy with college."

"Alright, but just log into your account as you would normally. And Ipshita, the only way we can help you is if you are completely honest about every aspect of the game. Even if it seems like a mundane, boring detail, we need to know."

Ipshita nods.

"There's just one more thing. Did you stamp each of the so-called actors during or after the game?" he asks.

Ipshita stares at him and nods. "A temporary tattoo was applied at the end of each game."

"Where?"

"Usually at the back of the neck."

"Why?"

"Why?" she repeats. "Well, the game is called Play to Kill. After each game is complete, the kill, I mean the success, is marked with a temporary tattoo."

"Why that design?"

"The spiral? I don't know. I just thought it was a pretty cool detail, a glow-in-the-dark tattoo."

"It was placed on a part of the body that the person is unlikely to notice. Didn't that seem odd to you?" Karan asks.

"It's just a game. I thought it was just a game," she corrects herself.

Karan looks at Sameer before leaving the interview room. The game was after something on Anya's computer—the one that was not connected to the internet. Karan walks out into the wide corridor and then makes his way up the stairs to the roof.

Anya picks up the call after a few rings.

"How are things in the capital, ACP Shekhawat?"

Karan grins. The woman has a weird way of answering calls. "As good as can be expected, and in Almora, Ms Aulakh?"

"Very interesting."

"Can you talk about it right now?"

"Not really. Do you want to speak with Antara?"

"I'd have called her if I wanted to speak with her," Karan replies sharply and then mentally kicks himself.

Anya tsks. "It's not like you to get impatient, ACP Shekhawat. So, I assume you found something that you don't like."

Karan sighs. "I'm sorry. You're the last person I want to snap at right now. And I thought we'd agreed to use first names."

Anya remains silent for a while. "You say I'm the last person you want to snap at. Does that mean the break in your case has to do with me?"

"I can't tell you much right now," replies Karan. "Is there anything on your desktop computer that anyone would want to break into your home for?"

"The desktop just contains copies of files that I want to keep for myself. Most of the files are for the photo bank, some are financial, and some hold photographs and documents from my childhood. None of them is confidential. I just don't want anyone else to have access to them."

"After you left Hisar, did you change your name?"

"Not really."

"That's not a good enough answer; it's neither here nor there," he retorts.

"I didn't change my name, officially or unofficially."

"But?"

"I continued using the nickname by which my hostel friends called me."

"So, on those papers on the computer, your name is ... ?"

"Saranya," she says in a low voice.

She was quiet, too quiet. He couldn't imagine what was going through her mind.

"So, you think this is about my family?" she asks. "Let me tell you, if they knew where I work or live, they wouldn't be playing cat and mouse. They have a more 'in-your-face' intimidation style."

"I agree," he says. "So, Saranya? As in the Goddess of the clouds, wife of Surya? Who would've known!"

"Most people who hear the name normally would ask if I have surrendered."

He snorts. "Then they don't know you very well, do they?"

"Goddess of the clouds? I'm surprised you know that," she says.

"My mother is a history professor. She specializes in Indian and Greek mythology. You'd be surprised how similar they are. Fun fact—Saranya is associated with Helen of Troy."

"Cool!"

"But your name is Anya, isn't it? I mean, that is what you respond to."

"Yes, it feels more 'me' than Saranya."

"So, is it from the Russian name 'Anna', or do you prefer the Sanskrit version? Knowing your penchant for research, I'm sure you know both meanings. So, are you Anya, the one who brings goodness, or the one who is inexhaustible?"

Anya laughs. "Why can't I be both? I'd have never taken you for a history geek."

He grins. "Well, it's good to know that I can surprise you. I'm not just a cop with a superhero complex."

"Touché!" she says. "You know, in a Nigerian dialect, Anya means 'the eye.'"

"As in the third, all-seeing eye?" he can't resist asking.

"That's for me to know and you to find out," she quips, then lets out a deep breath. She knows the playful banter is to help her not panic. "You think there is something on that computer that made someone drug me? That doesn't make sense." She thinks over the situation from multiple vantage points but still comes up empty. "You have the computer, and Kabir has the passwords to the files that are protected. You can take a look and decide for yourself. I signed the forms Kabir gave me, so it's all on the up and up."

"Okay. I'll—we'll see you soon," he says as he starts to hang up.

"Wait! Did you find the people who drugged me?"

"Sort of."

"Can't they tell you what they were looking for?"

"I'll explain when you come back. Take care," he says absentmindedly.

"You too."

His next call is to Kabir, and he adds Abhi to the conversation. Karan explains what they've learnt about PTK.

"Tell me you haven't opened the site from your computers," Abhi says.

Karan rolls his eyes. "Imran opened it on my laptop."

"It's fine, Sir. That device is fully protected. That said, I think we should use clean laptops. I haven't heard of PTK before. Have you, Abhi?"

"I have, but that was last year or maybe the end of the year before, when they were getting it set up. They were hiring programmers and designers at dirt-cheap rates. I passed on that not-so-bright opportunity. Besides, it seemed pretty shoddy."

"Shoddy, how?" Karan asks.

"From what I gather, they were asking programmers and designers to work on sections of the site. It was like a patchwork, mish-mash thing. That approach invariably causes glitches, and the programmer is always the first to be blamed."

"So, let me get this straight. A programmer or designer would only work on a small portion of the site and never really know how it comes up?"

"Yes, Sir," Kabir says. "It is mostly done to save money because neither the programmer nor the designer realizes the scope or span of the project."

"Considering the fact that no one has any idea of what the site is about, does it also keep the site more private and secure?" Karan asks.

Abhi snorts. "No! Only the site owners think it does. With too many cooks—in this case, too many programmers—in the kitchen, things are usually a mess, and that includes security. But I can tell you one thing for sure, they would not be blasé about the security of their players."

"Meaning what?" Karan asks.

"They probably keep a record of the players' identities. I'd think they'd allow players to use the site only when they can link back to their IP address, so no VPNs. Don't visit PTK or try to register on the site until we have a clearer picture of things. Let Kabir and I have a look at it, Bhai, and we should have an answer for you by the evening."

"Okay, I'll see you fellows then."

Karan is fairly satisfied he's done all he can with this line of investigation. He walks back to the observation room, sits down, and takes out his notepad to pen down details. Ipshita had said she started the game with social media searches and graduated to looking for people with only a photograph for a clue. Most of the games took her days—some even took weeks—to complete. Karan didn't think it was something a college kid would find interesting. *Unless...* He messaged Sameer and waited.

"How are you rewarded for the games you complete?" Sameer asks Ipshita.

"I get a better score and move to a higher level," she replies, looking down at her nails.

"And?" Sameer persists.

"And?" Ipshita replies insolently, then takes in the look on the officer's face. She sighs dramatically. "Okay, okay. For every win, you receive a gift card. The amount depends on the level of difficulty of the task. The one we were playing, apparently, has been in the works for weeks. Of course, it was on different levels."

"What do you mean?"

"I mean that the game moved to higher levels based on information that earlier games had brought in."

"You said it was difficult to find this television producer because of her lack of activity on social media," Imran says. "Then, how did you find her?"

"Look, I was not a part of that particular game, okay? All I know is they started the game without a photograph or a name. Can you imagine how difficult that is in the world we live in, both real and virtual?"

"How do you look for someone without basic information like that? You have to start somewhere," Imran says.

"I don't know the specifics, but I can check. I know one of the players on that team. We aren't supposed to talk about our games, but I am sure she'd tell me."

"Was she a part of this one, too?"

"No, the game likes to keep degrees of separation between the players. That way, people don't gang up."

Karan thinks it sounds like a pretty good strategy to compartmentalize the players. That way, they wouldn't have any idea of what exactly the game was up to.

"When you speak to her, you need to ensure that she doesn't tell anyone else you've been asking her questions, especially someone playing PTK."

"Obviously!" Ipshita replies.

"I am going to show you some photographs. Tell me if you've seen any of them," Sameer says as he takes them out from a file.

They go through the photographs slowly. She only identifies two photographs—one of them is of Mrs Naugiyal.

"Tell me about this one," Sameer says.

"This was an interesting one. The game itself was pretty simple. She was betraying the country and selling confidential secrets. We had to ensure she didn't board a particular flight. We were told we could choose where we wanted to set up the gameplay. Usually, these details are very specific—there is no deviating from them. Like the TV channel producer—we knew where she would be and where we had to take her," Ipshita says. "But in her case," she points at Mrs Naugiyal's photograph, "the players had to choose a location. We did a fair amount of research—her home, her store. Then we found out she parks her car in the Park N Fly at T3. That seemed like the quietest place to do it."

"Quietest?" Imran asks.

"I mean, some place we were least likely to be disturbed. The roads in front of her home and store are busy."

"She was drugged?"

Ipshita nods. "Yes, but it was just a game."

"Well, now you know it is more than that," Imran replies in a stern voice. "The drug caused her to have a respiratory attack, and she spent several days in the hospital. She missed that flight and the meeting she was scheduled to attend. As a result, she lost an international contract. These are not details from a gameplay but from her life—her real life."

Ipshita looks shocked.

"You did your research on her?" Sameer asks, and she nods her reply. "So then, you know her husband was an air force pilot who died on active duty. Mrs Naugiyal is a single mother—one who is trying to live her life in a way that would teach her children they can do anything they set their minds on. The store she owns sources all its products from a forest garden her husband designed and dreamed of creating."

Silent tears stream down Ipshita's face. Imran starts to reach for his handkerchief, but Sameer nudges him with his elbow. *Sometimes, letting things out is the only way forward.* They sit in silence for a few minutes before she starts to wipe her face with her hands and then accepts the handkerchief Imran offers.

She takes a few more minutes to compose herself. "How can I help?" she asks. "I can't undo the things I've done, even if at that time I thought it was a game, but there must be some way I can help."

"There is," Imran says and looks at Sameer. "First, we need to know what details were initially offered in the game to find the television producer. But I don't want you to rush off and start asking questions."

"You don't want me to raise any suspicions. I understand that. The player I talked about—the one who was part of the initial game that involved identifying her—I know her well. In fact," she says with a sigh, "I introduced her to the game." She rubs her forehead with her hand. "Can I tell her the drug part is real?"

Imran looks at Sameer, and Sameer looks at the message he's just received from Karan on his phone.

"Do you trust her?" he asks.

"She is my friend. I know her well. She would never want to be involved in something like this. Look, we were looking for good, clean fun. I should've known it was too good to be true. The IRL game setups are so elaborate, or so I thought. It never occurred to me that we could be messing with real people."

"I understand, but right now, don't tell her about the drug," Sameer says. "There is one particular person we are looking for." He takes out Raina's photograph from the file, places it in front of her, and begins to explain the case.

Ipshita shakes her head. "No! There is no way any of the players would have agreed to a game that involved snatching a child."

"But what if the players thought they were rescuing the child?"

Ipshita shakes her head but looks conflicted. "I understand what you're saying. If the story was convincing enough, you think someone may've tried. But you've to understand, most of the players are college students. I don't think anyone would've wanted to be involved with a case like that." She looks at the photograph carefully. "This baby is so small. I would be scared to even try to hold him. I can have a look at the Hall of Glory. It's a list of cases successfully solved on PTK."

"I need to check your devices to ensure they are safe," Imran says.

"You mean, they may be bugged or cloned? No way! I don't leave them lying around."

"Just as a precaution, okay? Let's ensure they are safe."

She nods and hands him her phone and iPad.

"I'll quickly check these out and bring them back," he tells her and leaves the room.

Ipshita stares at the door. Sameer is glad to see that the magnitude of the situation is finally starting to sink in.

"Please keep our conversation just between us. I assume you're going to tell your cousin," Sameer says, and she nods. "That's good. It'll be good to have someone to talk to. If you need to call or get in touch with us," he hands her his card, "you can call any time of the day or night. If you think something feels odd, or if you remember any detail you may've missed, however small it may be, message us or call us."

"Okay."

"I will expect to hear from you after you speak to your friend. In the meantime, if you are offered an IRL game, please inform us."

"Do I need to play it? I don't want to," Ipshita replies quickly.

"That's fine. Don't play if you don't want to. We only need the details."

"You understand, the basic details the game will offer will be sparse at best," she says. "It may involve several days of digging and following up to identify a person."

Sameer nods. The whole situation is convoluted. Whoever is planning the games has kept their hands clean of the whole situation. It is the players who do all the dirty work without realizing the trail of damage their games leave behind.

"Will it be odd for you to take a break from the game?"

"Not really. The IRL games take up too much time, and I have my end-semester exams coming up."

"Do players take a picture together at the end of the game—as something to remember the game by?"

"No, once the game starts, all phones are put into a bag so that there are no interruptions."

"Don't you need to check things while the game is in play—things like traffic in the area?" Sameer asks.

"Yes, of course. There is an iPad and a phone in the game pack for that."

"What all is in the game pack?"

"It's not the same for every game, but the iPad and phone are always there, as is the syringe in a small pouch. Sometimes, there are other things based on the game. Like for this one, there was a pen drive that was to be put into the computer at her house. Of course, we never got to that stage of the game; things got pretty chaotic as soon as we arrived at her doorstep," she says.

"So, you returned the pen drive to the game pack."

"I guess so," Ipshita says.

"'I guess so' is not good enough, Ipshita. I need you to think back. Is it possible that in the chaos of Neel getting bit by the bird, you didn't put the pen drive back?"

"Just give me a minute," she mumbles as she tries to retrace the memories of that night. "I got the first-aid stuff at the pharmacy. Then we drove to the hospital."

"Which one?"

"Ram Manohar Lohia. It was the closest to where we'd parked our cars."

"Where was that?"

"The hospital parking lot is open 24 hours. We were supposed to meet the rest of the team in front of the Sacred Heart Cathedral, but it seemed like a better choice to park in a crowded area."

"So, you walked from the hospital to the cathedral?"

"Yes, but later, the team just dropped us off at the hospital gate. By the time we finally got back home, it was close to dawn."

"What about the USB drive?"

She shakes her head. "I don't remember giving it to any of the players. I will check the bag I was using that day. I could have dropped it in the car or put it into the pocket of my jeans. I don't know. I'll check as soon as I get home."

Sameer nods. "We'll use your user ID to log in to the game. Imran will message you before he logs in—that way, there won't be multiple logins. He will coordinate the details with you." He glances at his watch. "Can we drop you off at home?"

"No. My friend is waiting in the parking lot."

"Oh! You could've brought him along."

She nods.

"Imran will show you out. One last thing—if you find the pen drive, we'd like to see it. Don't try checking it first," Sameer warns.

Ipshita puts her devices back into her leather satchel and nods. "I'll look," she says, standing up. "I'm really sorry. Can you please convey that to the lady? I just thought we were playing."

Sameer nods and watches Imran lead her out of the room before he looks towards the observation room, where he is sure Karan still sits. They have a lot of work waiting for them and are still playing catch-up.

CHAPTER TEN

"What did Cybercrimes say?" Karan asks Imran as he takes a seat next to Sameer in Karan's office.

"They haven't heard of it. There are no complaints about the website."

"Who is going to complain, Sir? The players think they're playing a game, and the victims have no idea of what is happening," Sameer says.

"Agreed," says Karan. "If it's all a game—a play set on the stage—who is behind the curtain? Who is pulling the strings? Who is directing it all? Mrs Naugiyal missing her appointment was important to someone. Anya's computer is important to someone. Someone is fixing these situations."

"We aren't going to open the website until Kabir and Abhi say it is safe, right, Sir?" Sameer asks.

"I thought it was safe to open it on my computer?"

"Let them check it out first, Sir. We don't want to warn off whoever is running PTK. Then we'll never know what this whole thing is about."

Karan nods. "I don't know what I was expecting. All these cases seemed odd, but I was definitely not expecting them to be part of a game." He taps his fingers on the desk. "What are your impressions of Ipshita? How much of what she told us do we take at face value?"

"A whole bagful of mixed emotions there, with disbelief being a strong one, but I think by the time she left, she was convinced," Imran says.

"Yes, but for how long? After mulling over things, people usually don't think they hold any responsibility in most situations," Sameer adds.

Karan nods. "If we can't look at PTK right now, we can, at least, check out where they parked and met the rest of the group. Let's try to create a timeline and see if we can pick up a trail."

Sameer rubs his eyes. "That means a lot of CCTV recordings. I will start requesting them. We know where they started and then picked up Anya before going to her place. Imran, you can chalk out the roads they would've likely taken."

"In the meantime, I'm going to try to identify the car used to kidnap Navin," Karan says. "Imran, make sure Kabir and Antara get a copy of Ipshita's interview and also the video you recorded this morning."

"Yes, Sir."

"Also, keep in touch with Ipshita, and continue digging into her life. Tell Kabir, by the end of the day, I want a spreadsheet of whatever Abhi and he find out about PTK."

After the officers leave his office, Karan clears the paperwork on his desk. Just the thought of watching fuzzy CCTV recordings is enough to give him a headache.

This once, just this once, give us a break sooner rather than later, he bargains with the gods that came up with Murphy's Law.

After being glued to the screen for over an hour, he is fairly sure of the three vehicles that had exited from the street next to the mall around the time Navin was taken. All three had Delhi licence plates. *So far, so good.* He's about to look up the details of the vehicle owners when he notices one of the cars has a mall parking sticker. *The car probably belongs to someone who works there. Did the other cars have any tell-tale stickers, too?* He pauses the image of the second car, a KIA. He can't see the driver or the passenger clearly, but the sticker with the insignia of a lawyer is clearly visible. The third vehicle, a white BMW, did not have any stickers that Karan could see from the limited view of the CCTV camera.

He accesses the RTO records. The system is slow, so he feeds the first set of details and pulls out his copy of the city's road map. His map, like the ones that each of his officers uses, has additional details that they've added over the last year. He looks at the relevant section and takes a moment to recall what he'd seen outside the mall.

As the cars exited from the side lane, they would've entered the main road. After the next traffic light, they could have moved in pretty much any direction, including taking a U-turn and heading back. He calls the SHO at the local police station. As he'd expected, the CCTV recordings from the traffic lights were collected, but no one had had the time to go through them. Karan asks the SHO to send them across to the Urban Crimes office.

The RTO search has finally brought up a result, and much to his surprise, the website loading has picked up speed. The first car belongs to a store owner in the mall, the second to a lawyer who lives in a neighbouring colony, and the third belongs to someone who lives on Pandara Road.

Karan glances at his watch and decides to look up the registered mobile numbers for each of the owners. He makes quick calls to them. Fortunately for him, two of them are minutes away from the office. He sends a message to Sameer and Imran to let them know he'll be out of the office.

***

After a brief conversation with the store owner, Karan is sure he'd just been going about his usual business on that fateful day and had arrived at the store early to take stock of a consignment. Instead of moving on to meet the next person on his list, Karan heads to the third-floor grocery store from which Navin was taken. He walks around the mall, taking note of the entrance and exit points, as well as the well-laid-out traffic paths.

He takes out his phone to call Antara. "Are you busy?" he asks as she responds on the third ring.

"No, Sir. You're on speaker. We decided to head back to Delhi. We spoke to everyone who was willing to speak with us," she says. "Mrs Naugiyal's in-laws are hosting some sort of a spiritual camp or retreat at their place. We were politely ushered away. Fortunately, we'd finished our conversation with Mr Naugiyal, but his wife refused to speak with us. Did you call to ask me something?"

"If you were kidnapping a baby from the mall, would you just walk off with the baby or take him in the stroller, pram—whatever it is called?"

"Hmm." Antara thinks about the options and looks at Anya.

Anya shakes her head slightly.

"If I were making a quick getaway, I would just pick the kid and move on. That way, the chances of being noticed with the baby would be much lower," Antara says.

Anya nods in agreement. "It's also easier and quicker to walk out than push a stroller or pram you aren't used to. Some of the high-end prams have a lot of complicated features," she adds.

"So, why did they take the baby, pram and all?" Karan asks.

"Because they intend to keep the baby—for a while, at least. The pram is convenient to have around," Antara volunteers.

"Also, it would've had a bag that had the basic things the baby would need—diapers, wipes, bottles, etc.," Anya says.

"So, do we agree it was a convenient option?" Karan asks.

"Yes, Sir. They obviously planned it well."

"The whole thing also seems like they were extremely confident. If you ask me, a mall is not a great place to snatch a baby or to drug a woman, with the CCTVs on, staff and customers around. It's just not a good choice," Anya says.

"Where would you do it?" Antara asks Anya inquisitively.

"What?" she asks, her eyes widening. "I'm not looking down that dark path."

"Humour me," Antara says. "If you were to plan this scene, where would you do it?"

"The parking lot, of course. It would be the perfect place to drug and kidnap people. And now, I can say that with an air of experience," she adds bitterly.

"Raina didn't drive to the mall, so the parking lot was out of the question. Other than family trips out of the city, she doesn't get out of the house much. Apart from taking a walk in the neighbourhood park or going out for groceries, I don't think she left the house often," Karan says.

"I can't blame her. Freelance work can take up more time than a conventional job, and then, of course, she has the baby," Antara says. "So obviously, these people knew her routine."

"They were more than just aware of it. They knew what time she'd get to the store. Sameer and I spoke to the neighbours and the maid. No one mentioned seeing a stranger around the house or anyone keeping track of Raina's activities."

Anya huffs. "You'd be surprised at the kind of information people volunteer about other people, even if it's none of their business. You don't even need to intrude—just listening to people discuss or talk about Raina would give someone the information they needed about her."

Karan and Antara remain silent. *It seems like Anya speaks from experience.*

"There are many ways to intrude into someone's life," Karan says.

"Exactly," Antara agrees.

"The other option, of course, is that someone purposefully shared the information," Karan adds.

"The maid?" Antara asks.

"It's unlikely, but we'll still have to check. It could be a neighbour, someone she worked with, a friend, or the landlady. It's not very difficult to get a clear idea of someone's schedule if they tend to follow it like clockwork. Raina had a fairly set routine. Okay then, drive safe, and message me when you stop for dinner."

"Does he do this often?" Anya asks when the call ends.

"What?" Antara asks, keeping her eyes on the road. "Oh! Put us in hypothetical situations? All the time. One thing this job teaches you is not to make up your mind about anything, and consider all the options—the obvious and the far-fetched ones."

"I guess a sounding board is important in your line of work."

"I'd think that is true of any line of work, but yes, definitely in ours."

"Like Watson for Holmes?"

Antara grins her reply. "It is a blessing to have a team that doesn't dismiss ideas at the outset or consider them trivial. Karan Sir runs Urban Crimes quite differently than most of the officers I've worked with in the past. No detail is considered too small or inane for the team. Since we usually work in pairs and approach the same case from different angles, it's crucial that we share these details, which is why Karan Sir's home is like a second base of operations for us."

"Does he often stow away people related to a case at his place?"

Antara pauses for a second before answering. "Never."

Anya nods. "It's best to keep work away from home."

Antara laughs. "You would think so, but it is difficult to do. For us, work and all its grimy details follow us home. Sometimes, it is a conscious decision, but most of the time, they just sneak in. When you are working through the muddled, murky details of a case, you can't just leave them on the desk after your shift is over."

Anya nods thoughtfully and stares at the long road ahead of them. "The house itself is incredible. Abhi told me there was no way anyone could see me from outside the compound, but I didn't take him seriously."

"Until you actually stepped beyond the garden, right?"

"Yes! I thought I was proud of The Tri's backyard..."

"And you should be," Antara interrupts.

"Yes, but his place is on a whole new level. If I hadn't wandered into it, I would've never known there was a jungle, forest—whatever is the right word for it—right there."

"Yes, it's amazing. Apparently, Sir's grandfather built the house. He used to be a senior officer in the forest department. Between Karan Sir and his grandfather, they planted each tree and planned how the whole area would come up."

"That way, even after he retired, he'd have a bit of the forest around him," Anya murmurs.

"Little stone paths run through the property, so you can walk around even when it is raining. There is a stream that flows through it. He'd never let you shoot there, if that's what's on your mind," Antara adds in a bland tone.

"Not at all! You don't need to convince me about keeping his privacy."

"I'm glad to hear that. Other than his immediate family and the team, I've never seen anyone else there—no other friends, colleagues, or relatives. I wish he'd come on this trip instead of me. The garden forest would've interested him. I've never seen anything like it before. Almost everything in that forest was edible! Absolutely incredible! And to have school kids guide visitors through the forest was brilliant!"

"Their sheer happiness and pride in the forest was apparent," Anya agrees.

***

Why would a team of PTK players kidnap a baby, Karan asks himself. According to Ipshita, the IRL games usually had four or five players in a team. In Navin's kidnapping, they could only see a couple walk out with the pram. *Had they meant to kidnap both the mother and her son?*

Karan shakes his head. *No.* From the start, the goal had been to kidnap the child and leave the mother behind. It would've been difficult to move Raina in a drugged state. They'd definitely planned to leave her there. *Why leave her somewhere she'd be noticed quickly? Something was off about the whole thing.*

He walks back to the grocery store and looks around. The entrance to the store is close to the corner of the building and the stairwell. It would have been smarter to take the child when Raina was walking in or out of the store, preferably close to the staircase or the bank of lifts. The whole thing seems odd—planned and yet, sort of rushed.

His phone rings. Karan notes it is a number he'd dialled a while ago. It is the owner of the KIA. A short conversation ends with more CCTV recordings to gather. The lawyer and his young wife had come to the mall, hoping that the pharmacy on the ground floor would be open, but it hadn't been.

When Karan asks him why they were in such a rush, there is an awkward pause. They were looking for a pregnancy kit, the lawyer tells him. They had to drive around a bit before they found a pharmacy that was open. Karan pens down the details of the pharmacy. He'd ask the local police station to check on it. He calls the third car owner again but receives an out-of-coverage area message again. Karan forwards Imran the number, certain the officer would be able to find more information than the RTO records had offered.

Back at the office, Karan studies the financial records Arjun shared with them, putting down details on his notepad. When he is done with the exercise, he goes through his notes. He still hasn't found anything that would raise a red flag.

The couple led a mediocre lifestyle. After Karan goes through their bank statements, it seems downright austere. They save most of their earnings, invest a large portion, and have more medical insurance than anyone Karan knows. They'd bought their house in Noida with their savings and hadn't taken a loan.

There had been no ransom note. The baby could have been sold off. This is always a cloud that looms over the kidnapping of an infant. The kidnappers may've wanted to keep the baby for themselves—that is yet another option to ponder over. The use of Rohypnol makes no sense in this case or in any of the PTK cases.

***

It is a little past ten at night when Abhi helps Antara and Anya with their bags and locks the main gate for the night. While Antara heads to Karan's home office to brief him, Anya goes to her room. Her plan is simple—unpack, take a quick shower, and go to bed. Something about the late hour and the sound of the falling water unexpectedly brings back a ripped fragment of a lost memory. She quickly dries herself and throws her clothes on.

In the living room, for the second time, Abhi patiently explains to Karan the coding issues with the PTK website and why the team shouldn't try to access it until Kabir and he are sure it isn't monitoring visitors to the website.

"Bhai, think of it like a patchwork blanket—some portions are beautifully done, some are shabby and rushed. We need to go through it all before I can give you a definite answer. As of now, I haven't come across anything to suggest that the game is keeping a watch on its players. We still have thousands of lines of code to go through. Besides, we haven't reached the level of the IRL games." He stops speaking as he watches Anya enter the room. She looks pale and sort of dazed. "Bhai," Abhi says as he gestures with his chin.

Karan turns around. The blank, distant expression on her face makes him wonder if she may be sleepwalking. He approaches her slowly.

"What do you want?" she asks him in a low voice. "What do you want?"

"Anya," Karan says gently as he touches her hand. She flinches. "It's okay." He lets his hand drop.

"What do you want? He asked me, 'What do you want?'"

"Who asked you?"

"The man on the phone. The one who called while I was asleep. I was taking a shower, and the words just came back to me."

"'What do you want?'" Karan asks.

"Yes, that's what he asked me," she says.

"Why do you think he was asking you that?"

Anya is quiet and then shakes her head. "I don't know."

"What do 'you' want, Anya?" Karan asks with more emphasis.

"I just want to be left alone to live my life," she replies listlessly.

Karan nods and then slowly reaches for her hand to guide her to the diwan. "Abhi, bring Anya a glass of water, please."

Once Anya sits down cross-legged on the diwan, he places around her shoulders the fleece throw Abhi keeps handy for when it gets chilly in the evening.

Karan sits down on the adjacent chair. "What do you think he meant?"

"I don't know. I don't know why I completely forgot about the call. It doesn't make sense."

"Let's focus on something else. What did his voice sound like?"

"It was low, sort of gruff. Barely above a whisper, but..."

"But?"

"It sounded intense and yet kind of restrained. Am I making any sense?"

It sounded like someone trying to hold back their anger.

"Let's think of this in a different way," he suggests.

She nods.

"When would someone usually ask a person that question?" Karan looks at Anya and then at Antara and Abhi.

"Obviously, when they want to know what the other person wants, Bhai," Abhi replies.

"Which is more important—the question or how it was asked?" Antara asks.

"Both," Karan replies. "Usually, when a person asks such a question and sounds angry, it's because they know they will not like the answer. Is there anything work-related that needs your consent or something you need to sign off on? Like a contract or a payment?"

Anya shakes her head. "No, the legal department and accounts section handle all that."

"Kabir mentioned some of your colleagues joke about you being something of a rainmaker. When you produce a show, sponsorships just fall into place."

Anya snorts. "Yes, I'm sure they think they just fall into place without any grunt work. It's nothing that any other producer doesn't do. You've got to keep your finger on the pulse of the market and pick the right brands and businesses to choose as sponsors."

"Could somebody be trying to bribe you?" Antara asks.

"Absolutely not. I've no influence that is worth bribing over."

"Could this be related to The Tri?"

"We handle a very select clientele and are careful with their privacy," she says and sees the look that Antara gives Karan. "It's nothing shady. We mostly get artists, authors, and business executives who just want a break. Think of it like a staycation."

"Then, there is only one other option," Abhi summarizes. "Who are you blackmailing, Anya?" he asks with a grin.

"What?" She sits up. "I'm not blackmailing anyone."

Karan thinks about it for some time. "It does make sense. Either this man wants something from you, or he thinks you have something on him. A bribe or blackmail—both scenarios could work."

"But I am not blackmailing anyone, and there is no reason for anyone to bribe me."

"It's on your desktop computer, or that is what this person thinks," Antara speculates.

"If the PTK thing and this call are connected, and it is most likely they are," Karan says before Anya can object, "then Antara is probably right."

"But how does he know it's on the desktop?"

"He knows because he already checked your computer at the office," Antara and Karan reply together.

Anya squirms with three sets of eyes on her. "You have my desktop. Do what you want with it."

"There are thousands of photographs in the photo bank database. We have to know where to start looking, otherwise it is like looking for a particular strand of hay in a pile of hay," Abhi says.

"Don't look at me. I have no idea what this is about," Anya says, raising her hands in apparent surrender.

"How about your investment in the startups? Could this be about that?"

"No, other than the initial investment and some personal contact with the owners, I've no role to play in them, and more importantly, I've no influence on them," she adds.

"Then, we have no choice but to wait for Ipshita to figure out how the players identified you in the game."

"So, essentially, we wait and watch?" Anya sighs.

Karan rubs his face. "Yes."

"Anya, can I sleep in your room tonight?" Antara asks as she stands up. "In case you remember anything else at night, it may help to have someone there."

Anya doesn't miss Karan's barely perceptible nod at the idea. *He is probably worried about me having a panic attack.*

"Are all of you worried I might forget some important clue in my sleep? Okay, roomie, let's go to sleep," she says as she pats Antara's shoulder and walks past her. "Goodnight, everyone."

Once she has left the room, Karan looks at Antara and Abhi. "We need to figure out how the PTK players found her. I have a bad feeling about this whole situation," he says as he goes back to his room.

"Can I ask you something, Antara?" Abhi asks in a low voice.

"You're going to ask me if I think Karan Sir has any idea of how much he likes Anya, right?"

Abhi gestures with his hands and makes a soft 'boom' sound. "I can't even tease him about going all googly-eyed around her."

"You dare not, Abhi! Let's just see how this goes. If he needs a little nudge on the way, the team has his back," she adds with a loud yawn.

CHAPTER ELEVEN

The next day, the team takes turns watching the CCTV videos. Too many hours of watching bad-quality video are a pain but also a crucial part of the job. There is also the risk of looking away at the worst possible moment and missing out on a vital clue. When they aren't watching the videos, they take turns searching through the files on Anya's computer. Karan is reading one of her write-ups for 'High Tea' when Kabir comes into his home office and stands behind his chair.

"She writes well," Kabir mumbles. "From the first sentence, it feels like she pulled up a comfortable chair and invited me to sit down to high tea with her."

Karan nods. "Some of the travel articles I read made me feel like she had reached out and grabbed my hand—sometimes, it felt like it was my shirt collar—and dragged me off on an adventure in a distant land. How does she do that?"

"There's nothing controversial that would get her into trouble," Kabir adds unhappily.

"Yes. It's all about food and travel—stuff people enjoy reading. If she were writing about politics or finance, I'd still understand that she may've rubbed people up the wrong way. I don't see anything worrying here."

"As yet," Kabir says.

"As yet," Karan agrees.

"When does she find time to write so much?" Kabir asks as he continues to read the article. "Sir, did you know, a few years back, she did a series for a public transportation company that was bleeding?"

"Public transportation?" Karan asks, giving Kabir a sidelong glance.

"State transportation, to be precise."

"No way!"

"Yes. She developed a show for budget travel, basically focusing on college students, people starting their careers, and without personal transportation. Then, she chose a range of homestays and small but quality guesthouses, along with restaurants and *dhabas* dotted on those routes."

"I watched that series with Abhi. In fact, he and some of his friends even went on some of those trips. I thought it was brilliant."

"What if a business or company decided that they could turn their fortune, and Anya refused to work on the project, or let's say, she couldn't work on it? Would they be offended enough to threaten her?"

Both officers think for a while before Kabir continues, "It doesn't explain their interest in her home computer." He shakes his head. "I'm overthinking the whole thing, aren't I?"

"No, it was a good line of thought. It could explain the 'what do you want' kind of phone call. I'm moving to the photo bank now."

"They have an extensive collection. I had no idea people stocked pictures of nuts and bolts and whatnot."

"She said they had permission from all the people in their photographs, didn't she?" Karan asks.

"Yes, Sir. They get paid every time a photograph is used."

"This is a waste of time," Karan growls. "At least, until we know how the PTK team found her. Where are we on the three vehicles leaving the mall?"

Kabir walks around the desk and sits down. "The storeowner's and the lawyer's stories check out. The third car is registered to Rajendra Singh of Jor Bagh."

"I thought the RTO records said Pandara Road," Karan interrupts.

"Yes, they do. Strangely, the address options for the records club neighbourhoods. I tried the number, but there was no response."

Karan glances at his watch. It's just short of noon. "Let's go meet this fellow."

"Now?" Kabir asks.

"Yes, now. I need a break."

Kabir grabs his bag as they walk out of the house, simultaneously running a quick map search for the address. "It's close to the Jor Bagh market. Maybe we should park there," he suggests.

Karan grins and shakes his head. "You just want to shop at ChicPo."

"It's a win-win, Sir." Kabir laughs aloud.

On any other day, Karan would have called the entire trip a waste because Rajendra Singh's home was locked up. Though they could see the car parked outside the house, they saw no sign of a driver. The vehicle looked clean and almost sparkled in the afternoon sun. Karan peeped in through the windows. The interior was also well cared for.

Kabir says, "I spoke to some of the people living in the servant quarters. The driver, Ram Singh, had to go to his village—some sort of a family emergency. We missed him by about an hour. He'll be back the day after tomorrow. He is also the caretaker. He opens up the house twice a week for the maids to clean it. Rajendra Singh and his wife are visiting their daughter in Dubai."

Karan smiles at Kabir. The young officer has a way with people. Before they realize it, they often spill both important and inane details of their lives with ease. Kabir is smart enough to sift through them to decide if any of the odds and ends are relevant to their case.

"Phone number?"

"I got it, but it's out-of-coverage area right now. I'll try again in an hour or so."

They walk back to the vehicle. Kabir's gaze is set on the far end of the market. "Do you think we may have time for... ?" he asks and gestures towards a quaint café.

Karan nods, and they walk over. A few minutes later, Karan sighs as he takes the first sip of his coffee. There are two good reasons why the team frequents this café whenever they are in the area. The coffee made with freshly roasted and ground beans competes with the almond croissants that melt in the mouth. Kabir is nowhere in sight. Karan has a fair idea of where he's vanished. The owner of the café is a young woman Kabir is clearly interested in, but for some unknown reason that baffles the rest of the team, he's yet to express his affection for her. In a world that chooses partners at a swipe right, Kabir stands out.

Karan closes his eyes as he takes yet another sip of the coffee. Somewhere between his fourth and last sip, something about Arjun and Raina's case suddenly becomes so clear and apparent that Karan wants to kick himself. Rather than making innumerable suppositions, it just makes sense to focus on the facts, as laid before him. Keeping an open mind and considering all possibilities is one of the cornerstones of investigation, but when they've considered all the details of a case, Occam's razor wins, more often than not.

It, quite literally, shaves off the unnecessary to get to what truly matters in a case. And in this case, if for a while, Karan kept the presence of PTK and the use of Rohypnol aside, what it left them with is the kidnapping of an infant in the most peculiar way. Karan goes through the many scenarios that need consideration and comes to a decision. He has to check on a few things before he changes the focus of the investigation into Navin and Raina's case.

After paying their bill and waving goodbye to the hostess, they walk out.

"Do you have everyone's orders?" Karan asks Kabir.

"Yes, Sir. I messaged ChicPo earlier. They have our orders ready. I'll just go pick them up," Kabir says as he walks ahead. When he returns, he finds Karan sitting in the passenger's seat of the vehicle and talking on the phone. Kabir beams. *This day keeps getting better and better.* Karan hands him the keys and continues with his conversation on the phone. Kabir drives them back to Karan's house. An hour later, when the team sits around the dining table with their cups of tea, Karan shares his thoughts.

"So, what you are saying is that we can't rule out Arjun and Raina's families simply on the basis of what Arjun said," Antara concludes.

"I've gone through Arjun and Raina's financial and other papers," says Karan. "Arjun said Raina kept track of their investments and such. She is meticulous and seems to have planned for most eventualities, including hospitalization. It is not merely by chance that she is hospitalized in this particular hospital. I'm convinced she chose it after doing her due diligence."

"Sir, you are right. From Arjun's interactions with the doctors and nurses there, it seemed like they were familiar with the family," Sameer says.

Abhi and Anya return from a walk, and while Abhi joins them at the table, Anya smiles and walks past them. She has caught the last bit of the conversation and cannot help but wonder to herself.

Anya's quiet 'hmm' to herself didn't go unnoticed by Karan or the others. His officers look at him curiously. He returns their glances before nodding and following her into the kitchen.

"Hey!" Anya says. "*Chai*?"

Karan nods in response. "What was that?"

Anya looks perplexed. "What was what?"

"The deep, thoughtful sigh you let out when you walked past us."

"Maybe I was just tired or thinking to myself."

"Oh, you were definitely thinking to yourself. I know that, but was it in reference to our conversation?"

Anya leans back against the counter and watches him before she replies, "I've been trying hard not to eavesdrop, but I cannot tell you how difficult it is not to because at virtually every hour of the day, all of you are working on this case and coming at it from different angles. So, I didn't intentionally try to listen in. I need you to know that."

"That goes without saying," Karan replies.

"So, from what I gather, this man, Arjun, thinks that because he wasn't attacked, the family is not involved. Is that right?"

"Yes, that sums it up."

"Hasn't he been in that hospital pretty much night and day since the incident?"

Karan nods.

"Then, that basically cannot eliminate anyone from your suspect list because that hospital has the best security I've ever seen." She looks at his face for a reaction, but when she doesn't get one, she continues, "A while back, Samaira was looking to make a change, and this place was on top of the list of hospitals she was considering. Rohan and I visited it a few times to get a feel. The company that handles security for the hospital is owned by a group of retired army officers, and the on-ground team includes handpicked ex-servicemen. Every floor of the hospital has a QRT. Since Arjun's wife's 'accident'—although it seems too casual a word—he has been in one of the most secure places in the city."

Karan considers her words. "And that is why Raina chose this hospital."

Anya nods. "Even in a coma, she is still protecting him."

Karan rubs his face. "If something strikes you about our cases, or if you have any ideas, I need you to tell me or one of the others. Am I clear?"

"Okay."

He walks back to the living room. It is time to move beyond the hypotheticals and get down to the specifics. They need Arjun to come clean on the family dynamics.

Karan makes a call to Arjun. The conversation keeps going back and forth, as before. Finally, Karan decides that enough is enough.

"Arjun, you told me if your family was involved, Raina and you would've been dead. But what if they never got the chance? What if your wife took every possible step to protect you and Navin? What if the only reason the two of you haven't been attacked is because you are in the hospital that she chose after careful consideration?"

"Let me think about this, ACP Shekhawat. Just give me a little time. If we open this door, there may not be any going back for us."

"We may not have a lot of time, Arjun. Call me back soon."

CHAPTER TWELVE

The next morning, when Karan walks into his office, he can hear Kabir having an animated conversation with someone on the phone. Curious, he walks to the door that connects his office to that of his team. A map of the city is spread out on Kabir's table as he verifies details.

Karan returns to his office and goes through the daily SitReps from officers handling Rohypnol cases in other parts of the country. They've made no progress; in fact, Bangalore has added another case. He logs into the Zonal Integrated Police Network (ZIP Net) on his computer and checks the status of the missing children for Navin. Next, he logs into the National Tracking System for Missing and Vulnerable Children.

Karan looks at the calendar and tsks. It's been weeks since Navin was taken.

How does a three-month-old infant deal with being snatched from his parents? With every passing day, the chances of finding him dwindle. *Something's got to give.*

Kabir knocks and enters. "Sir, I was finally able to get through to the driver, Ram Singh. There was a death in his family. He won't be back for at least another week. So, it turns out, he did drive a couple to the mall from where Navin was taken. He drove them there and back with a baby." Kabir can't wipe the smile off his face. "We've got them, haven't we?"

"Start from the beginning, Kabir. I thought the homeowner was away."

"Yes, Sir. Ram Singh got a call from his boss. He was told to make the home and car available to a couple who'd be visiting Delhi. He was told they had his mobile number and would be in touch with him. Anyway, the couple apparently changed their mind and didn't stay at the house but requested Ram Singh to ferry them around the city."

"Does he know where they were staying?"

"No, Sir. He only took them around twice. Both times, he picked them up close to the traffic lights on Aurobindo Road—the ones just before Safdarjung's Tomb." Kabir hands him the map on his iPad, and Karan zooms into the view. *There are some private residences and a few diplomatic missions in the area.*

He changes to a satellite view, and a blue rectangle catches his eye. Lutyens Veranda, a 4-star hotel on the edge of Lutyens Delhi, has a swimming pool. The couple could've stayed in one of the private residences or a hotel. The latter seems to be a likelier choice.

"The first day, he drove them to Hauz Khas Village and Khan Market and dropped them off close to where he picked them up. The next day, he drove them to the mall. He confirmed that they returned with the baby, pram and all. He offered to drop them at their hotel, but they refused."

"Did he say anything about the baby?"

"Just that he cried for a while and then slept off."

"Did he, by any chance, notice which direction they headed towards after he dropped them off?"

"He did. He was driving towards Safdarjung's Tomb, and they were headed in the opposite direction."

"Let's go check out Lutyens Veranda. If that doesn't work out, we'll start ringing some doorbells."

Kabir frowns at the map. "In that neighbourhood?"

When Karan parks the car in the side lane next to Lutyens Veranda and turns off the engine, Kabir tells him the sprawling colonial building houses the Sharma family and offers only eight rooms to visitors. It is listed on most of the travel websites that offer premier lodging and has great reviews.

Karan knows that great reviews also mean that the family goes out of their way to make their guests as comfortable as possible. A word with the guard at the gate, and they are quickly invited in. They wait on the veranda and take in the meticulously maintained gardens around them.

"I can see why people would want to stay here. It's a side of Delhi most of us only get to drive past."

"It's not really the kind of place I'd expect kidnappers to choose, Sir."

"True." Karan turns to see an elderly couple approach them. He makes the necessary introductions and decides to cut through the usual polite conversation.

"We want to check if a couple stayed with you sometime around the 4th of October. They would have arrived by themselves and left with a baby."

The hotel owners share a look of confusion. "Yes, they did. It was quite sad. The gentleman lost his brother, and his sister-in-law was in the hospital. They had come to take responsibility for the baby."

"I assume you keep records of your guests?"

"Of course. Would you like to see them?" Mr Sharma nods to the young woman dressed in blue jeans and a grey T-shirt standing beside them. She returns with the visitors' book and a rather thick file that holds copies of guest identification papers. She hands the file to Mr Sharma, who flips through the pages before handing it to Karan.

Even before he gets to the first name, Karan groans inwardly. He is not expecting the words 'The United Kingdom of Great Britain and Northern Ireland'. As if things are not already complicated, now they'd have diplomatic issues to deal with.

Why on earth would Kamal Singh Chauhan and Deepti Singh Chauhan drug Raina and take Navin?

He hands the file to Kabir and reaches for the visitors' book. The couple had checked in on the 2nd of October and checked out on the 5th. Karan takes out his phone to take a picture of the page.

"What can you tell me about them?" he asks.

"They were good guests and gave us no trouble. Of course, the circumstances of their visit were unusual. May I know why you are asking these questions?" Mrs Sharma asks.

"Well, it seems they kidnapped the baby."

"What! No, no, they were here to take care of their nephew. It was just so sad. That little baby lost both parents in a matter of days," Mrs Sharma says.

"No, Ma'am. His parents are alive, though his mother is hospitalized. She was injured when the baby was taken from her."

Mrs Sharma looks at Mr Sharma and back at Karan. "Are you sure?"

"Yes. Anything you can tell us could help find the child."

"Well," Mr Sharma says, "they mostly kept to themselves. We can get you the payment information for them."

"Yes, that would be useful, but what I want is your personal opinion of the couple."

"Most of the guests we host like to interact, so we have an opportunity to get to know them a little. This couple was courteous but kept their conversations brief. We try to accommodate any requests our guests may have. The only one they made was for a babysitter," he says as he looks at the young woman. "Disha is our granddaughter. She helped with that request."

"I told you that couple was trouble," Disha says.

"Yes, you did," her grandfather agrees.

"Why did you think they were trouble?" Karan asks.

"Please take a seat." Disha gestures to the easy chairs placed across the veranda. "They wanted a babysitter almost as soon as they returned with the baby, which was weird considering that it was the first time they were seeing their nephew."

"Why do you find it weird?"

"I am a psychology student. I am doing my Masters from DU. Normally, in times of emergency, people like to keep their loved ones close. This couple was here to get their orphaned nephew. Would you not want to hold that child close? Offering comfort is a basic human instinct."

"How did the baby look to you?"

"That is the weird thing. Initially, I thought he was asleep. I assumed he was exhausted with all the changes in his life, but this baby was still, too still. I was with him for several hours. In that time, I checked his diaper twice—he hadn't even passed urine. He didn't even react to my touch. It didn't seem normal, so I conducted an online search. Dadi said the body reacts differently to extreme life changes. The baby's breathing rate was also low. It just didn't feel right. When the Chauhans returned, I asked them if they wanted to take the baby to a paediatrician." Disha looks at her grandmother.

"They didn't really want to take the baby to the doctor, but I told them how unpredictable a baby's health can be, so they agreed to take him. We sent them to a well-known paediatrician on Pandara Road; Ajay even made the appointment with the clinic," Mrs Sharma adds. "The doctor agreed to see them even though it was already about eight in the evening—after clinic hours."

"They checked out the next day," Mr Sharma adds.

"Can you give me the details for the doctor?" Karan asks and scribbles them on his notepad. "Anything else?"

Mr and Mrs Sharma look a little uneasy.

"It's nothing really," Mr Sharma finally says as he looks at Disha. "Disha agreed to babysit if they would fill in one of her project questionnaires."

"I am using a personal inventory for my project and trying to include as random and large a sample group as possible," explains Disha. "Are you, by any chance, familiar with personality inventories? I don't mean the kind of personality test you can take from a magazine."

"We are, Disha. Which one are you using?"

"The MMPI."

"This is why she is perpetually helping guests and friends with chores," Mrs Sharma adds with a smile.

"Anyway, by the time I calculated their scores and sat down to write an interpretation, the Chauhans were gone," says Disha. "MMPI doesn't give a clear diagnosis; it just helps identify maladaptive behaviour. According to my professor, the Chauhans need to speak to a therapist—separately, of course. They are not the kind of people who should have guardianship of a baby."

"Would it be possible for us to see the room in which they stayed?" asks Karan.

"It's unoccupied right now, but it's been cleaned many times after they left," Mrs Sharma says.

"That's okay. I just want to see it. Also, Disha, could you send me the MMPI scores and interpretation to this email address?" He hands her his card.

"I don't know if I should do that. I'm still studying the subject—the interpretation may not be accurate."

"The manual would've given you a very specific interpretation."

"Yes, but it's not a diagnosis, you've to understand that," she repeats.

"I do. If it would help, we could fill the MMPI for you," he volunteers.

"Really?"

"Yes. Now, can you show us their room, please?"

Disha gestures for them to walk down the veranda. "Each of the rooms opens out to the veranda. That way, guests have their privacy and can come and go at their ease." She stops in front of a room and points towards it. The wooden door is open, but the mesh door is closed. Karan walks in, while Kabir stands outside with Disha.

"So, what was your initial impression of them?" he asks her.

She smiles. "They have the '*hum*' syndrome."

"The what syndrome?"

"You know, the '*hum*' syndrome—when people refer to themselves as '*hum*' instead of '*main*'. It makes them sound distinguished—like a '*main*' isn't enough for their personality."

Kabir chuckles. "Do you see a lot of people with the '*hum*' syndrome here?"

"More than our fair share. We get a lot of PIOs and NRIs. If they've been gone for more than a decade, they also catch the '*sanskar*' syndrome," she adds with a grin. "It's when you expect people to live up to the stereotypes you left with when you moved out of India. Coming back to the baby, do you really think they kidnapped him? They didn't seem particularly happy or thrilled with him."

"Why would you think they'd be thrilled or happy?" Karan asks as he stops at the doorway.

"Well, I can only think of two reasons why someone would kidnap a baby—either they want a ransom or they just want the baby. Either way, wouldn't they be happy to get their hands on the baby?"

Karan nods. "Send me the MMPI forms. We will fill them and send them back to you. Now, what can you tell me about this paediatrician?"

"Oh, she's good. She is a no-nonsense kind of doctor."

"What do you mean?"

"She was in the army medical corps before she retired and has an awesome nonsense detector. You'll see."

Disha walks them to the gate and waves goodbye.

"Do you think you could develop her as a contact?" Karan asks Kabir, and he nods.

"How far is the doctor's clinic from here?"

"It shouldn't take us more than a few minutes," Kabir replies as he walks to the driver's side of the car.

"I have a call to make first. Let's make it a video call for confirmation," Karan says as he calls up Arjun.

"Kamal Singh Chauhan," Karan says as Arjun picks up the call and watches the colour drain from his face.

"No!"

"Yes, Arjun. The chief security officer of the hospital will come to speak to you. Please listen to him, and don't try anything on your own."

"He took Navin?" Arjun asks in a whisper.

"Yes. I'm going to call you back in about an hour. Then, you and I are going to have a long conversation. Please don't go anywhere, stay with Raina, and listen to the CSO."

Arjun barely manages a 'yes' as Karan ends the call.

"Bad?" Kabir asks Karan.

"Sometimes, knowing is worse," he replies as he searches for the number of a close friend and batchmate who is posted in Jaipur. He's barely given him the details of the case when the other officer interrupts him, and Karan listens without adding a word.

Kabir parks in front of the doctor's clinic and waits. He runs a search for Kamal Singh Chauhan on the ZIP Net on his iPad. It comes back blank. Next, he checks on the PIO database and notes down the details.

Karan ends the call and stares out of the windshield for a while before nodding. "Let's go."

Dr Bhattacharya is expecting them, and so the receptionist quickly ushers them through the still crowded waiting room. Karan makes the required introductions and asks the doctor if she remembers Kamal and Deepti Chauhan.

"It is difficult to forget morons like them. In my line of work, I see all kinds of parents and caregivers—the anxious kind, the patient and supportive type, and occasionally, the really stupid kind. This couple falls in the last category. When they brought the baby to me, he was not asleep—he was sedated," she huffs. "Those idiots gave Phenergan to a three-month-old baby. It is not recommended for children, and most definitely, not for those under the age of two. The drug affects the chemicals in the brain. I think that should tell you how dangerous it was for this baby. He was barely breathing and hadn't passed urine in several hours. I recommended that they take him to the closest paediatric hospital, but they refused. We got him set up for a drip and ensured that Mr and Mrs Chauhan waited until the baby was somewhat stable." The doctor's face is pinched. "I asked them to come back the following day for a check-up. When they didn't, I called Lutyens Veranda and was told they'd checked out. Even if there was a tragedy and the baby was orphaned, the use of Phenergan is unacceptable. It is the kind of thing people did in the 1980s and 1990s when they didn't even think of the side effects and damage caused by a medicine. Since the police are involved, I assume things have taken a more serious turn."

"Yes, Ma'am. The baby was kidnapped. We're hoping to find him soon."

Dr Bhattacharya rubs her forehead. "Something felt off," she says.

"When we find the baby, is there anything we should keep in mind?"

"I hope someone is taking care of him." She sighs before she continues, "Make sure he is well hydrated. This baby was on breast milk, so a sudden change to formula would've affected him. I can only hope, given his age, that he'll not have any memories of this time. If possible, please let me know when you find him. I'd appreciate it."

"Of course. Is there anything else you can tell us about the Chauhans?"

The doctor shakes her head. "I'm sorry. I was so angry with them, and my focus was entirely on the baby. His breathing was so shallow. With infants that young, things can go from bad to worse very quickly."

"Thank you for your time, Ma'am," Karan says as he stands up and hands her his card. "If you want to contact me or remember anything else, please don't hesitate to reach out."

She, in turn, hands him a card from the stack on her table, and they leave. Karan goes through the whole scenario in his mind, again and again, over the next few hours, until it exhausts him. His batchmate has given him plenty to think about. Now, they finally know where Navin is, and yet, he is well beyond their reach.

CHAPTER THIRTEEN

When they return home, Karan changes into his running gear. Half an hour later, as the day settles into night, he stands leaning against one of the many boulders that serve as landmarks on the property.

"Who sent you?" he asks bluntly as Anya walks towards him.

"Antara," Anya replies as she comes to stand beside him and watches the changing colours of the sky. After a few minutes of silence, she says, "You found who took the baby, and yet, here you are. So?"

"So, I'm stuck. I know where Navin is and still…" he leaves it at that.

"Ah! It's someone powerful, isn't it? That couple was perfectly correct to be so terrified of their families?"

"His family," he corrects. "I thought Arjun was exaggerating. I spoke to a friend in Jaipur. He's going to handpick people he can trust—people who have no connection to Arjun's family—before he even considers looking for the baby."

"At least you know where he is. That's a beginning."

Karan makes an acrimonious sound. "A few days ago, there was a write-up in the editorial section of a newspaper. It was titled 'India, Bharat, and *Sarkar*'. There is the urban India that you and I know; there is Bharat, the backbone of the country; and then there is *Sarkar*—seemingly above it all. I don't think I've read anything more depressing and yet, spot-on."

"There are more sides to this country than any of us would ever care to admit, Karan. In which of those worlds is Arjun's father powerful?"

Karan sighs. "All three."

"Is that even possible?"

"He isn't a political leader but backs the party that's in power."

"He is essentially a 'maukatarian.'"

"'Maukatarian'?" Karan asks with a laugh.

"*Har mauke ka faida 'tarian',*" she replies.

"Yes, that seems to be an accurate description," he says, smiling.

"What are you going to do?"

"Find Navin, of course, but I'm having trouble dealing with a scenario where the people who took him go unpunished."

"That is not going to happen, is it?" she asks.

"It's quite likely," he replies. "If I even try, it is likely that Arjun, Raina, and Navin will bear the brunt of it."

"May I say something?" she asks.

"I assume Antara sent you here for a reason, so go ahead."

"You've got to decide what is most important to you in this case. Far too often, our need to be right muddies the waters. Take a breather, step away, and relax. When you get back to the case, you may just find a way to make it all work. It doesn't have to be conventional; it just has to work."

"Is that what you do?"

"Absolutely. I believe all of us have at least one specific trait that makes us truly unique. Some people solve problems, some heal, and some support. I find answers. It's what I do. I've this unwavering faith that I can find the answers I'm looking for. No, that's not the right way to say it. I know the answers will find their way to me," she grins. "I just back off, relax, garden, read, or listen to music at a volume that feels like I'm immersed in it. When I come back to the storyboard, the answer is usually right there, like it was waiting for me. Usually, the solution isn't far away. I've just not been looking at it in the right light."

"So, your advice is to just leave it alone?"

"For now," she says. "Can you do that?"

The air around them seems to have stilled before a tug of breeze releases something inside him. "I think so."

"It'll come to you." She starts to walk back towards the house. "Just let it."

"How come you've not asked me about this?" He stretches his arms.

"Your little forest in the city?" She glances back. He nods. "I thought you'd tell me when you were ready."

"Are you always this patient?"

"No, but I'm sure you like your privacy, as I do. Your place is incredible. I'm surprised local schools are not queuing up to picnic here."

He snorts.

"I guess they tried and probably left behind a trail of empty packets of chips and biscuits. Do you cook?" asks Anya.

Karan frowns at the question that comes out of nowhere, then nods.

"The process of marination cannot be rushed. If you rush it, the dish never tastes as good as it could have."

"You want me to marinate?"

"Not you, your thoughts." She grins. "Just let the odds and ends sit for a bit. Do you know what helps in the process? Good food shared with friends. What do you want to eat?"

"What do you eat when you marinate your thoughts?"

She lets out a short laugh. "I'm easy that way. Butter chicken is soul food for me."

"Okay. Let's do this your way and see how it works."

"What is more important to you right now—finding the baby and protecting this family, or making sure the people who kidnapped him are punished?"

Karan tsks as he walks alongside. "It frustrates me that I'd have to consider an either-or option. It should, naturally, be both. But I understand what you're saying. Keeping this family safe is more important."

"Nonetheless, you won't let those responsible go unpunished?"

"Do you know why the usual suspects are called so?"

"I assume because they're likely to commit the same crime again."

"Something like that."

Later that night, Karan shuts off his laptop and looks around the living room. Abhi is fast asleep on the diwan. Sameer and Antara are still going through CCTV footage. Kabir and Imran sit on opposite sides of the dining table, filling out the questionnaires for Disha. Imran's phone rings. He quickly picks the call, listens carefully, and asks a few questions before ending it.

"That was Ipshita. She was finally able to speak to her friend. The clue that the team looking for Anya was given her column for *Fly with Me*. Did she give a restaurant or café a terrible review? That doesn't sound like her," Imran says.

"No, she isn't a food critic. Maybe she chose one restaurant or café over another," Antara says.

Karan shakes his head. "No. The purpose of the game that Ipshita was part of was to delete all the data on the computer. Imran, what did she say about the USB drive?"

"She found it in the pocket of her jeans. She will bring it across tomorrow. Luckily for us, the jeans weren't washed."

"Was a specific 'High Tea' column shared or just details of the magazine?" Karan asks.

"The first game had to identify the author of the column. It wasn't so easy because the column doesn't carry her name, and no one at the magazine was willing to talk about her. The PTK team hacked into a computer of the magazine's accounts section and followed the electronic payment trail to Anya," Imran says.

"Okay. We'll follow up on this tomorrow. Let's call it a night," Karan says.

"Are you going to sleep, Sir?" Sameer asks as he glances at the rest of the team.

"No, but you all are. The three of you have bloodshot eyes from too much screen time. I'm going to have a look at Anya's computer again, specifically, the files for the column."

"So, after *all* the work we've put into her case, you want the glory all to yourself?" Antara asks with an exaggerated sigh.

Karan smiles, shaking his head. "Okay, have it your way. So, we are starting with the presumption that someone read one of her columns, and something about it annoyed them. The first question is, which one? This person doesn't know her; otherwise, he wouldn't be on PTK, trying to figure out her identity. So, it is not the café or restaurant owners with whom she came in contact. How did she anger someone without even meeting them?"

"It's a special skill I have," Anya replies from behind him. "If I put my mind to it, I know I can accomplish pretty much anything." The uncomfortable expression on the officers' faces is difficult to miss. "You guys are a noisy bunch when things start progressing on your cases."

"The request on PTK is dated two months ago. So, let's start with your columns going back to three or four months." Karan picks out the printouts and hands them to her.

She flips through the printed sheets. "That is Udaipur, Kasol, Darjeeling, and Mumbai—two newer cafes and two golden oldies. Now, sometimes, I may've written a column months before it was published, but I always confirm the details before it goes to the printers. I don't think there were any issues with these columns."

"Does the column ever get complaints?" Antara asks.

"Rarely, but it happens. Sometimes, a reader is disappointed that their favourite café wasn't covered—that kind of thing. Nothing serious."

Karan takes the printouts from Anya and walks to a corner of the room. "Can you open the files for these columns on your computer?" he asks Anya.

He reads each column before passing it to Sameer and then moves to the next. There isn't anything offensive in her writing.

And then he sees it. *No, no, no!*

"Move." He nudges Kabir from his seat next to Anya and takes control of the mouse. He flicks through the files and goes back to the Darjeeling article. "When did you visit Darjeeling? Can you tell me the exact date these pictures were taken?"

"May I?" She gestures at the mouse. She opens a folder and then, after a few clicks, finds the sub-folder she is looking for. "It was in the end of July. It's not exactly tourist season, but it has its own appeal. What exactly are you looking at?"

"This photograph." Karan points to a table set for high tea against a large glass window and the rainswept street behind it. The lighting makes the whole thing look ethereal. The adjacent table is occupied by blurry figures, and only a black curved walking stick with a generous dragon handle is in focus. "Show me this one."

Anya clicks on a few pictures until she finds it. "The photographs pay more than the text, but I'm not a professional photographer, so I need to shoot a fair amount to get a few that are just right. Luckily for me, the light that day was incredible, and this man's walking stick just struck an interesting note."

"Show me the other photographs," Karan says in a gruff voice.

Anya opens the folder and returns the mouse to him. Karan clicks through the photographs until he finds what he is looking for. He'd been hoping he was wrong, but the photographs on the screen don't lie. Even if Anya didn't go looking for trouble, it had found its way to her.

"By any chance, did you speak to the man with the walking stick?"

"No. They were almost ready to leave when I got there. I just saw the table all set up and the light coming in and couldn't resist taking a few pictures."

"USB drive," Karan says and keeps clicking on the mouse until he finds what he is looking for. Kabir hands him the pen drive. "I'm copying this whole folder." He also emails himself the dozen or so photographs.

"Okay," Anya replies. "It's this photograph that has me in trouble?"

Karan makes a noncommittal sound. "I'm going to my study to make some calls. When I have some answers, I'll tell you." He finally looks at Sameer, the only other person in the room who could've recognized the walking stick.

"Do you think so?" Sameer takes another look at the photograph on the screen. "No way! What are the chances of running into him?"

"We'll see. Get some sleep, people," Karan adds as he leaves the room.

Back in his office, he emails the photographs to his contact in the Intelligence Bureau (IB) before he calls him. "Check your email, and let me know if this is of interest to the bureau," Karan says as he hangs up.

About five minutes later, his phone rings just as Sameer walks into the study. Karan notes down a few details as he listens, and a few minutes later, ends the call.

"It's the dragon cane man from the IB?" Sameer asks.

"It looks like it."

"What are the odds? No one other than his immediate superiors knows what he looks like. The cane became his calling card of sorts."

"He was an ex-director who was not pleased with the idea of his voluntary retirement," Karan adds.

"It wasn't really voluntary, was it? All that power—I'm not surprised. The stories about him…"

"Hmm. He was an effective agent. As long as he got the results, they chose to look the other way," Karan says.

"That's just an excuse for not taking responsibility, Sir."

"Of course, it is, and look at where it has got them. They don't know where he is or what he has been up to. They suspect him of selling vital security details, but that's about it—just suspicions."

"And now?"

"And now, thanks to those photographs, we know he was in Darjeeling when a senior agent died on duty. Anya thinks she isn't a good photographer and takes more pictures than she needs, so we have photographs of both—the dragon cane man and that senior agent."

"Are they clear photographs?"

"They are clear enough to make an identification. The cane man's last official psychological evaluation diagnosed him with paranoia."

"To some extent, in his line of work, it is understandable, isn't it?" Sameer asks.

"Maybe, but there are suspicions he may have killed more agents. In fact, three of them were supposed to be close to him—the kind who were rooting for him despite all his issues."

"I guess it makes sense. You'd be paranoid of those you interact with the most," Sameer says.

"The so-called IB legend claims he had the dragon cane crafted in Japan. It's one of a kind; it's not wooden but made with tamahagane steel," Karan says.

"Like katanas?"

"Right. While it is molten, the steel is fused and folded many times to make it more durable. The handle of the cane can be pulled out and becomes a dagger—a poisoned dagger."

"Is that how the agents died?"

"All three died of a heart attack, but the postmortem found large doses of aconite in their bodies. The IB suspected the dragon cane man, but there was no evidence."

"Until now."

"Until now," Karan agrees.

"When he saw that photograph in the magazine, he would've gone into full-blown paranoia. But why go through PTK and all the trouble of involving others?" Sameer asks.

"I guess when he couldn't find out who wrote that column, and more importantly, who took the photographs, he must've been desperate. Once he found out who she was, he probably got someone to check her office and home. The DNI on her record and the security system at her home would've most likely driven his paranoia to a whole new level."

"There has been nothing suspicious at Anya's home or workplace since the accident. So, I guess we can assume he was behind the wheel of the vehicle that hit her."

"Hmm. I don't know how long the 'in the hospital, cannot have visitors' bit will work."

"They want to use her as bait?" Sameer asks as he picks up a squishy stress ball from Karan's table and squeezes it.

"Wouldn't you?"

"I guess so, but these IB fellows only want to get rid of this man. They won't care about what happens to her."

"That is where we come in."

"Okay. Do you want me to tell the team?"

Karan nods. "They'll have a look around her office and home and get back to me tomorrow."

"That soon?"

"The sooner the better, isn't it?"

"I guess so. Why is it when cases start opening up, it's everything all at once?" Sameer asks with a laugh, then sobers quickly. "Will you tell her?"

"Of course. Tomorrow," Karan says.

"Not being able to look into PTK is really killing you, Sir, isn't it?"

Karan frowns. "Are you trying to pacify me, Sameer? It's not helping."

Sameer laughs. "It's just that Kabir and Abhi have been going through it, but they can only view the games and players on the lower levels. The IRL games are either hidden or the site is partitioned. That's why they're being careful not to set off any warning bells."

Karan nods. "Are they creating a list of players?"

"These kids are either stupid or extremely naive. The registration asks for everything—from a photograph to personal identification details."

"So, we have all that too?"

"Yes, but no trace of the IRL games."

"Whoever is running PTK doesn't seem to have much of a tech background. All the work is done by the players, unknowingly, or at least, that is what we think right now. The IRL games are an entirely different ball game," Karan adds.

"That is why Kabir is looking for a partition or a hidden section."

"Can Ipshita access the IRL games that she has played before?" Karan asks.

"Yes, Sir."

"Ask her to take a screenshot of the whole screen and send it to Kabir. Let me know what you find on the USB drive she brings in."

"I'm guessing it's going to be some kind of malware. Sir, do you think the IRL games are not on the website?"

"If you were running an operation like this, wouldn't you want some degree of separation from the PTK site? The security of the site isn't as strong as we thought it would be; that is the only option that makes any sense. Let's get some sleep. Tomorrow promises to be interesting."

"I'm not sure I like your definition of 'interesting', Sir. It's like that Chinese curse: 'May you live in interesting times.'"

"That's not Chinese or oriental in any way, Sameer. It was made up by a Western politician."

"That's nothing new. They love to make up stuff, and then, just so it sounds wise, they say it is from the Orient," Sameer laughs.

CHAPTER FOURTEEN

"Let me get this straight," says Anya. "The photograph from my article identified someone the IB is looking for, and because of the photograph, this man wants to kill me?" Anya asks.

"He is not right in the head, Anya. It seems the photograph may have set off an obsession," Antara explains.

Karan laid down all the cards—well, almost all because the IB wouldn't let him share all the details with her. To make matters worse, they want to take her into custody.

"That, the DNI, and the lack of information available about you may've made him paranoid."

"Paranoid?" Anya's eyes widen. "About me? Does he think I want to harm him?"

Karan watches her carefully. Her expression tightens, and he can see just when the gravity of the situation sinks in.

"The IB intends to handle things now," he informs her.

"What exactly does that mean?" She looks at Karan, then Antara, and back again. "We'll see about that. I've a call to make."

Karan sighs as he watches her walk away.

"You lit a fire under her," Antara comments. "She isn't going to trust them—you know that." She turns to look at him. "*You do know that!* Sir, what are you playing at?"

"I got a call this morning. Her case is out of our hands, Antara. No amount of reasoning helped."

"Sir, as long as they get their man, the IB won't care what happens to her."

"It's time to see how powerful that DNI is," Karan says.

Ten minutes later, Anya returns, looking calmer. "You can't tell me the specifics of the case because they don't want you to," she states and watches their faces. “But they want to use me as bait to get him. Who is this man?”

There is complete silence.

“The officer in charge should be here in about half an hour,” Karan adds.

“I’m going to ask you a clear, simple question. Do you want me to leave?”

Karan looks at her and shakes his head.

***

Soon after the IB officer arrives and begins to question Anya, things go from bad to worse, very quickly. From the get-go, the officer is aggressive and on the offensive. Anya holds her phone tightly on her lap as she listens to the man blame her for photographing people without permission, and then moves on to the DNI.

“I don’t care who you’re sleeping with, but this DNI charade is not going to protect you. You started this whole stupid episode; now, you’re going to help end it.”

“I’m not going anywhere with you,” Anya says.

“Then who is going to protect you? The Urban Crimes team is out of this mess now. Believe me, the last thing I want to do is to have to protect you, but that is what it comes down to. Without the IB’s protection, you are as good as dead. You will also tell me everything about this DNI.”

“I’m not going anywhere with you. I’d rather take my chances on my own,” she says as she looks down at her phone. “You know, officer, if you want someone to help you, threats are not the best way to go. You might be from the IB, but this isn’t the most intelligent move.”

“I can have you detained.”

“On what grounds? That picture in the article doesn’t show any faces. You and I both know I’ve done nothing illegal.”

The IB officer gets up, walks over to Anya, and bends down so they are at eye level. Karan forces himself to remain still.

“Look, lady, you have secrets, and I’m going to enjoy bringing them all out. Your column is written anonymously. You’ve no social media presence. It's obvious you are hiding from someone. Let's see," he pretends to be in deep thought, "how about I make you famous overnight—half-page photographs of you in all the national newspapers. Let's see how you deal with that on your own. You've been drugged once. Wasn't that enough for you?" he says as he comes inches from Anya's face.

Karan isn't sure who is more shocked, him or the officer, when Anya flicks him on his nose, and he stumbles backwards.

"Do you know who I hate most in the world? Bullies like you." She picks up her phone from her lap. "Is that enough?" She listens to the response and says, "Okay." She places her phone on the side table and watches the officer stand up awkwardly. Before he can get another word out, his phone rings.

"Sir, yes, Sir. No, Sir. She must have misunderstood me," the officer explains but is cut off. He listens for a while before he says, "Yes, Sir," and ends the call.

He turns to Anya. "I seemed to have pushed more than I should have." He looks at Karan. "You understand. It's for her own safety, after all."

"The only way I'm going to be any part of this plan is if Urban Crimes is involved. Otherwise, it's fine by me to disappear for a few months. I have plenty of leave," Anya says.

"Look, Ms Aulakh, it's my job to push and investigate," he explains.

"But it isn't your job to bully and threaten, is it?" she counters. "If there hadn't been someone listening to our conversation, you would've just continued. Let's just get this straight. I did not go looking for trouble. The cane looked interesting, and that is the only reason it found a place in the photograph. Just let me know what you need from me. I will be involved in this only if Urban Crimes handles things. I'm not dealing with you again."

He nods and then gestures for Karan to see him out.

"Her DNI seems to be genuine. That was the director himself on the phone. She is obviously important to someone powerful, so you better be careful if you value your job. If you ever figure out why she has the DNI, let me know."

Karan smiles. "If the IB doesn't have access to that information, do you really think Delhi Police will?"

"That's true," the officer concludes. "I'll be in touch. She is a handful. I'm glad she is your headache and not mine."

Karan wasn't going to tell him he is more than glad.

"So," he asks Anya as he enters the living room and lets the word hang.

"So," she replies.

Antara looks at them both before she sighs. "Sit down," she says. "How do we do this, Sir?" she asks Karan.

"We let them decide the plan, and we'll figure out what we want to do with our part of it. In the meantime..."

"Please don't say CCTV cameras," Antara interrupts him. "My eyes can't take any more screen time."

"But this time, we know who to look for," he says.

"That means nothing, Sir. From what Sameer says, this man could walk past us in disguise, and we wouldn't recognize him."

"Except," Karan says and waits for her to catch up.

"The cane!" Antara huffs. "I don't remember seeing anyone with a cane, but okay, we'll look."

"Why don't we all look?" Anya asks. "It would be faster. Also, it may be easier if I sat down with them. Considering it is my workplace, I may be able to spot something odd."

"Okay." Antara rubs her eyes. "Let's get started."

Karan takes out his phone and redials. "Kabir, pull up the CCTV recording from Anya's office around the time when her computer was hacked. Yes, I know that they only cover the outside area. Also, check if there was anything special happening in the building that day."

Anya looks at him curiously.

"What?" he asks.

She points at the ceiling. "He's in your study upstairs, and you're still calling him on the phone."

"That way, by the time I walk up, he would've found what I want," he explains.

Anya sighs and shakes her head in mock dismay. "You are lucky you have a team that loves and respects you as much as they do."

"That's true," Karan says, noticing the way she rubs her nape with her hand. "Are you fine with all this?"

She nods. "I have no choice, do I?"

"There is always a choice."

She shakes her head. "I'd rather get it over with. I'm done with hiding."

"I wouldn't call it hiding as much as taking a timeout."

"A timeout from someone trying to kill me," she replies. "Also, I'm sure the conversation with the IB officer shed some light on the DNI situation."

Karan remains silent.

"You should go. The team is waiting for you."

"Anytime you want to talk…" He leaves it at that and is about to walk away when he says, "You don't have to do it all alone. You know that, don't you? Somehow, you've got to stop living as if there is a disaster at every turn." She looks away, and Karan wonders if he has overstepped.

"What if I don't know how to?"

"You could start with the basics."

"And that is?"

"We have your back. I have your back."

"Until this case ends. I understand that."

"No, apparently, you don't. There are more people on your side than you realize. I know the DNI protects you in a unique way, but whether you accept it or not, you've made a few new friends in the last few days. They are the kind who don't walk away, even when you want them to. So, think about it."

She nods.

"If you are not fine with how the IB plans to proceed, we can try to find an alternative."

"It's best to get it over with," she repeats.

Karan nods. The IB plans to lure him out by placing her back into her normal routine as soon as possible. There is something that has been bothering him for days, and now, finally, a clearer picture has started to develop.

Back in his office, he goes through the CCTV videos with Kabir. They don't find anything that seems out of the ordinary.

"Go back to that morning," he tells Kabir. More than half an hour later, he points at the screen. "Stop. Go back. There."

"I don't see him, Sir," Kabir replies as he looks closely at the picture on the screen. Then he notices the man walking away at the far end of the screen. "He is not going out through the main door. There is one main entry up front, and the door at the back is for deliveries. Honestly, the building must have passed fire inspection with top marks. At the back, each level can be accessed via the fire escape. Ironically, these fire escapes also double up as smoking corners."

"Does Anya use it?"

"She doesn't smoke, but during an editing session, she usually takes a break there with the editor to get some fresh air and perspective—her words, not mine," he clarifies.

"How busy are the editing rooms?"

"They are very busy. These people begin work in the afternoon, and one can book slots late into the night."

"How late?"

"Until three, maybe four o'clock in the morning."

"That late?" Karan asks sceptically.

"Or early, based on how you look at it. Anya usually gets to work much earlier than the rest and leaves earlier, but if she needs to, she'll go back for an editing session, depending on when the editor is free."

"I want to see this area. Let's go," Karan says as he picks up his phone to make arrangements.

"Now?" Kabir asks, but Karan has already left the room. By the time Kabir catches up with Karan, he has taken the bike out from the garage.

"The company that handles security for the building and the whole complex was bought over last month," Karan tells Kabir.

"Like you asked," says Kabir, "I checked for anything unusual that happened in the building around the time that Anya's computer was hacked. It turns out the security company ran a new security check that night. The owner of the company was also on the premises to oversee it, but we don't see him in any of the CCTV recordings."

"Let's go find out why. When we get there, I need you in the security office. Do whatever you need to keep me off the CCTVs."

Kabir had spent a fair amount of time with the recordings and is certain they've not been doctored. The dragon cane man had not been in any of the videos, and yet, they were sure he'd been on the premises. It was a strange situation, and it was driving him a little crazy.

Once they arrive at The Channel, Karan calls Mr Shah again. He tells him all he can, without going into too many details. The owner of the network isn't happy about using Anya as bait. "Just get this over with, and keep her safe," he says.

Rohan meets them at the reception and walks them through the office. He answers Karan's questions and adds details of his own. Karan takes a few minutes looking around Anya's office before they move on. When they enter the narrow corridor lined with editing rooms, he is fairly certain this is where the cane man would potentially target Anya. At the end of the corridor is the door to the fire escape. Rohan uses his card to swipe it open. "You need one of these to get in or out. The door locks on its own."

"What happens if you are out for a smoke and forget to carry your card?"

"You call someone to open the door because even if you walk down and enter through the reception, you'd need your card there."

"So, no card, no entry," Karan says. "Can we see one of the editing rooms?"

"Sure." Rohan leads the way and opens a door. Large screens and keyboards dominate the wide table, and recessed lighting leaves most of the room in darkness. Black insulation panels cover the walls, making the room look smaller than it is. There is just enough space for two chairs at the workstation and a narrow bench placed against the wall next to the door.

"Does Anya favour any particular editing room?"

"Yes, this one."

"Do people know about this?" Karan asks.

"Most producers and editors have rooms they prefer to work in. So, yes, people know."

"Okay. I need you to do me a favour, and of course, keep this only between us," Karan says and proceeds to tell Rohan exactly what he wants done. "Message me when you have it ready."

"How soon do you want it?"

"How soon can you have it ready?"

"It depends on how good a job you want. It can be done in the next two hours. If you want it perfect, then by tomorrow, I guess," Rohan adds.

"How about we do both?"

Rohan raises his eyebrows.

"We don't have a timeline, but the way I see it, the minute she is back to work, he should make a move. Message me when it is done."

Rohan nods, and they part ways. Kabir calls Karan from the security office of the complex.

"Okay, Kabir, let's see how this man seems to keep off every CCTV camera here."

Once Karan is outside the building, he does a complete turn to identify the location of each camera in the vicinity.

"I can see you on three different cameras," says Kabir.

"I'm going to walk around a bit, and you need to tell me when and if you see me," Karan says as he puts the earpiece in. He walks at a steady pace, taking careful note of the multiple cameras in the parking lots. There is almost no public spot that is not within the view of the CCTV cameras. *Almost.* Despite the tremendous developments in security gadgets and stringent protocols, there are always a few blind spots. One just has to know where to look.

"Sir," Kabir's voice comes through the earpiece. "I just saw you turn a corner on the main road, but I only saw your back, and now, I can't see you again."

Karan continues to move and sometimes backtracks his steps when he spots more cameras ahead. He is glad to see that the security company made the parking spaces a top priority, but he notes that if he walks closer to the office buildings themselves and weaves his way through side roads, there is a clear path that avoids surveillance.

"I can't see you anywhere, Sir. Where are you?"

"I am close to the main gate," Karan replies as he pauses at the corner to identify the last section of the path that escapes the cameras. He can only find two parking spaces that fit the requirement. The black beamer that is parked at the far corner looks oddly familiar. He wonders why. Neither is it the latest model, nor is it an odd colour that would stand out. *Where have I seen it?* "Anything?"

"No, Sir, where are you?"

Karan looks around and identifies the spot he is looking for, out of the path of the CCTVs and not too close to the black beamer. He tells Kabir where to park and wait for him. Since the beamer is parked in a blind spot, it gives him an opportunity to examine it. Then he stops in his tracks. Even from a distance, he can see the tiny red light of the dash cam. *Oh no!* Karan retraces his steps.

"How did you find the blind spots, Sir? I thought they'd designed the CCTV paths well," Kabir asks as Karan gets into the car.

"They have, Kabir, and their entire system is closed—backups are only on location."

"Someone designed a good system, and yet, this fellow managed to bypass it. So, do you think it is the cane man who owns the security company now?" Kabir asks.

"Possibly," Karan answers, as he clicks a few photographs of the car and the registration plate. "Kabir, check the registration number with the RTO and anything else you can without raising any flags."

As they drive out of the office complex, Karan's phone rings.

"Hi Sameer, we're just leaving Anya's office." He listens to the other officer before gesturing for Kabir to park on the side of the road. Karan listens to Sameer for several minutes before he finally responds, "Do you want us to come there?" He looks at his watch and says, "Give us about forty-five minutes."

A message chimes on Kabir's phone. He checks it and asks, "Are we going to Gurgaon?"

"Yes. We may have a break on one of the cases Sameer was following through. Do you remember Mr Sinha, the lawyer who was found unconscious in the office parking lot?"

"Yes, Sir. He was lucky his colleagues found him when they did. I thought he was fairly blank about why he may've been drugged."

"Sameer has been in touch with him, but he didn't really volunteer any other details. Anyway, his executive assistant called Sameer this morning. She thought something weird was going on with her boss."

"Weird?"

"He was turning up for work with bruises. Also, a cousin started dropping him and picking him up from work, and today, she noticed the same man hanging around the reception."

"So, he got into a fight with someone?"

"Not a fight. His bruises are more colourful than expected."

"He's been thrashed over a period of time," Kabir concludes.

CHAPTER FIFTEEN

By the time they reach Mr Sinha's office in Gurgaon, Karan has gone through his file. He studies the photograph Sameer has added to the PDF file. Although in his mid-thirties, the senior partner looks younger. Professionally, he is doing well. He owns the apartment in which he lives in an expensive neighbourhood of Gurgaon and drives a Porsche.

Sameer asks them to park behind the office building and enter discreetly. He is waiting for them at the reception and quickly fills them in on a few more details about the case as they take the elevator. The law offices are opulent and remarkably quiet. Sameer knocks on the door of a corner office before they enter. The first thing Karan notices is the drastic amount of weight Mr Sinha has lost. There are dark circles under the eyes and tell-tale bruises on his chin and neck. Karan watches the man for a few moments before nodding.

"Coffee? Tea?" the assistant asks.

"Let's start with some answers," Karan says as he takes a seat.

Mr Sinha looks at his assistant and then at Karan.

"You *have* to speak to them," she says in a hushed voice.

Mr Sinha shakes his head.

"Tell me a story, Mr Sinha," Karan says.

"A story?"

"Yes, tell me a story of what may have been if you hadn't been drugged that day."

Mr Sinha considers Karan's words, then shakes his head in resignation. "I am gay."

"Okay."

"Okay?" Mr Sinha asks.

"You are gay. Fine. Does that have something to do with you being drugged in the parking lot?"

"Earlier, I wasn't sure, but now, things are bad."

"Tell me how we can help."

"I don't think anyone can help me now."

"Let's see. Just tell me how things stand."

Karan doesn't have his notepad out for a change. Right now, the emotions involved are more important than the details.

Mr Sinha says he isn't out, and Karan can only imagine the pressure the man is under. Mr Sinha tells them that on the day he was found in the parking lot, he should've been on a connecting flight to Mumbai and then flown out to Sweden. He was emigrating and had hoped to make a clean break from his family. His partner had taken an earlier flight on the same day. They'd planned their move meticulously to avoid being caught by his family.

"I know you think I'm being too dramatic, but two years ago, a cousin of mine was beaten to death by my mother's family when they discovered he was gay."

"They don't know you are gay?"

"Oh! They know now, that's why I have been given the royal treatment." He gestures at his face. "They've fixed my marriage. It's in a week. Do you know why they haven't killed me?"

Karan shakes his head.

"I'm worth more alive than dead, and that's despite a very large life insurance policy. Apparently, the dowry my profession will bring in is much more than the value of my life."

"Do they know about your emigration plans?"

"No. All my paperwork was kept in the office. My colleagues even had a farewell dinner the week before. Imagine their surprise to see me come back to work. But I had to keep the façade going."

"Are you sure your family didn't know about you leaving the country?"

"Absolutely. My bags were in the boot of the car. They were still there when I returned to work two days later. My family has a blunt, in-your-face approach to handling things. This drugging thing makes no sense. It was just pure bad luck."

Karan looks at Sameer and then at Mr Sinha.

"You don't think so?" Mr Sinha asks.

Karan shakes his head. "How many people knew of your plan to fly to Mumbai that day?"

"Just my partner and Rhea, my assistant. It should've been a very ordinary day. I was going to lunch at the place where I usually meet some friends."

"I think your family has known about you longer than you think. But that's irrelevant now. What do you want to do now?"

"I don't know. I am being watched day and night. Obviously, I can't go through with the wedding."

"There is a late afternoon flight that he is tentatively booked on," Rhea says.

"Rhea, how am I supposed to get on the flight when I can't get out of the building?"

Karan turns to Rhea. "That is why you finally decided to trust us. If we can get him on that flight, is he sorted in terms of paperwork and other details?"

"Yes," Rhea replies and leaves the room to return with a small carry-on case and leather bag. "This contains everything you need to make a new start," she says to Mr Sinha. "Buy new clothes and anything else you need when you get there. ACP Shekhawat, all his paperwork is in order. All I need to do is confirm his booking on the flight."

"Can we give you a ride to the airport, Mr Sinha?"

"It's not as easy as you think. My mother's brother is a senior IFS officer. Even if I could get out of this building and reach the airport, I'm pretty sure he would've flagged my passport."

Karan looks at Sameer.

"I'll take care of it, Sir."

"Let me know if you need me to speak to anyone. Also, to be on the safe side, run a check on Interpol flags, too. When he reaches the airport, there should be nothing in the system that could pose a problem," Karan says as Kabir and Sameer move to the far side of the room to make their calls.

"What else do you need to tie up here before you leave?"

"It's all done. I was prepared to leave weeks ago."

"Are there any financial transactions you need to make or any papers to sign? You should take care of all that right now. Also, my suggestion is that you let Sameer have a look at your phone to ensure that you aren't being tracked."

"I checked. It's clean," Rhea says. "We scan all our electronics regularly. We handle a lot of mergers and acquisitions, so we can't be too careful in our line of work."

"In that case, if you're ready to make a clean break, I suggest you leave your SIM in the office, and we'll get you another one. Now I need you to think about the last few weeks. Was there anything odd or anything that stood out? No detail is too small."

"Do you think my family had me drugged? I thought I was being paranoid. Honestly, this really isn't their style—a fist in my face is more like it."

"I agree with you, Mr Sinha. They may not have drugged you themselves, but they are linked somehow, and I need your help to find out how," Karan says.

Three hours later, once the flight has taken off, Karan turns to Sameer. "We need to know everything we can about the family."

"The others are already working on it. Honestly, Sir, when he mentioned how devoted his uncle is to Mataji, I almost choked on my coffee."

"Yes, that's the second time someone has mentioned that name. It's time to start connecting the dots. I'll speak with Mrs Naugiyal. Hopefully, she'll know more about this woman."

"Do you know what this sounds like, Sir? A weird version of the 'Agony Aunt' column that my mother read in her magazines when I was a kid—the kind of column where you told her your woes, and she suggested solutions. Some of them were just common sense, but most had a fun, interesting twist. It's like people are reporting their issues to this Mataji, and she is snapping her fingers or waving her wand and resolving them."

"Hmmm."

"Does that sound stupid? It was just a thought I had."

"No, it sounds quite accurate. So, what are her motives?" Karan asks the younger officer.

"Money, power—the usual reasons, I guess."

Karan nods.

"I don't know why people can't mind their own business and let others be. I mean, what was the purpose of interfering with Mr Sinha's life?" Sameer asks. "Why can't people just let other people lead their own lives?"

"Sameer, if we look into his financials, I'll bet he supported most of the family. That is why they chose to look the other way about his sexual orientation. Something changed recently. Maybe this marriage would've brought in a large dowry or built connections further than Mr Sinha could have known. His family didn't know he was emigrating, or things would have gotten far worse. By the way, was his passport flagged?"

"No, Sir, it wasn't, but I took the necessary precautions. If someone checks the system, we'll be the first to know. His travel arrangements will not show up."

"And he'll send us a message once he arrives."

"Yes, Sir."

***

Since there's been no communication from his batchmate in Jaipur, all Karan can do is wait. Abhi and Kabir have been monitoring the PTK website for days now, but neither has given the team the go ahead to open the website.

Karan is surprised to see Abhi walk into his office, settle down in a chair, and just stare at him.

"Abhi, just tell me what you know, without any of the tech jargon."

"Okay," Abhi says, standing up and pacing around Karan's home office. "So, the site was set up about two years ago. It mostly catered to bored high school and college students who wanted a little excitement in their lives without actually breaking any laws. In the beginning, it offered free games, but later, it added paid ones that also carried rewards. The games themselves seem harmless enough.

They usually involve finding information about people online—sort of like creating a directory of sorts. I couldn't identify any set profile that they may've been looking at. The lists include people of all age groups and backgrounds."

"How did they find the information?"

"Bhai, you know how much information people share online. From what they ate for lunch to what they plan to do on the weekend, finding information isn't difficult. If you are willing to spend some time on a focused search, you can find out pretty much anything."

Karan nods.

Abhi continues, "The information collected for each person is carefully docketed. Once a file is complete, it is sent to an anonymous email address. I think someone paid PTK to find information about people. I'm not sure why it would be so valuable because even though some of the information is sort of personal, it doesn't seem particularly important."

"Can you access one of these files?"

"Of course." Abhi opens a file on his iPad and hands it to Karan.

The PDF file offers details about a young designer. It lists her personal as well as professional details. From her favourite films to her hobbies and the projects she has worked on—it includes it all. It goes on to offer information on the route she takes to work and her likely plans on weekends.

"That's a lot of detail," Karan says as he swipes through the pages. "Collect enough data, and trends and habits become visible. If she tends to shop at a particular market every weekend, she is likely to go there this weekend too—that kind of thing."

"But why all the effort?"

"Imagine you're interested in her, Abhi. Wouldn't it make quite an impression if you're at the right place at the right time and have a lot in common? She'd probably think it is destiny. On the other hand, if this is about her work, the same information can be used by a head-hunter or a competitor."

Abhi nods. "After a while, they added an image section. Players had to first find the person online and then search for all the information they could find. This one is rather curious because most pictures look like the person didn't pose for them."

"Can that be done? Like a Google search for images?"

"It's not as easy as it sounds. Also, as of now, there isn't a legitimate photo search engine that does an accurate enough job, but..." he pauses.

"But?"

"If you are willing to spare your computer for hours at end and give it access to a black site, you have some chance of finding the person. Even then, the search parameters require specific parts of the face to be visible—the eyes, nose, and ears."

"Are you telling me I can click a picture of someone on the street, and PTK will find them for me?"

"Theoretically, yes, but it all depends on whether there is a corresponding image online with which it can be compared."

"And most often there is?"

"Right. Day in and day out, people give away parts of themselves online. They don't even realize when they're doing it. On the surface of it, they're sharing photographs and experiences with friends, but once these are online, they are on the internet forever. It's just a matter of looking for them. After focusing on some of this information, even I can predict what someone is likely to do on a weekend and who they will be with," says Abhi. He continues, "Coming back to the timeline for PTK, a few months after they added online searches, the offline version was added. These were designed like missions. They mostly required players to find people offline, take pictures, record routines, and get signatures—that kind of thing."

"Signatures?"

"Most of us end up signing for couriers every day, right? We even give away our phone numbers, and sometimes, more details like PAN or driver's licence number. If you keep collecting all these little pieces, you can create a bigger picture that gives you a close-up view of the person's life. I checked. The air force officer's wife," Abhi refers to his notes, "Mrs Naugiyal, was on the signature collection list."

This sort of explains why someone risked trying to sell off a piece of her land. Did they really expect to get away with it, or was it just a ruse to cause more confusion within the family?

"There's more," Abhi says.

"Of course, there is." Karan sighs as he put down his pen and gives Abhi his complete attention.

"So, PTK has been making money from both sides—from the players and also from the people who are looking for this information. But something changed about eight months back. Their games and missions became more focused. The database they created in the last two years looks sort of random—like every time someone put in a search order, it was added to their database. But in the last few months, the information they started looking for became very specific."

"Specific, as in how?"

"Well, in the earlier searches, we found hardly any connections between people. Sometimes, the girls were from the same college. Did I mention that about 70 per cent of photo searches were for women? But the search logs in the last few months have connections—close ones. They are mostly familial."

"So, someone is searching for information about the whole family?"

"Yes and from a wide range of angles—from basic information to professional and personal relations. Initially, we thought it was a one-off, but in the last few months, PTK has tagged as many as twenty-five families. We call them cluster searches."

"Do they have anything in common?"

Abhi pauses before replying, "I assumed they would've had, but not really. Some have a business background, others are in government service, but what I did find interesting is that they are focused in only about eight cities." He looked at his iPad before rattling off the names, "Patiala, Chandigarh, Delhi, Mumbai, Bangalore, Pune, Kolkata, and Gangtok."

"That's an interesting list. Were there offline searches at each city?"

"Yes. We also have a list of players from each city and information on who played which game. I don't know if that helps."

"It does, Abhi. We can't arrest them for playing a game, but I think we are lucky to have caught this at a nascent stage."

"Bhai, they've already drugged so many people, and you say we're lucky," Abhi shakes his head.

"Abhi, the person who administers the drug thinks it is a part of the game. If there is no motive for foul play, the PTK cases will go nowhere. The ones who are planning and running the show have their hands clean."

"So, now?"

"So, now we find out who is behind this before things get worse. Are there any offline missions coming up?"

"Not the IRL team games, but the Watchlist games are on."

"Watchlist?"

"It's pretty much as the word describes. People are watched on specific days, and their activities are recorded. Most of it is mundane stuff, like how someone travels to work, where they tend to go for lunch—that kind of thing. Do you think it is important?"

"Yes. When you put all that information together, it creates a much bigger picture. Can we create something like a mind map for all this data? Abhi, I know it's a lot, but I really need to see these connections. PTK is all about making money, isn't it?"

"They get paid by both parties," he says.

"How was the search for Anya paid?" Karan asks.

"Firstly, it was not one search but multiple ones. There was neither any picture to identify her with, nor was her name shared. All payments were made with cryptocurrencies. Before you ask, they can't be traced back."

"Even I know that, Abhi," Karan replies.

"Sure, you do, Bhai, but you were still going to ask me," Abhi says, grinning like a Cheshire cat.

"Are there any searches that are unpaid?"

"Yes, a fair number of them are. I assumed they are paid for with a payment channel that doesn't connect to PTK directly.

"I need you to identify these unpaid searches first."

"Okay, but it may take some time, especially this mind map you want."

"Send me the information about these twenty-five families that searches have been focused on. Also, I need you to check on these families first." Karan writes down the names on a piece of paper and hands it to him.

Abhi looks at the paper, touches his iPad a few times, and says, "Sent."

"Did Ipshita send you a screenshot of the IRL games section?" asks Karan.

"She did, but it wasn't very useful. The URL is masked. To players, it looks like they are on the PTK website, but they aren't. The system is probably redirecting players to another website or portal, but it looks like they are still on PTK."

"So, we can't trace it?"

"We can, but it is a little complicated. When an IRL game link appears for a player as an invite and they use the link, that's the only time the system redirects them to the other website. The only way we can explore the IRL games is if we can access that other site when the player clicks that link. Once a player agrees to play the game, they can't go back to that section again. The system automatically creates a private group on PTK for instructions and communication. The group is deleted once that game is completed."

"Let me get this clear. The gateway to the IRL games section opens only when the players click the link with the invite. Does PTK have any information or data stored for these games?"

"It sort of does. The player profile indicates the level they play on, including IRL games, but doesn't give details. Players have usernames, and until players meet for an IRL game, they don't know each other's identities. From what Ipshita tells me, even during the game, the players are completely focused on their so-called mission, and once it's done, they break off quickly. Unless they know each other before they started playing PTK, the players don't seem to interact in the real world," Abhi says, rubbing his chin with his fist.

Karan watches him. "What is it? Just spit it out."

"You won't like it."

"There are a lot of things I don't like, but I still deal with them. So, spill."

"I found Akansha on the list, too."

"Akansha? As in the PC's daughter, Akansha?" Karan sits up.

Abhi nods.

Karan rubs his face. "I knew something was off there."

A few months ago, Akansha was all set to go to Rome for her Master's programme in design. A week before her departure, she was supposed to meet a few friends for dinner. When she didn't turn up, her friends began to worry and later found her in the parking lot outside the restaurant.

When she'd been taken to the hospital, being asthmatic, the doctors assumed her respiratory distress was because she hadn't had her inhaler with her. That small detail had irked Karan. Even as a child, Akansha had carefully managed her condition. He knew there was no way she'd leave the house without her inhaler.

This was a conversation Karan would need to have face-to-face with the PC. The worst part was that he was quite sure he'd find a connection to Mataji, and he knew the PC's mother was probably the link to her. Akansha was the eldest grandchild, and the PC's mother had been pressuring him and his wife not to send her to Rome but to marry her off.

Had the old woman decided to take matters into her own hands?

"PTK keeps photographs of its players, doesn't it?" asked Karan. "Can you get the team and Anya to have a look at those pictures?"

"Do you think one of us may have seen someone from the game? How? Where?"

"Maybe it's just wishful thinking. There must be a direct connection between this Mataji and PTK."

"So, followers make their requests, and she blesses them with interventions. Is that what you're saying?"

"It looks like it."

"So, in each of the PTK cases, someone wanted to steer the victim away or towards something?" Abhi asks.

Karan shakes his head. "I don't think it is in each case. Some cases would've been on the request of paying clients."

"Like the cane man in Anya's case."

"It seems like it."

"That's some weird level of intruding into people's lives, but I guess it makes sense, doesn't it? The more people think someone can resolve the issues in their lives and sweep away the obstacles in their path, the more they come to depend on them. What does Mataji gain in the process?"

"The usual, I guess—money and power. Was there a cluster search on the PC's family?"

"No. I was surprised at that."

"It's not surprising. They wouldn't risk digging into him and his family."

"Yet, they interfered with Akansha?" Abhi points out.

"Hmm. The PC's mother must be an important person for them."

"From what little I know, the PC is not the kind to look the other way, even if it was his mother telling him to do so," Abhi mumbles.

"True. His father is something of a legend in the department. He passed away last year. Maybe this Mataji stepped in when the PC's mother was going through a difficult time."

Abhi nods. "Maybe."

CHAPTER SIXTEEN

Two days later, Imran walks into the living room after his run, wiping off the light sheen of sweat that covers his face with the sleeve of his T-shirt.

"Where is Anya?" Karan asks him.

"When I left, she was near the rock."

"Okay."

"She got a call from that IB officer when I was there, Sir. It was short and curt. She told him to contact her only through the team. Basically, it was a polite version of telling him to go take a walk."

"Did she look troubled?"

"If she was, she didn't show it," he says. "Sir, how is the PC taking it?"

"He is furious and basically avoiding all contact with his mother. He and his wife are still trying to convince Akansha to consider joining the design programme. You know, when the whole incident happened, her confidence took a real beating. She's happy at her new job, so I'm not sure if she'll decide to study abroad after all."

"And the Mataji bit?"

Karan rubs his chin. "Apparently, his mother was introduced to her more than a year ago. The PC still hasn't been able to get too many details. Mataji's gatherings are only by invitation. He's looking into it quietly. I'll see you in a while," he says, leaving the house.

He finds Anya leaning against the last boulder that sits on the side of the narrow path. He stops a foot away from her and leans against the rock, taking in the view of the trees around them. The days have grown shorter. It isn't six yet, and the sun has already set.

"So, do you have any questions for me?" he asks her.

She shakes her head and continues to watch the sky change its colours.

"Aren't you curious? What did the IB officer say?"

"He asked if I was willing to put my life in the hands of someone who'd had a nervous breakdown."

"And?"

"And, I said, at this point in their career, if an officer had not come close to one, they probably weren't doing their job right. He said you threw someone out of a building. He did clarify that it was out of a window."

"Oh, it was nice of him to clarify that," Karan says with a laugh. "First, I didn't throw him—he fell out. And second, it was just one floor, and he didn't break anything." He didn't like explaining himself, but this was Anya, so he hoped she'd understand. "I was with the Interpol in Paris at that time. We were tracking a human trafficking network. My partner and I had just come on duty and were relieving two other officers," he continues. "We were watching a mid-level member of the network who was staying in the hotel across the street. I put on the earphones and heard screams. It was a nine-year-old that this piece of scum decided to keep for himself. The officers had been sitting there, listening to her. By the time we got to the room, she was dead—sliced open in ways I never thought imaginable. There was nothing we could do. The officer who had been on duty kept telling me to look at the bigger picture. Anya, this kid was just nine, but she looked like a six-year-old. I couldn't for the life of me understand what kind of bigger picture needed her to bleed all over that room."

He rubs his face. "You can imagine what happened next. Anyway, I finished my tenure with the Interpol, came back, and put in my papers, but the PC at that time refused to process them. He sent me on a sabbatical. I got my Master's degree in psychology, came back, and set up the Urban Crimes team. The IB officer wasn't really lying—I did have a breakdown of sorts. For months, I could hear the shrieks of that little girl." He doesn't tell her that sometimes he still wakes up to them.

"You wouldn't be human if you didn't," she says. "For months after I escaped from Hisar, I would have the weirdest nightmares. It was only the sound of the wind I heard as I got out of the house and cycled to the bus stop. I never thought such a calming sound could be terrifying. I'm sure, at some point, Rohan has told you about the volume at which I sometimes listen to music."

"It drowns out that silence," he says, and she nods. "How was your day at the office today?" he asks, appreciating the way she changed the direction of the conversation.

"Pretty good, I think. It was productive workwise, and everyone knows I'm back, so I guess it was good in terms of the psycho cane fellow, too."

"We think he'll not be able to wait any longer. Increased patrols around The Tri will force him to make his move at the office."

"What if someone else gets hurt?"

Karan shakes his head. "No, this man likes to do things at his own pace, without people around. Did you put in a request for the editing room?"

She nods.

"I think you'll be allocated an editing room late tomorrow night or the next day at the latest. Kabir said the new online security system is now connected to the scheduling programme. The IB has a plan in place, but we're going to be there, just in case."

"We?"

"We," he replies and holds his hand out to her. Anya stares at it for a while before taking it. "Let's take a quick walk before it gets dark," he suggests.

"It's already dark," she replies.

"Well, then darker," he says with a laugh.

They walk in companionable silence for a bit.

"This truly is an incredible place you have built."

"I didn't build anything. My grandfather designed the whole thing. Abhi and I helped him plant each tree. The rest was all nature."

"Your grandfather was a forest officer, wasn't he?"

Karan nods in response. "He started off as a botany professor, then joined the Forest Service. He was fortunate to find his soulmate in my grandmother. He'd joke that she tolerated him when most relatives kept their distance. Soon after she died, he was diagnosed with Alzheimer's disease. It was the first time I saw fear in his eyes. He didn't want to stay locked up at home just so he wouldn't get lost. So, we decided this was a good way for him to be happy and safe. He did everything possible to postpone the inevitable. Crosswords, Sudoku, origami—you name it, and he'd tried it. However, over time, it became difficult for him to adjust to the lapses in his memory. On good days, he'd remember us all. On bad days, he'd retreat into his forest. Emotional memories remain—that is a blessing. Abhi and I were the only ones allowed around him on his bad days—me, because he trusted me to take care of all the details."

"And Abhi?"

"At that time, Abhi was the spitting image of one of Dada's brothers—the one who had died in his late teens. With the age difference between us, Abhi and I had never been close, but the last few years changed that. Sometimes, I wonder if Dada insisted on creating this little forest for himself or for us."

"A bit of both, I'd think," she says.

"So, tomorrow," he swiftly changes the subject, "the IB people have a plan in place. The team has been chosen based on people who know him, or rather, knew him well."

"But," she emphasizes the word, "I hear you've made some arrangements of your own."

Karan smiles. "You hear too much."

"Is there anything I can do?"

"Just try to get back to your usual routine at work like you did today."

"Why didn't you let me move back home? He may be watching."

Karan shakes his head. "No, he's already tried that. This man is paranoid. He is now going to make a move only when he is sure he can control all the factors involved. Besides, planning to make a move near your home or even when you are on the road would mean that he'd have to admit that things didn't go his way the last time. He is not going to do that," he pauses to look at her before continuing. "The advantage we have is that not only is he paranoid, but he also has a delusion of grandeur. He thinks he is better and smarter than everyone around him. A few years back, that was true, but now, not so much. He takes great pride in his tech skills, but I have faith in our officers. I think, in the end, this whole thing is going to come down to that."

"You have some idea of when and where he will try," she says.

"It has to be at your office. It can't be with too many people around. He likes to use poison on many occasions, but in his head, you've tormented him for weeks, so there can be only one resolution."

"Face-to-face?"

"Yes. He shouldn't try anything in the daytime. But, if you see him or even catch a glimpse of his cane, turn around and walk away in the opposite direction, without making it too obvious, of course."

"Of course," she repeats. "Because, of course, meeting a paranoid killer with delusions is no big deal."

"Just keep an arm's distance."

"You mean a cane's distance," she quips, and he shakes his head, smiling.

"One more thing. I suggest you stay on with us for a few more days," he says and continues speaking even as she tries to interrupt him. "The logical brain will know the threat has been taken care of, but emotions take longer to process." He sees impatience in her eyes. "Just stay," he adds gently. "At least until the PTK cases are done." *And until you're sleeping better.*

Now that the darkness has closed in, there is barely any light around them, but he can see the confusion on her face. "Let me just put this out there, just so you and I are clear," he says. "I like you. I like you a lot. Just saying it out loud feels good. But there is no pressure on you. They are my feelings, and I just want to be clear about them."

She shifts her weight slightly from one foot to the other. "Despite my best intentions, it seems I like you too, but I'm not someone you want to be involved with, believe me. I've never been in a relationship. I wouldn't know where to start, and to top it all, I'd probably get most of the stuff wrong."

"What stuff?"

"All the things it takes to make a relationship work. I work too much, I like my space, I'm pretty much a homebody, and I have trust and control issues. Should I go on? Oh yes, I couldn't tell you about the DNI even if I wanted to. I come with a lot of baggage."

"Don't we all?" he replies, but she looks unconvinced.

"Let's just take it one step at a time. I wanted you to know how I feel; we'll take the rest as it comes. Is that fine with you?"

"I guess so."

"Well then," he smiles, and they walk back home. "You meditate, don't you? I assume you do breathing exercises, too. Can you focus on box breathing for the next few days?"

"You want me to control my breathing even if I am panicking."

"Something like that."

***

The next day, Anya catches glimpses of Rohan in the office, but since they are working on different projects, their paths run parallel. She messages him to let him know she's booked an editing room and gets a quick response. Kabir and she manage to shoot several episodes of 'Living Solo' with the help of two other interns. She spends the rest of the day finding the right sponsors. It's past nine when she finally shuts down her computer, closes her eyes, and leans back in her chair. *It's been a productive day.*

She is on her way out when she gets the message. The editing room she requested will be available at 11 p.m. She looks at her watch. There is no point braving rush hour traffic only to return. She quickly adds her name to the dinner list and is glad to see Rohan and Kabir's names on it.

***

A few minutes before eleven, she knocks on the door to the editing room and walks in. Instead of the editor, she finds Karan in his seat.

"Is it happening?" she asks. Karan nods. "So, are the IB officers here?"

"Yes."

"I didn't see them anywhere in the building."

"That's the idea—like you didn't see the Urban Crimes team the whole day, too."

"Were all of you here?"

"Did you really think we were going to leave you by yourself?"

"No. I knew Kabir was here. I guessed the rest of you would be close."

"Put your phone on DND, or better yet, switch it off. I don't want it to ring or light up at a crucial moment," he says as he gets up to show her the false soundproofing panel Rohan had made. Since it's placed in a dark corner, its presence is virtually undetectable. "This man has years of experience, Anya. He trusts his instincts and pays attention to the slightest change in a room. When he enters this room, he has to believe that he just missed you."

"Why would he come here if he knows the editor will also be here? I thought the IB was going to catch him on the fire escape."

"That's the plan."

"Why do I feel like there is a but at the end of that sentence?"

"Because there is. Each time you people use this room and take a break, the editor goes outside for a smoke. You usually join him, but only after you've been to the restroom."

"What do you want me to do?"

"I need you to start working on the project you are editing. It should look like you paused midway. Would it be normal to leave the music playing when you take a break?"

"Yes, especially if we are trying to pick one for the theme."

He watches her work and explain things to him as she views segments and makes changes, her fingers tapping furiously on the keyboard all the while. The faint sound of cymbals and bells plays in the background.

"Okay. Showtime," Karan says abruptly as he takes her by the elbow and stands up. He removes the false panel and looks around one last time. "I need you to just breathe and not move until I tell you it's safe. Okay?"

"Okay."

They stand side by side, enclosed between the soundproof panelling and the false panel. In the darkness, Karan reaches for her hand and gently presses it.

All I need to do is breathe. I can do that, Anya tells herself.

A gentle shift in the air is the only indication of the door opening and then closing. To her, for a few seconds, it feels like she has forgotten to breathe. She gently takes in a breath of air, then out, and in again, until there is another shift in the air. *Has the man left?*

Karan presses her hand.

Patience is a virtue, Anya reminds herself. *And sometimes, it can keep you alive.*

A few minutes later, Karan moves the panelling and gestures for her to sit. After a minute or two, he finally says, "It's over. We'll stay here until they take him away."

"You missed out on all the action," she murmurs.

Karan grins. "Thankfully, we didn't need any action here. Antara tasered him in the restroom. The IB officers will take him away."

"And then?"

"Our involvement ends here, as does yours."

"So, that's it?"

"Pretty much. Do you need to save your work?" He gestures at the computer screen with his chin.

"Are you crazy? If the editor knew I'd worked on it, he'd ban me from his editing room for weeks."

"Let's go home. And before you begin arguing, no, you can't go back to The Tri until we solve the PTK cases."

"But you said there is no threat to me now."

"You are a threat to yourself, Anya," Karan says, humour twinkling in his eyes. "You even photographed one of the most elusive agents the IB has produced."

"I didn't know that," she counters.

"Exactly. You didn't know it. Imagine the kind of chaos you could create if you did."

"That's complete nonsense," she huffs.

"If you say so."

***

Early next morning, the jarring sound of Karan's phone wakes him up. He may've been groggy, but it takes only seconds for the gravity of the message to sink in. He grabs his notebook from the bedside table and starts jotting down the instructions. He makes his batchmate in Jaipur repeat them again.

"It has to be this way, Shekhawat. Do you understand? This is the only way she'll meet with you. Be very careful of who you trust with this information; at least four lives depend on your discretion. One last thing. If you want this family to survive, they have to disappear. I don't know how you will do it, but there is no other way."

"Thanks. I know this wasn't easy."

"It was sheer luck that you called me and not someone else in the department."

"Integrity and luck aren't interchangeable words," Karan replies, and the other officer laughs as he ends the call.

The atmosphere at the breakfast table is more boisterous than usual. The relief of getting the dragon cane man out of Anya's life is apparent. Karan watches Anya at the other end of the table. She sits back, watches the team converse animatedly, and just smiles when one of his officers or his brother teases her over something. From the far ends of the table, their eyes meet. Karan nods, and she nods back. He is glad to see she is at ease with his people. When breakfast is finally over, he clears his throat and has their attention.

"So, we found Navin. He is with Arjun's aunt. Arjun's father handed the baby to his late wife's sister on the day Navin was brought to Jaipur. Arjun's father has not visited Navin since then, neither have the uncle and aunt who kidnapped him."

"I'm sorry," Anya breaks the silence around the table. "Obviously, I'm missing something you all understand. Why kidnap him if they didn't want him?"

When no one answers, Karan speaks up. "Just because they could. There is no other answer. They want the child because he is the only heir. If things had gone as planned, Arjun and Raina would've probably been in a fatal accident the same day."

"Now?" Sameer asks.

"My batchmate had a conversation with the aunt. She is expecting us to come pick up the baby tonight."

"Just like that?" Kabir asks.

"Yes."

"But what will happen when Arjun's father figures out the baby is gone?" Sameer asks.

"Apparently, Arjun's aunt is ready for this situation. Before you ask me any more questions, I don't have the answers."

"But, Sir," Sameer starts to object.

"Sameer, let's first get the baby back. Then we'll deal with this 'India, Bharat, and *Sarkar'* issue again."

***

It is well past midnight when Karan turns off the headlights as he parks the car on the quiet tree-lined side street. Kabir is fast asleep in the passenger seat. Choosing him to pick up Navin is a no-brainer. Kabir is a doting uncle to his two-year-old twin nephews. When his sister, his fraternal twin, was close to full term, Kabir had rented the apartment next door so he would be at hand whenever she needed him, and yet, have his space and privacy. Unlike the rest of the team, he didn't wince at the thought of changing a dirty diaper. In Karan's book, that places him higher than most people. Karan looks towards the small bungalow that sits amidst a tidy garden. He's been told the main gate and the side door would be open. The whole setup makes him itch. There are too many things he can't control, but if they can walk out of the house with Navin, he is willing to take the risk.

He nudges Kabir gently with his elbow. "We're here."

Kabir nods as he wakes up in stages. Karan rechecks the house number and looks around the quiet neighbourhood.

"Ready?" Karan asks.

"Yes, Sir," Kabir replies as he touches the backpack at his feet for reassurance. It has the essentials they'd need to take care of Navin on the trip back home.

"Then I'll see you in a few minutes," Karan says as he puts the earpiece in and places a call to Kabir.

"Any sound of trouble, I'm coming in," he tells Karan and holds his fist out.

Karan shakes his head but bumps fists. "Forget about the first sign of trouble; if Navin starts crying, you're coming in."

Karan opens the wooden gate and walks down the brick-lined path. The fragrance of night flowers fills the air. A faint light comes from a room on the side of the house. The fly mesh door is closed, but the wooden door behind it is open. He doesn't want to startle the woman inside, so he clears his throat.

"Come in," calls a soft voice. Arjun's aunt sits on a chair, reading. She is dressed in jeans and a light jacket. Despite the salt and pepper hair, she doesn't look much older than Arjun.

"ACP Shekhawat?" she asks, looking up from her book.

"Yes, Ma'am."

"Will you take him straight back to his parents?"

"Yes, Ma'am."

She watches him for a while and then nods. "Would you like a glass of water?"

"No, thank you, Ma'am. We'd like to get back as soon as possible."

"We?"

"My partner is waiting outside. He's more accustomed to taking care of babies," Karan says. There is something about the woman that makes him want to reassure her. He looks around the neat, sparsely furnished room. Moonlight streams in from the windows. Only the area around her chair is pooled in light from the table lamp next to it. Closer to her chair is a low table. A singing Tibetan bowl sits next to several small boxes wrapped in fabric. A deck of cards lies spread open on a silken cloth. There is just a hint of incense in the air.

"Pick a card," she tells him.

"Tarot?" he asks.

She nods.

"I'd rather not," Karan says, his eyes on the cards.

"You don't believe in them?"

"On the contrary."

"Pick five for me, please. I insist," she says.

Karan knows the routine. He closes his eyes and focuses on his breath before bending down to gently pick each card with his left hand and place it on his right palm. He hands the lot to her, and she spreads them on the table.

"In the last few weeks, I've been trying to do readings for Arjun and Raina," she says in a low voice.

"I assume the cards haven't been good?"

She nods. "The Death card and the Tower appeared at each reading."

"It doesn't have to signify death. You'd know that better than me, Ma'am."

"Hmm. That is what I'd normally tell someone I am reading for."

"But?" Karan asks.

"But, Arjun's father will have them killed, ACP Shekhawat. They escaped his clutches, and no one gets to do that. If you truly want to help this family, they must vanish completely—no trace, no trail."

"How did he find them?"

"That's the thing. He looked for so many years and found no clue or sign of them. Believe me, he has the resources to search the length and breadth of this country, or so he thinks. Then, out of the blue, someone writes to him and tells him where they are. What kind of a person does that?"

"Someone wrote to him? A friend? A relative?"

She shakes her head. "A letter came for him. He says it's a sign from God that he has a right to..."

"Right to?"

"Take the child and kill his son and daughter-in-law."

"Why take Navin?"

"Is that his name? Arjun's father decided to call him Suraj. Why did he take Navin? I guess because he could. Arjun's brother can't have children—a childhood illness left him impotent. When I first heard about the letter, I wanted to warn Arjun, but there was no way for me to reach him. When the baby arrived, all I could do was make sure he was taken care of. Will you help them?"

"Yes, Ma'am."

"It won't be easy." Her eyes move to the cards he'd picked. "Getting justice is important to you. What if you must sacrifice that to keep this family safe?"

"I don't understand."

"Yes, you do. Whatever charges you bring up against my brother-in-law, they will disappear even before you can prove them. That is the kind of power he holds in this state. So, what will you do?"

Karan remains silent.

"You don't want the reading?"

"I picked the cards for you," he replies.

"Yes, you did. Thank you."

Karan takes out a business card from his wallet. This one only has his personal phone number and email address. "This is in case you ever need to contact me or if you want to check on Arjun, Raina, and Navin."

She nods. "I know you don't want a reading, but I'll still tell you that the Queen of Swords is reversed. Do you understand what that means?"

He shakes his head.

"Usually, it represents repressed feelings, lack of centre, and lack of inner voice. It can also mean not having all the information you need to decide on something vital. But I think, in this reading, it is someone who betrayed them—someone older and wiser, but someone who is lost in their world and yet, determined to ruin theirs."

"I think I know who that is."

She shakes her head. "But there won't be any justice."

"Maybe justice will find another way."

"Do you really think so?" she asks, eyes sparkling.

"All I know is when people think they've got away with a crime, retribution always comes. It's just not as obvious as it should be."

Arjun's aunt laughs. "Yes, I think you are right. My brother-in-law, Arjun's father, is dying—slowly, painfully, from the inside out. So yes, maybe there is justice." She stands up. "Come, meet Navin."

It is only when they walk to the far end of the room that he notices there are two cradles set side by side. "There are two babies?"

"If Arjun's father realizes that he doesn't have his grandson, he'll begin looking for him again, won't he? So, soon after I heard his ridiculous plan, I adopted the other baby."

"I see. I have one last question. Do you know how Arjun's brother got Navin?"

Her eyes hardened. "Did that idiot take Navin? With Kamal and Deepti, everything is a perpetual adventure. You won't find a more self-involved pair. Kamal wouldn't have cared that he was taking a baby from his parents, just that there was an heir to the family."

"Does Arjun's father know someone called Mataji?"

"There are so many Matajis around, ACP Shekhawat, but I guess you are talking of a spiritual or religious guide. No, he wouldn't seek counsel from anyone, especially not a woman."

"So, you've never read for him?" he asks.

"The cards don't look kindly on those who manipulate lives, do they?"

"I don't read, Ma'am, so I wouldn't know. But a long time ago, I knew someone who did."

"When the time is right, I think the right deck will find its way to you. Thank you for taking Navin home," she says as she places the sleeping baby into his arms. She gently puts her hands on the baby's head. "Be well."

"We'll be on our way then, Ma'am," Karan says with a nod.

She holds out a card. "This is in case you ever need to get in touch with me. There is also a number on the back for Arjun, in case he wants to call."

Karan nods and leaves.

CHAPTER SEVENTEEN

The journey back is relatively uneventful. They stop once so that Kabir can give Navin his bottle. They sit in silence as the baby happily sucks on the bottle.

"On the Delhi-Jaipur highway, with a baby enjoying his midnight feed," Kabir says in a low voice from the rear seat.

Karan chuckles. The 'never did I think I'd be here' game is something the team often plays. Sometimes, it is after they've been a part of the worst day of someone's life; sometimes, like today, it is after the unexpected closure to a case.

"Did you ever think we'd find him, Sir? After the visit to the paediatrician, I wasn't sure if it was a good or bad thing that he was taken by a relative."

"Kabir, you know that with kidnappings, most often, it's someone known to the family. It's never a good sign."

Once the baby is patted, burped, and safely harnessed in the baby seat, they get back on the road. A message chimes on both their phones. Karan keeps his eyes on the road while Kabir reads out an update from Sameer.

"Raina regained consciousness last evening. The doctor is going to continue monitoring her for a few more days. Arjun hasn't told her about Navin being taken. The doctor wants to avoid any kind of shock at this point."

"We'll take Navin straight to the hospital. Get in touch with the CSO, and ask him how he wants to handle this," Karan says.

"I'll message him now, and call him a little later, Sir."

Karan looks perplexed.

"Sir, not everyone is awake at this hour."

Karan glances at his watch and laughs. "That makes sense."

"So, Raina and Navin were never on PTK. Then, how did Arjun's brother get his hands on the drug? It can't be a coincidence that they used the same drug on Raina."

"That one answer could help us understand what's going on with PTK, but we aren't going anywhere near that family—at least, for now."

"Do you know what has been troubling me, Sir? Why would someone risk getting involved with the PC's mother and Akansha? The PC is not someone who would look the other way on something like this."

"Maybe his mother has more influence than we think. I've met her a few times, and she makes quite an impression. From what I hear, she has had a hard time adjusting to her husband's passing away."

"Do you think someone took advantage of a vulnerable moment?"

"I don't know, Kabir, but there was something the PC's mother could do for this Mataji that she was willing to risk being even remotely connected with the PC."

"Do you think it is money?"

"I am sure it is, but not just money. It has to be more."

"How did the PC respond when you spoke with him?"

"Not well," Karan says and leaves it at that. The only reason the senior officer had not gone charging home and confronted his mother was that his wife had been there to calm him down. It had taken Karan, the PC's wife, and later, Akansha, to make the PC back off. Finally, he'd promised to investigate the situation quietly.

At the hospital, Kabir hands the baby to Arjun. Tears of relief stream down his face. Kabir can see his hands tremble, so he gently guides the man to the closest chair in the visitors' lounge. Karan stands at the door, giving the father and son time to themselves. Later, he explains the plan to Arjun. If they are to disappear, they would have to uproot their lives completely, and they'd need all the help they could get.

"Don't worry about your home—we'll take care of it. Everything will be packed and put into storage, and you can decide how to handle it. Once your family thinks you are dead, I'm hoping you will have a clean start. But we'll wait for a while to see how things unfold."

Arjun nods.

"Are you fine with this plan?" Karan asks again.

"We planned to emigrate eventually. So, this is just a little sooner. Are you sure we can use the same identities?" Arjun asks.

"I can't help you get fake ones, Arjun, or even have a discussion on that. But I can ensure that you can't be traced. We'll have to move fast, most probably by the end of the day, if Raina is discharged."

"So, Mrs Sharma will think we are dead, and Navin is with my father?"

"Yes."

"Okay, let's do it your way, ACP Shekhawat."

While Kabir spends the day at the hospital, Karan oversees the movers and packers meticulously pack Raina and Arjun's home.

"Is it true? Are they dead?" Mrs Sharma asks as the last package is placed in the small truck.

"Yes, Ma'am. Raina died last evening, and Arjun had a cardiac arrest soon after."

"I guess, in a way, it's a blessing, isn't it? I mean, after they lost the baby and all."

"They didn't lose the baby, Ma'am. He was taken away."

"That's what I said."

Karan stares at the woman. "There are lines that shouldn't be crossed, Ma'am. Ever. And once you cross them, there is no going back."

"What do you mean?"

"I mean, the post office has records of your letters to Arjun's father."

Her face turns pale. "So what? It's not illegal to send someone a letter. Nor is it illegal to tell someone where their son and grandson live."

"True. You did nothing illegal, but how will you live with yourself when there is blood on your hands?"

She looks at her hands and lets them drop. "My conscience is clear. I did the right thing."

"Why did you do it? They treated you like family."

"Really? Then why did they buy a house?"

"First, the house was an investment—they weren't planning to move. Second, it is not unusual for children to move away from home, as your children did. I hope you are satisfied with the result of your actions."

"How dare you speak to me like this?"

"How dare you ruin three lives, Ma'am? Two dead, one orphaned. That's all on you," he says, handing her the keys to the *barsati*.

"I did nothing illegal."

"Only immoral," Karan counters. "Maybe not today, but you will be held accountable for your actions."

"Is that a threat?"

He shakes his head. "It's faith."

***

"How are things going?" Karan asks, pulling up a chair to sit behind Abhi and Kabir at the dining table. They have three large screens before them, one of which shows the PTK website.

"So, we were able to sort of access the IRL games page but only for a very short time," says Abhi. "Ipshita got a game invite. She went to the page to view the details and then declined. Like we thought, that page was not on the PTK website. A link rotator simply directs the traffic to different pages. This means that each IRL game has a different landing page."

"Sir, a player cannot go back to it, irrespective of whether they choose to play it or decline," Kabir adds. "The URL is also masked, but we managed to follow it. It's a static site. Players just come to check the game details, after which they are linked back to the PTK website, where a private group is formed until the game is complete. The files are on a server abroad. There is no way to track who owns or runs PTK."

"Good work!" Karan places his hands on their shoulders and gets up.

"Good work? It's not something we didn't know, so we didn't really contribute anything new," Abhi grumbles.

"No, but you just confirmed a lot of details that tell us we won't find these people through the website. We've to go into the IRL games. Can we track if a new game pops up soon?"

"Actually," Kabir turns to face Karan, "there is a game coming up soon, but all the details haven't been shared as yet. It's the one Ipshita declined. I was hoping..."

"Let's do it, but we can't let anyone get drugged on our watch. So, you can plan it accordingly. Can you send me the updated data from this?" he waves at the screen.

"It's already in your inbox."

"We could avoid all this if the PC would let us speak with his mother," Sameer says from behind them.

"She'll just warn this woman or whoever is behind PTK, Sameer. He's looking into it, too. Hopefully, he'll have something for us soon." Karan's phone rings. "Speaking of... I'll take this in my office."

Karan patiently listens to the PC speak and keeps noting down details. It is too early to decide which detail is small and which will split this case wide open.

"So, your mother's friend only came to know about Mataji after Akansha was drugged?" he asks.

"Yes, she noticed a difference in my mother, but since she seemed happier and more at peace, she didn't push it," says the PC. "Apparently, only when you are a part of the inner circle can you introduce one family member or a close friend to Mataji. My mother wanted to introduce this friend, but she didn't like the idea. It was then that my mother told her about how Mataji worked a 'miracle' with Akansha."

"I assume she didn't know Akansha was drugged."

"No, she thought it was fate. Akansha was hospitalized," said the PC, his voice rising, "and my mother thought it was *fate*. I'm not sure how I'm supposed to deal with that. This is not right."

"Does Akansha want to consider the Master's programme, or does she want to continue working here?"

"She wants to go, Karan. She is sorting those details out, while my mother is searching for suitors for her," he says with exasperation.

"Just find this Mataji soon. I don't know how long I can pretend everything is fine."

"Sir, we'll find her," Karan promises. "In the meantime, please send your mother's financial and bank statements."

***

"What's going on?" Anya asks as she walks into the house and finds Abhi, Kabir, and Antara in front of three screens on the dining table.

"She's home!" Antara yelps. "Wash up quickly, and come back. We need another set of eyes." She fills her in on Karan's conversation with the PC.

"Just give me five minutes, and then I'm all yours," Anya says. She looks at the empty mugs and bottles of eye drops on the table. "Tea? Coffee?"

"*Masala chai,* please, pretty please," says Kabir, his eyes still on the screen.

She delivers the steaming mugs first to the living room, before taking the other mugs up to Karan's office.

"*Chai*!" Imran exclaims and stands up to take the tray from her.

Karan clicks 'pause' and looks up. "Did Antara tell you?"

"Yes. How can I help?"

"We're going through CCTV camera footage from anywhere the PC's mother used her cards to pay in the last six months. Apparently, the woman is a true believer in retail therapy."

"You are hoping she met Mataji somewhere during her retail therapy."

"I'm fairly sure she wouldn't have met her at her house. She may have been introduced to her at a friend's place, but I'm hoping the following meetings happened in a public space."

"Why not at a quieter, more private place?"

"That does make sense, but she wouldn't have invited Mataji home. She is more likely to have met her in a public place that seems private. The PC's mother is pretty careful about these things. Of course, none of this seems to match anything I knew about her."

"The intervention with her granddaughter made a true believer out of her, I guess. Okay, I'm off to see some CCTV videos. Do you all want something to eat?" Anya asks.

"Some people refused to stop for a bite," Imran says from the corner.

"I told you to take a break," Karan huffs.

"Yes, but you weren't going to take one."

"Okay, okay, go back to your screens. I'll take care of dinner," Anya says.

A meal and two hours later, Anya can't look at the screen anymore. "Have all of you been doing this the whole day?"

"Sir went through her bank statements last night and found certain changes in her spending behaviour. He's fairly convinced we'll find Mataji in one of these recordings. The question is, which one?" Antara says, leaning back in her chair with her eyes closed.

The next morning, when Anya leaves for work, the team is mostly asleep, but she doesn't find Karan and Sameer anywhere in the house. *Weird!*

As Karan and Sameer drive to the five-star hotel where the PC's mother has charged the cost of a tea room to her card on a weekly basis for the last few months, Karan is fairly sure they are on the right track. He messages the PC with an update, and promptly, his phone rings.

"Are you telling me my mother has been meeting this woman every week? For how long?" he asks.

"Months, Sir."

"When will she meet her next?"

"The day after tomorrow."

"I really think I should speak with my mother now, Karan. Enough is enough."

"We're long past enough, Sir. The way I see it, if this woman is Mataji or the go-between—I'm not sure of that—she has your mother's confidence. If you speak to your mother now, there is no doubt in my mind this so-called Mataji will vanish. Her whole operation is about manipulation; she doesn't get her hands dirty. Also, Sir, even if we approach her, we still have to link her to PTK.

Not all the IRL cases involve the drug. We are still trying to figure out whether PTK started with the specific motive of intruding in people's lives, using them like pawns, or whether Mataji is just hiring out the games, as and when required."

"You know what the most important thing in this is, don't you, Shekhawat? We need to find out where that drug is coming in from," the PC points out.

"I spoke to a few colleagues at the Interpol. They haven't heard of it. This refined version of Rohypnol hasn't entered the market."

"As yet."

"I didn't want to say that."

"The players can't be prosecuted because they have no motive, Karan. They didn't know they were using an actual drug. What will you do?"

"I'll find a way, Sir. Even if nothing breaks in the next two days, we'll still be able to follow her when she meets your mother."

"Okay, we'll do this your way. I don't understand one thing. My mother got her wish—Akansha didn't go abroad," he says bitterly. "So, why is my mother still connected with this woman?"

Karan remains silent.

"Just say what you want to, Karan."

"When someone does you a favour, Sir, something no one else could do, that's a very different connection. This woman is basically a fixer. She fixes situations—sometimes quietly and sometimes with more flourish. She is always behind the scenes, directing things—not really in the forefront. But when the job is done, it's all her. I'll not be surprised if your mother now seeks her counsel over all small and big matters."

"Why does it sound like you have more to say?"

"There is, but you won't like it."

"Is there any part of this case that I like, Karan?" the PC sighs.

"When you are indebted to someone, it's a lopsided balance of power. It makes people uncomfortable, and they tend to back away."

"But not in this case."

"Correct, Sir, which suggests that Mataji's clients are not just paying her but also doing her favours that keep the power balanced."

"That's some warped logic, but it makes sense."

"Sir, I've sent you the report on the information collected on PTK so far. The information that involves IRL games focuses on certain families. On the surface, they seem to have little in common—some of them are rich and politically connected, others have power that is not as apparent. The fact that each of them can only introduce one more person to Mataji is rather interesting," he adds. "She chooses a small group of people in each city. This is interesting on several levels, but mostly because self-declared gurus usually want to reach out to a larger audience. She is restricting her followers to a select, small group—one on which she'll have a strong influence."

"Families do weird things in the name of love and concern. Carry on, Shekhawat. Let me know if I can help with anything. Before you say it again, I'll stay out of my mother's way for now."

"Sir, one last thing. If your mother didn't introduce her friend to Mataji—the one you spoke to—who did she introduce her to?"

"I've no idea, Karan. Right now, I'm more worried about what favours my mother did for her."

"We'll close the case quickly, Sir. Jai Hind!"

"Jai Hind!"

The officers watch the CCTV footage with the hotel security chief. In each meeting, it shows the PC's mother entering the so-called tea room first—actually an alcove with large potted palms, set away from the rest of the coffee shop—and then being joined by a younger woman. Karan wasn't sure what he was expecting of Mataji, but it was definitely not *her*. Dressed in a saree, the woman looks poised. *Maybe she is the go-between?*

"Can you rewind and show it to us again?" asks Karan. "Also, can you pull up footage from the same section for the same day and time for the last few weeks? We'll need all of that on a USB drive." He turns to Sameer. "Let's try to clear up the images as best as possible. Does she look at all ... ?"

"Familiar?" Sameer completes his sentence. "She does, and yet, she doesn't. Does that make any sense, Sir?"

"Maybe she changed her appearance. Or, maybe we are seeing her in a different context." They watch for another half hour, with both officers paying keen attention to the interaction between the two women.

"When was the last time you saw someone leave their home without their cell phone or wallet, Sameer?" asks Karan. "Her hands are free, and her focus is completely on the PC's mother. I wish they had another camera that covered the same spot from a different angle. Let's talk to the staff who attended to them."

No CCTV, no smart trackers can ever give them the input that can be given by people on the ground.

A while later, a young man enters the security room and introduces himself. "Hello, Sir. I'm Rajat Saxena."

"Hi, Rajat. Has your manager mentioned what this is about?"

"Yes, Sir, the tea room ladies. How can I help you?"

"Did you take care of them every time they met?"

"Yes, Sir. I'm responsible for that section of the coffee shop. Besides, when we have regulars, they usually prefer the same people to wait on them."

"Can you give me your impression of them?"

"Well, they meet every week at the same time and order the same things from the menu. The bill is paid by card. But I think you want to know more about their interaction, don't you?"

Karan nods.

"Initially, I thought it was work-related. Some people do that—have their meetings over a cup of tea. But these meetings didn't seem official in that sense. The older lady always arrives first, and she is joined by the younger one later. They chat for a while, have tea and something to eat, and leave."

"How long do they sit there?"

"About forty-five minutes, sometimes a little more. The older lady does most of the talking."

"Anything else?"

"The younger woman somehow seems—I don't know how to put this—more in control of the situation. It's just a feeling I got. They stop talking when I am at the table, but the thing is, while that part of the coffee shop appears sort of private, it's really not. So, I usually catch snippets of their conversation. But it's just family stuff."

"What kind of family stuff?"

"The usual, Sir—what the older woman's granddaughter is doing, that her son and daughter-in-law are travelling."

"Rajat, I noticed the younger woman never carries a purse or even her cell phone."

"Yes, Sir. I noticed that too and thought it was a great way to give a person their complete focus."

"I agree, but you rarely see anyone move out of the house without their cell phone. Most women I know carry a purse whenever they're out of the house."

"I guess, since she was staying here, she didn't really feel the need to do so."

"Wait! She was staying here?"

"Yes, Sir. Didn't the manager mention that?"

"No, I just spoke with him on the phone. He was handling some kind of an emergency."

Rajat smiles. "Our emergencies are a little different from yours, I guess. I'm sure he'll come speak with you before you leave. Coming back to our tea room ladies, I did find it strange that they pay the bill on the table each time instead of charging it to the room. Most people find it more convenient to do that. But then, of course, the older woman pays."

"Is the younger woman still staying here?"

"I'm not very sure whether she has checked out or not, but I haven't seen her around in the last few days."

"Is there anything else you could tell us about either of the women?"

Rajat considers the question. "Are you only interested in the meetings she had with this lady or with the others, too?

"Others?"

"She pretty much meets someone daily at the same time. In fact, some of the interns call her 'the 4 p.m. woman'. She chooses different items from the menu on each day, but it is always the same order based on the person she is meeting."

"Is that odd?"

Rajat shrugs his shoulders. "People usually eat things they like. It could be nothing, really. From an F&B point of view, it is strange."

"Each meeting is set for four in the afternoon? Any other time you may have noted her in the hotel?"

"Honestly, Sir, I can only tell you about the coffee shop. I'm not so sure about the restaurants."

"Thank you so much, Rajat. You've been very helpful."

As Rajat gets up to leave, an older man in an immaculately tailored suit and a hint of salt and pepper at the temples walks up to the table. He smiles as Rajat leaves.

"Sanjay Ranjan," the manager introduces himself, extending his hand, and Karan shakes it. "I'm sorry I couldn't meet you earlier. I believe this is about one of our guests."

Sameer shows him some of the footage the security team had given them.

The manager nods. "Ah! The Canadian. She has been staying with us off and on for the last few months."

"Could we see the documentation she submitted when she arrived?"

"Sure," he says as he types on his phone and puts it down on the table. "Is she in trouble, or is *she* the trouble?"

Karan smiles. "Why do you put it like that?"

The manager smiles. "In my line of work, as in yours, I'm sure, we see all kinds of people."

"Your hotel receives hundreds of guests, Mr Ranjan. Why do you remember this one?" Sameer asks.

"Some guests just stand apart. She is polite, well-spoken, and gets all the ticks on the standard guest checklist of each hotel manager. And yet, something seems a little off. When she speaks to you, you have her complete attention. Not too many people do that. She seems to genuinely listen and not just hear you. I guess, people open up to someone like that."

"But isn't what you say a good thing?" Sameer asks.

"Yes, I guess it is. Except, how do I put it, she seems to be storing away all those details, all that information, as if she may find use for it another day. Look, maybe it is nothing. Maybe I'm too suspicious. I shouldn't have even mentioned this."

"No, Mr Ranjan, there must be a valid reason why you did. You're right. In both our lines of work, we constantly meet people and have to deal with them and then move on. Some of these skills we come by naturally, but most are earned with experience," Karan says.

"She travels lighter than most of our guests," adds the manager. "She dresses well, mostly in sarees. She's attractive and polite and makes an effort to establish a connection with people, but she has this sort of veneer that makes it obvious she keeps people at an arm's length. It's pretty odd."

A hotel employee walks into the room and hands the manager a few sheets of printed paper. "We have her passport details. Will this be enough?"

"What else can you tell me about," he refers to the papers, "Kamaal Karna?"

Was that a real name? It was the kind of thing grownups said to a child before an exam or competition.

"Well, when Ms Karna stayed with us, she seemed quite at home in the hotel—like she is used to staying in one for long durations. She used the hotel gym, sauna, and pool. She ate all her meals in her room, even though her room came with a complimentary breakfast. We've given you the dates of her stay with us. Is there anything else we can help with?"

"I know your security team is busy, but we'd really appreciate it if they could give us all the footage of her afternoon teatime."

"Absolutely. Anything else?"

"Any other details, like if she hired a vehicle from the hotel or any special service, would be useful, too."

"The high tea bill is usually paid for by her guests. That is a bit unusual. You can have a chat with our people at the door, but I don't think she used our taxi service. Let me check and find out if she requested for any special service. Do you want to wait for the footage? Or we could send it to you as soon as the team has it ready."

"Hopefully, it shouldn't take long for them to gather it. We'll have a chat with your people and wait in the lobby. Anything else that struck you as off?"

The manager shakes his head.

"Well, if you think of anything, please get in touch with me." Karan hands him his business card and takes the card the manager offers in return.

"Sameer, will you speak with the doorman? I want to make a few calls," Karan says as they leave the security room.

"Kamaal Karna?" Sameer asks. "Is that a real name? It sounds like a character from a television drama."

"Let's find out what we can about her."

On a hunch, Karan sends Kabir a picture of the woman along with her passport details and asks him to check with Disha from Lutyens Veranda. His next call is to an RCMP officer he worked with during his Interpol deputation. The conversation is long, with the other officer doing most of the talking.

Karan's next call is to the PC. "We have a problem."

CHAPTER EIGHTEEN

"Where is everyone?" Karan asks Sameer as he hands him the car keys.

"They are all in the office. Do you want to call a meeting?"

"You drive, Sameer. I'll call them." Before he has a chance to do that, his phone rings. It's the PC. Karan listens to what the senior officer has to say. "It's already done, Sir. There is nothing we can do to undo it now, but it ends here. My request to you is to stay away from your mother for the time being. I'd really like to arrest this woman with minimal fuss. But you do know she is going to start throwing out names once we have her. At some point, I'll have to have a conversation with your mother."

He listens to the PC's response.

"Jai Hind, Sir."

His next call is to Antara. "I'm sending you a name and profile. Deep dive, please. Fast!"

"How fast?"

"An hour. We'll have a meeting as soon as Sameer and I get there."

"This passport is clean, Sir," Antara says. Karan can hear her clicking away at the keyboard.

"Keep digging," Karan replies and ends the call before opening his iPad.

Sameer glances at him, then looks back at the road ahead.

When they arrive at the office, it's quiet but for the soft sound of clicking and typing on keyboards. Karan begins to speak, but Kabir raises a finger in the air. Karan knows better than to interrupt his team in the middle of a tech storm.

Five minutes later, Kabir looks up at him with a grin. "Someone is going to be in a world of trouble soon. And 'who took the Interpol flag off this passport' is the name of this game."

"Really?" Sameer interrupts and moves to stand behind Kabir's desk to read the details on the screen.

"Kamaal Karna is wanted in Canada for multiple counts of fraud and attempted murder," Karan says. "My Interpol contact there was obviously quite shocked that I didn't know about the red flag. Apparently, they've also been in touch with the embassy there and have been coordinating with the MEA. None of that means anything when someone takes the flag off the passport."

"She is a fixer," Antara says, "plain and simple. They can trace her hand behind many cases going back several years. It's only in the last year that they finally managed to get enough evidence to charge her with, at which time, she left the country. From what I understand, she was not using the drug there, and the Canadian police have no knowledge of a game like PTK."

"Sir, I don't think the PC's mother would've been involved if she knew an Interpol red flag was involved," Imran says.

"It all depends on what cock-and-bull story she gave her. The older woman was in a vulnerable position to begin with, and the right story, most probably of abuse, would have made the PC's mother sympathetic enough to introduce her to someone who would get the job done. Do we know who removed the flag?" Karan asked Kabir.

"Yes, Sir. He didn't take the flag off because only the Interpol has the authority to do that, but he did take the passport details off the Indian Interpol system. The system was accessed from the PC's office—not his actual office but the computer used by his admin. We know how particular that man is. If I can check his computer, I can give you a picture of who used his computer."

"A picture?"

"Yes, Sir. A while back, the PC's admin reached out to us, quietly, of course. His computer cannot have a password so that it can be used even when he isn't in the office. He was worried about it being misused," Kabir says.

"So?"

"So, we wrote a little programme for him that takes a picture whenever the computer is used by someone other than the admin."

Karan is silent for a bit. "This is brilliant! Does the PC's computer also have the same programme?"

There is silence in the room.

"Come on. No one is getting into trouble for this."

"Yes, Sir, but he doesn't know it," Sameer says. "His admin insisted on it. He said the PC was too trusting of visitors to his office. The programme simply detects if someone other than the person who works on the system uses it, takes a picture, and saves it."

"Okay, Sameer, get everyone up to speed on what we found at the hotel. Then you and Kabir can go and retrieve these pictures from the admin's computer."

Karan and Antara are still going through the CCTV videos from the hotel when Sameer and Kabir walk into the office.

Karan looks confused. "I thought both of you left."

"We did, and then we came back," Sameer says. "Kabir got a call from the Lutyens Terrace girl."

"Lutyens Veranda, Sameer Sir, and her name is Disha," Kabir corrects him.

"Okay, Disha from Lutyens Veranda called Kabir," Sameer says and looks at Kabir to continue.

"She is there. Kamaal Karna is staying there. Disha just sent me a picture to verify that it is the same person." Kabir hands Karan his phone.

"Disha confirmed the passport details?" Karan asks.

"She did."

"Antara," Karan calls out. "Sameer and you head to Lutyens Veranda. I'll get to work on the arrest warrant. As soon as I have the warrant, arrest her. Is her passport flagged on our system now?"

"It is," Imran replies.

"What time is sundown today?"

"5:30," Kabir says, checking his phone.

"Don't let her get away. Make sure you get her phone and electronic devices. Don't let her call or message anyone until we've gone through her devices. Now go."

"What if the warrant doesn't come in time?" Antara asks.

"It will come in time, but just in case it doesn't, make sure she isn't warned off. Kabir, make sure Disha doesn't give the game away."

"She won't. We can count on her."

"Okay, then, go, go, go!" he shoos them out of his office and calls the PC.

"We found her. We need the arrest warrant quickly. Her passport is now flagged on our system." Karan glances at his watch. "Yes, Sir, Antara and Sameer are already headed to the location." He listens to the PC. "Are you sure, Sir? I can go speak with him. I have all the documents ready—the Interpol red flag notice as well as her links to the people connected with PTK. We're also asking for a search and seizure warrant for electronic devices. Once the arrest is made, we'll let the Interpol deal with it, but I want a few hours with her." He listens to the PC before he says, "I'll see you at his chambers then."

***

Kamaal Karna's arrest is quicker and smoother than most arrests the team has made. They do everything by the book—dot their i's and cross their t's. When she's brought into the interrogation room, she is calm, and other than the odd smile on her face, she shows little reaction.

She's only spoken to Sameer once, given him the visiting card of a high-ranking police officer, and asked that he be informed of her arrest. She reassures Sameer that she understands they have no choice but to arrest her, but that they'd have to let her go soon. Sameer and Antara exchange glances.

"Lady, your passport has an Interpol red flag on it. You are their headache, not ours," Antara says. But other than her eyes widening for a few seconds, Kamaal Karna gives no other response.

While Kabir and Imran work with her electronic devices, Sameer deals with the paperwork. They now know the red flag was removed much before Kamaal Karna was introduced to the PC's mother. Karan assumes the introduction was arranged to leverage the PC, if and when the whole story came out.

They let Kamaal Karna stew for a while. When Karan and Antara enter the interrogation room, the stage is set. Karan has his fingers crossed, hoping things play out the way they've planned. The PC is in the observation room.

They know Kamaal is in her late thirties, but she can pass for a woman in her twenties. She is pretty, fitting the conventional image of the frail and fair damsel in distress that they've seen repeatedly. But when you look at her eyes, they are hard and cold.

"A lot of people have been looking for you," Karan says as he flips through the pages of the file before him.

"I'm not speaking to you until you call the person I asked you to."

The door springs open, and the officer who took the red flag off comes charging in. "How dare you?" he says to Karan.

Perfect! I couldn't have timed it better myself. Let the games begin!

"Mataji, I'll sort everything out," the officer says and then turns to face Karan. "I'd like a word with you outside. Now!"

"No, Sir, I think someone else is waiting outside to have a word with you," Karan says, gesturing at the PC standing by the open door.

"Sir, this time, he has really overstepped his boundaries," the flustered officer tells the PC.

"Come, Sharma, let's talk about this. Shekhawat, carry on."

"But, Sir," the officer interrupts.

"Now, Sharma." The PC walks away, and the other officer has no choice but to follow.

"Okay, now that we are done with that, let's talk about your connection to PTK," Karan says, turning to Kamaal Karna.

"Is that what this is about? Go ahead, ask me what you need to. I didn't do anything wrong. I just helped my people a little bit."

"You paid PTK," he refers to his notes, "thirty-six times in the last few months. Each time, someone was drugged, and their life was affected in some adverse way."

"I didn't do anything wrong. I just steered them towards a better life."

"A better life?" Karan asks.

"Of course. Each of them needed a little direction—guidance, if you will."

Karan refers to his notes, even though he doesn't need to. "Do you remember Mr Sinha of Gurgaon? What kind of guidance did he need?"

"What he *needed* was a wake-up call. He owed his family and was trying to run away from his responsibilities," Kamaal says scornfully.

"He is a grown man. As far as I can see, he has no dependents in the family. Why should he not choose his own direction?"

"Towards another man? That's not normal! All he had to do was get married, and then everything would've been fine." Her words are terse as she spits them out.

Karan and Antara go through the details of each of the PTK games, why she'd paid for them, and who'd benefitted. Three hours later, when they've gone through most of the details, they're ready to stop for a break. Antara places Raina and Navin's pictures on the table.

Kamaal Karna smirks. "What do you want to know about them? I didn't pay for this game."

"But you do know them?" Antara asks her, but Kamaal doesn't respond.

She only looks at Karan and says, "How does it matter now? They are dead, and the baby is where he was always meant to be. Your surname is Shekhawat? You're a Rajput, aren't you? You, of all people, should understand what honour means."

"Where did you meet Kamal and Deepti Chauhan?" Karan asks.

"*Kya farak padta hai*?" Kamaal replies.

"You are right. *Ab kya farak padta hai*?"

"I just happened to be staying at the same place as them. I knew the PTK games couldn't handle taking the baby. So, I told them to do it themselves."

Karan tsks. "Oh, you did more than that. You connected them with whoever is supplying the drug."

Kamaal stills, before relaxing. "I don't know anything about that. The game takes care of it," she says as she nonchalantly gestures with her hands. "I would like a lawyer now."

"You don't need one. The Interpol officers should be here in a few hours. You should get some rest. You have a long flight back," he tells her and is pleased to see her face lose all colour.

The team sit in Karan's office, cups of tea in their hands.

"How did she know they were supposed to be dead?" Sameer asks. "The hospital just dealt with all the paperwork on that. There was even a cremation and everything."

"Obviously, Arjun's father's reach is as strong and wide as we were told. But you are right, if she knows about it, she has been in touch with them. Where are we on the phone dump and on her other devices? We only have custody of her for another few hours."

"The dump is complete. Now, the programme is sorting through it, Sir. It will take at least a couple of hours. We'll check for phone calls and messages she recently received to find a link to Arjun's father or his brother. Then we'll begin with her emails, photographs, and all the apps on her phone. Do you think we'll find something on every person she 'helped'?"

Karan nods.

"So, every time a follower had a problem, they told her, and she resolved it?" Kabir asks.

"Not each time; sometimes, she would simply offer advice. Her services were only for the ones who could pay her and had so-called big requests—issues that couldn't be resolved through conversation or emotional manipulation. Whether it was a parent wanting to change their gay child's sexual orientation, a grandparent trying to prevent a grandchild from leaving the country, or a family member disapproving of their son or daughter's chosen life partner, Mataji dealt with them all," Antara says.

"That's seriously messed up," Imran says.

"What's seriously messed up is that we may actually have to let her get away with this," Kabir says as he looks at Karan.

"Yes, but apparently, the cases against her in Canada are airtight. Her brother was sixteen when he was found dead close to their home. Initially, the cops thought it was a hate crime, but as they dug deeper, they discovered he'd been thrashed in his own home. Kamaal, or whatever her real name is, discovered her brother was gay and told her parents. They asked her to deal with it, and she apparently did. The kid escaped while he was being roughed up, only to die outside on the street in front of the house. The cause of death was head trauma. At that time, the parents were at work. When they realized what had happened and that the police had caught on, they committed suicide."

"That's horrible!" Antara says.

"That was the last time she had physical contact in a case. Since then, she has been something of a puppet master, working behind the scenes."

"What's with the name, Sir?"

"Apparently, that was something her father was known to have said to encourage his kids. After her parents died, she sold the house and their business and changed her name. It's been years since her brother died, but there was enough trace evidence on his body to convict her. Unfortunately, she slipped out of the country before the final hearing."

"So, now?" Sameer asks.

"The Interpol take over tomorrow, and we'll continue looking for whoever is running the game. More importantly, we need to find the person who is supplying them with the Rohypnol. Anything new on PTK?" Karan asks.

Imran checks his phone. "Abhi just messaged on the group chat, the private group for the CP IRL game just opened on the PTK site. Right now, only basic information is offered. Once players acknowledge, more details will become available. The game is scheduled for the day after tomorrow," he says.

"Once we know the game details, we'll follow the team, but obviously, we can't let someone get drugged on our watch. We need to be ready with an intervention," Karan says.

"How about a 'long time no see'?" Antara suggests. "One of us gets the target out of the PTK team's way, and then the rest of us can follow the game players. From what Ipshita said, if the game is interrupted, they should walk away."

The 'long time no see' ploy, like the name suggests, is when the intended target suddenly meets someone they think they knew in the past—someone who gently moves them off their path or schedule.

"For the 'long time no see' to work, we'll need enough information on the target," Imran says.

"We'll get that when we know the game details," Kabir reassures him. "Do we bring them all in?"

"When they can't get their target, they should disperse. We'll each take one player, and of course, one of us will stay with the intended target. At least one of the players has to have a direct link to the PTK admin. I don't think they would trust the drug in just anyone's hands."

"But this person will not be the one to administer it, will they?" Antara asks.

"Exactly. We'll have to play it by ear. I'm hoping we'll get the player as well as the drug," Karan says. "Also, I want the PTK players to be separated when they are brought in for questioning."

"So, separate entrances?" Sameer asks, and Karan nods. "I'll make sure everything is ready, Sir."

Having their offices in an old colonial building always helps. The building sits on a corner plot, and the boundary has as many as four gates for them to use. The building itself can be accessed from several points. That way, they can ensure that the players don't have any contact with each other.

"It looks like we are going to be here for the night, so get comfortable. Sameer and I will deal with the paperwork for the Interpol to process Kamaal Karna... After that, she is their headache. Nonetheless, I need all three of you to start working on the information on her devices. If we have any more questions for her, we need to ask her before she leaves. We're specifically looking for any contact she may've had directly with the person or persons running PTK. We need to find the source for the Rohypnol."

"Okay," Sameer says as he gets up. "Let's get started."

Before dawn, they have the name and face they are looking for. After they hand Kamaal Karna over to the Interpol officers, Karan sends everyone home. They need to be fresh and ready for what he hopes will be the last piece in the PTK puzzle.

Despite a few hours of sleep, he is still groggy when Abhi hands him a cup of tea.

"Thank you," Karan says as he takes a sip of the *masala chai.*

"Linner?"

"Lin what?"

"Breakfast plus lunch is brunch, so lunch plus dinner is linner," Abhi says.

"If you say so," Karan replies.

"The dictionary says so," Abhi insists.

"Nonsense!"

"Check it," Abhi says, looking it up on his phone. "Other options are lupper, dunch, dinch."

"Let's eat a late lunch."

"Check," Abhi teases him, and Karan does.

"You silly kid, it's a word suggestion, not a word accepted by the dictionary. And before you say it, the Urban Dictionary doesn't count." They both laugh.

"So, it's almost done," Abhi asks as he transfers the food from the meal bags to plates.

"You know there is no such thing as 'almost done'. It'll be done when it is."

"Have the kid and his parents safely moved away?"

Karan makes a sound in acknowledgement.

"How did the uncle and aunt who took him get the drug?"

"Kamaal Karna gave them a phone number. They made a bitcoin transaction online and received the syringe at their hotel."

"That's crazy! Once it is all done, what will you do with PTK?"

"The cyber unit will take over and make sure there are no mirror sites that come up. Right now, we are basically focusing on the source of the Rohypnol."

"That database PTK created is scary because it shows how easy it is to get all that information," Abhi says as he chews on his food.

Karan nods. "There will always be people who keep giving parts of themselves away and others who will use those parts to take advantage of them."

"You're a ray of sunshine—hope and rainbows all the way," Abhi says, and Karan laughs.

By the time Anya gets home from work, Abhi is busy digging into the name Kabir sent him. The photograph of the third-year commerce student looks innocuous. Nothing in his online profile would've suggested that he runs PTK.

Why is it always the quiet ones? The fellow doesn't even have a background in computers, Abhi thinks.

"Did you find the person who runs PTK?" Anya asks from behind him.

"Did I say that out loud?" he asks.

"Is it a secret?"

"No, nothing like that. I didn't realize I spoke aloud."

"Is he home?" she asks.

"Yes, 'He Who Shall Not Be Named' is home," Abhi jokes.

Anya shakes her head and can't help but laugh as she goes up to Karan's home office. She knocks on the closed door and enters.

"You're home," Karan says as he leans back in his chair. "How was your day?"

Anya slips her shoes off and sits cross-legged on the couch against the wall. She tells him all about her day. She knows he's had a few hours of sleep in the afternoon, but he still looks tired.

"Can you take a break from your work, or do you have more to do?"

"There's nothing for me to do right now. Abhi, Imran, and Kabir are snooping into this fellow's online life. What do you want to do?"

"Have you watched *The Holiday*?"

He nods. "Do you want to watch it?"

"Only if you have the time," she says.

He nods, and they walk downstairs to ask Abhi if he wants to watch the film with them. When the popcorn is ready, the doorbell rings. Karan carries big bowls of popcorn into the living room and shakes his head.

"Don't you all have lives outside work?" he asks his team, handing a bowl to Sameer and one to Antara.

"*Su casa es mi casa*," Imran says.

"My mistake. I thought it was '*mi casa es su casa*'," Karan says.

"No, Sir, your house is definitely our home, too," Sameer insists. "Abhi, play the movie."

***

The plan is simple—get the target out of the way, follow the players, and hope the PTK fellow has more Rohypnol on him for them to arrest him. That is where the simple part ends. The target is to be drugged in a Connaught Place parking lot; she is a doctor, expected to offer testimony in an ongoing medical negligence case. It doesn't make much sense to drug her in broad daylight in a fairly crowded parking lot.

Antara gets the target out of the way, and the players disperse rather quickly. If the team did not have information from the PTK private chat room, they would never have picked the four players as people who'd drug a woman. Individually, they look harmless—three college students and a high schooler.

Karan follows Rakshit Arora, a third-year commerce student, to his car, parked in the adjacent parking lot. He waits for him to open the boot to place the bag he carries in his hand and then orders him to freeze. He handcuffs him before he calls out to Antara. He is tempted to check the boot, but he knows he should wait for her to arrive.

"Sir," she calls, and he turns to see what looks like an insulated lunch bag. Inside are rows of tiny syringes like Ipshita had described. He can see at least fifty syringes and is fairly sure there is another lot under it.

"Let's take him in."

It takes hours of conversation, coaxing, and the appearance of the prosecutor to get the whole story out. They let the other three players off with a warning, but Rakshit Arora is going to jail.

***

It's been a week since Anya returned home. She and Karan keep in touch through the days with messages, but it is not quite the same. On Friday evening, Karan arrives at her place with a big order of food from her favourite *dhaba*.

"Are you bribing me with good food?" she asks as he closes the door behind him.

"Is it working?"

She looks into the paper bags. "Butter chicken will always work," she says, as she takes out plates and cutlery.

"The others should be here in about an hour," he says and watches the expression on her face. "I thought you might be more comfortable with them around."

She looks at him in confusion, then grins. "Oh, my God! Is the Urban Crimes team going to chaperone us?" She laughs aloud.

He grins back. "I wasn't sure if you were comfortable. I mean…" he fumbles with the words.

"Relax, Karan. They're always welcome, but we don't always have to meet in a group. You're welcome to come over any time—by yourself, I mean."

"So, we're good?"

"I don't know. You tell me," she says, as she takes out glasses from the cabinet.

"Just put me out of my misery, Anya. Are we dating?"

"Of course. I have no clue, whatsoever, what that will involve, but yes, I think we're dating. If there are any rules, please just tell me. I don't want to overdo or…" The rest of her words are lost as their lips meet.

Karan finally lifts his head and says, "That's the first time I've heard bells chime when I kissed someone."

Anya stares at him for a while, then shakes her head. "I don't think we can take credit; it *is* the bell. The team is here."